Secret Places

Vivian Kay

This book contains an excerpt from the novella *Knit Together.*
Copyright © 2017 by Vivian Kay

E-Book ISBN: 978-0-9950361-8-5
Paperback ISBN: 978-0-9950361-7-8

Ayoka Books, Ontario, Canada.
Copyright © 2015 by Vivian Kay
www.viviankay.com

Other Books by this Author

KNIT TOGETHER

ADVANCE PRAISE FOR SECRET PLACES

In *Secret Places*, Kay pens a unique and redemptive tale about what happens when we bend our values to fit our carnal desires. You will find yourself in a love hate relationship with Moni and Sam as they try to pull themselves out of their web of deceit. It kept me turning pages to find out what's next. I can't wait to see more from this author. ~ **Rhonda Bowen**, author *Get You Good* & *Under Covers*

Secrets Places is an amazing story of restoration and redemption. I was quickly pulled into Moni and Sam and Debo's story and Kay held me there until the very last line. She is an anointed storyteller and a master at characterization. Readers will not soon forget this book or God's message of forgiveness between the pages. ~ **Rhonda McKnight**, author of *An Inconvenient Friend* & Romance Slam Jam Award winning novel, *Unbreak My Heart*.

In her debut, *Secret Places*, Vivian Kay takes readers on a shocking but no less entertaining ride into the lives of two couples who decide to fix their marriage by any means necessary. Their journey takes them to places they never imagined. *Secret Places* is a story of redemptive love that readers won't forget in a hurry. You think you know but you have no idea. ~ **Unoma Nwankwor**, Author of the NWA Award winning novel, *When You Let Go* and the National Bestseller, *He Changed My Name*.

DEDICATION

To Jehovah Tsidkenu, The Lord, Our Righteousness.

ACKNOWLEDGEMENTS

First thanks to the Lord Jesus Christ for the gifts of life and inspiration. Writing this book was a journey for me, and I'm grateful for His grace and faithfulness.

My sincere thanks to family and friends, near and far, who support my dreams through prayers and encouragement. I appreciate every one of you.

To Unoma Nwankwor, Rhonda Bowen, Tyora Moody, Karen Rodgers, Joylynn Ross, Melanie Freeman and Rhonda McKnight, I say a big thank you for the invaluable critique and support.

Can any hide himself in secret places that I shall not see him? saith the LORD. Do not I fill heaven and earth? saith the LORD. Jeremiah 23:24 (KJV)

Chapter One

At first, Moni Badmus thought she needed to get her forty-four-year-old eyes checked because surely her vision was failing her. Either that or she was hallucinating, so she closed her eyes tight and opened them again. She realized she didn't see double. Her vision wasn't blurry, and her mind was as sharp as the blade of a chef's knife. That was her daughter, Shekinah.

Dressed in the too-tight camouflage pants she was supposed to add to the Goodwill pile; Shekinah stood outside the strip mall with a group of teens. Moni recognized some of them as Shekinah's classmates. Her eyes widened at the sight of their multiple tattoos and piercings.

Long, gold braids piled on top of her head, untied high top sneaker laces trailing behind her, Shekinah didn't look like she had dressed for school. In fact, Moni knew she wasn't because she'd been wearing a different outfit when she left home that morning.

Moni stepped out of her car and took rapid steps toward the little group. She willed Shekinah not to turn around and see her. She wanted her to nearly throw up as she had almost done when she heard Shekinah's unmistakable laughter.

She thought Shekinah was going to faint when she turned to see who had given her a light tap on her back. "Mom!"

Since she was only five-feet-two, Moni was forced to tilt her head. Her blood pressure shot right up when she saw Shekinah's heavy kohl-lined eyes and bright red lips. She and Miss 15-going-on-30 just talked about not wearing heavy makeup to school. Did this child listen to anything she said?

"Let me guess? You are on a field trip, and any moment now I'm going to see a teacher?"

Shekinah bit down on her lip, smearing her teeth with the ridiculous lipstick she was wearing. Even in the freezing Brampton cold, Moni thought she saw beads of perspiration forming on her forehead. *That's right be afraid,* Moni thought. *I need you to be afraid of me or we'll never get out of the cycle of rebellion.*

"We're allowed to leave the school grounds during our lunch hour."

Shekinah's friends began backing away from them. Soon, they were alone.

Moni raised an eyebrow. "You're several blocks away from your school."

"We came to see someone working here," Shekinah said as she looked around her.

"Your friend works at a tattoo parlor?"

"No." The scowl on Shekinah's face was identical to her father's. "Mom, you're embarrassing me."

"I'm sure your lunch is over," Moni said. "I'll drop you at school."

For a minute, she thought Shekinah was going to run after her friends. Instead, she stormed off toward their minivan.

Moni took a deep breath and counted backward from ten as she hurried after her. If Shekinah knew what was good for her, she would not say a word during the ride.

"Who were those kids?" Moni asked, pulling her seatbelt around her. "I don't even recognize most of them."

"That's because you don't pay attention to anything that's not work-related," Shekinah replied in a nasty tone.

"Excuse me." Moni snatched her head back. "I don't pay attention? How could I not pay attention to you…you're like a neon sign at a cheap motel. Who could miss you?"

Moni, a soft answer turns away wrath.

She ignored the familiar voice in her head. It would be easy to give soft words if the child had not developed an allergy to the word "no."

"Well, dad isn't wearing makeup, and you don't pay attention to him either."

"And who told you it's appropriate for you to talk to me like that about my marriage?"

Shekinah had been facing the window, but she turned to her and looked her square in the eyes. "I live in the house, too."

Moni realized she did. And a cold house it had become. But still, that didn't give her the right to mouth off and be disrespectful. "Your father and I will work things out."

Shekinah guffawed before saying, "Good luck."

Moni was going to scream at her to stay out of grown folks' business, but the tears that welled in her daughter's eyes stopped her. They were familiar tears, and Moni was struck by the fact that this was her child and she wasn't even sure if they were real anymore. Shekinah turned on the waterworks every time she got in trouble. But Moni knew she couldn't let things go because her daughter appeared to be hurting.

"When did you start changing in the middle of the day?" She didn't get a response. "Do I need to make random visits to your school to check out your clothes?"

Shekinah shrugged. "Dad doesn't have a problem with my make-up and clothes."

Good Ole' Daddy Sam. Of course, he would support his daughter's marginal choices since she could do no wrong in his clouded eyes. "I'm not going to let you ruin your life on my watch."

"You just like making my life miserable."

Moni shook her head. "If not getting your way is what's making you miserable, you can consider this practice for adult life."

Shekinah rolled her eyes upward. Moni realized that hadn't come out quite the way she wanted it to. Her bitterness over the state of her marriage had leaked into her conversation with her daughter. Not good. "What I meant was, you have to learn that you can't always get what you want. Believe me, not everything you want is right for you."

Lips pursed, Shekinah turned away.

Moni turned the key in the ignition. She had to get back to work.

When they arrived at the school, Shekinah got out of the vehicle and slammed the door. What had happened to the precious child she'd fasted and prayed years for, Moni wondered as she watched Shekinah's tall and lean figure march off. It was as if someone broke into their home, stole her real daughter, and left an angry, defiant teenager at their doorstep.

Chapter Two

Moni dragged herself up the carpeted staircase. The afternoon's incident with Shekinah had cost her time as she had been unable to stay focused despite the urgent deadline.

She paused in front of Shekinah's bright purple, bedroom door. Hopefully, Shekinah was asleep and not surfing the Internet on a school night. It was too late for another fight, Moni thought as she headed down the hallway.

Seated in her rocking chair, Sam looked up from his laptop when she walked into their bedroom. "Hey, how was your day?" he asked.

Moni dropped her purse on the dresser. "It was brutal. I hope you got my message?"

"Yes." Sam put the laptop down. "Were you able to finish the presentation?"

"No. Thanks to your daughter." She unclasped her bracelet. "Did Shekinah tell you about her educational visit to the tattoo parlor?"

"She said you lost your temper in front of her friends."

Moni snickered. Their daughter knew how to tell a good story. "I can assure you that given the circumstances, I was very well-behaved. I don't understand why she is fixated on getting a tongue ring."

"It's nothing," Sam said as he reclined back in the chair. "Kids in my class have piercings."

Sam's calm countenance made her clench her hands in frustration. "Is that what you told her?"

"No. Listen, I don't think Shekinah would get one. You know she gets queasy at the sight of blood. If you don't nag her on the issue, she may drop it."

Moni flexed her tense shoulder muscles. Sam's words made sense. She wasn't in the mood to hear them. "I'm going to take a shower."

"I know something else which might help you relax."

She recognized the look on Sam's face. *Don't even think about it.* Moni escaped to the bathroom.

Moni came back to find Sam sprawled on the bed. Stripped down to his boxers, he had Charlie Wilson's "Without You" playing through the surround sound speakers. Sam meant business. So did she.

"Are you feeling better?"

Moni feigned a loud yawn. "I'm sure an uninterrupted night's rest will help." She mumbled a quick prayer of thanks before getting into bed.

"Babe, you don't know how much I've missed you," Sam whispered as he reached for her.

Moni swatted his hand away before pulling the comforter up to her chin. "Sex is not on my agenda for the evening."

"Well ma'am, how about you pencil me in your schedule?" Sam said in a tight voice. "Or do you need my people to call your people? Moni, it's been two whole months. I don't want to cheat on you."

Her words were clipped and bitter. "It wouldn't be your first time."

Sam glared at her. "How long are you going to punish me? I've said I'm sorry. Several times, too. Moni, you're a pastor's daughter. Don't you have a forgiveness gene?"

Moni turned her back. She would never forget the day Sam came home and confessed to an affair with a fellow teacher at his former school. Sweating profusely, he'd said it was a momentary lapse in reason.

Nothing was fleeting about a three-month affair. And because Sam had pretended everything was fine, she'd been blindsided by the news.

They had attended counseling, and she had told Sam he was forgiven. But, stabbing feelings from the betrayal grew until they controlled her mind. Sam's touch began to repulse her as she imagined his fingers caressing the other woman's skin.

Behind her, she heard him sigh. "Moni, I'm trying to make our marriage work. I can't do this on my own."

Moni faced him. Sam's dark eyes reflected the despair she had heard in his voice. She refused to feel sorry for him. "You think this is easy for me?" she asked.

"I don't. Moni, I can't say more than I'm sorry."

She looked away. "I need time."

"Moni, I need you."

The whispered words made her heart ache. A part of her wanted to let Sam hold her. She missed the Sam she married. The man who had made her feel secure in his love. It was better not to touch this Sam, she decided. This one offered less and wanted more than she was ready to give.

"I'm exhausted," Moni said as she turned away and curled into a ball. As she squeezed her eyes shut to keep in her tears, she knew it was going to be another sleepless night.

Chapter Three

Debo Ajala sang along to Jill Scott's "Golden" as he drove his Mercedes through the gate of his estate home.

He and a group of men from Faith Assembly had spent the morning organizing and delivering groceries to nearby food banks. He hadn't always been enthusiastic about spending Thanksgiving morning away from his family. However, each year it reminded him of how lucky or blessed he was. Either word worked for him.

Debo turned into the wide, stone driveway of his six-bedroom, Tudor-style home before pressing the garage door remote.

He parked inside and closed the retractable hardtop before getting out of the vehicle. He was tired and hoped he'd be able to get some rest before their guests arrived for Thanksgiving dinner.

The aroma of good cooking met him at the door and filled his nostrils. Debo took a deep breath. On so many levels, his wife Adele knew how to tantalize his taste buds.

Adele looked up from stirring a pot when Debo walked into the kitchen. Her face was make-up free and with her long, blonde hair pulled in that loose ponytail style, Adele could pass for a twenty-year-old. "Hey, Honey," she said. Debo never tired of her French accent or soft, sweet voice. "You guys finished early."

He walked up to Adele, wrapped his arms around her waist and drew her close until her head nestled under his chin. "I told them I had to leave because I was missing my wife."

"Aww, that is so sweet," she said. "I doubt Pastor would have let you go just because of that."

He kissed the side of her head. "Pastor knows how much I love you."

"You do?"

Surprised by Adele's question, he turned her around. He noted a flicker of sadness in her eyes. "Yes. Is everything okay?"

Adele took a deep breath. "I guess."

His French was limited to a few sentences. *"Je t'aime ma femme."*

Adele returned Debo's hug. "I love you too, husband." She stepped away from him and raised her voice. "Boys, your dad's back."

Debo braced himself as four, screeching boys came through the basement door and ran across the white marble floor.

They were still asleep when he left home. The youngest, their two-year-old, fell on his bum as he tried to keep up with his brothers. Their chorus of, "Welcome, Dad" and hugs warmed his heart. Debo sent them back downstairs. They would only get in their mom's way.

He looked around the kitchen. "Is there anything you need me to do?"

Adele gave him a grateful look. "I do need the table set. The fancy plates are on the top shelf of the china cabinet. Please, and thank you."

"I'll take a quick shower and get to it." After stealing a kiss, he headed upstairs. He was living life like it was golden.

***

By the time his best friend, Sam and his family arrived, the table was set, and the Ajala family were decked out in their Thanksgiving finery. Debo would have preferred comfortable slacks and a Cashmere sweater, but Adele loved dressing up for the holidays, so dress up they did.

"Hello, Mrs. B. Happy Thanksgiving." Moni had always been one of his most favorite people.

Moni hugged him. "Happy Thanksgiving, Bro. Thanks for the invitation."

"Our pleasure. You look beautiful as always." He gave Sam a wink. "My friend is doing a great job of taking care of you."

Moni gave him a half-smile. "Thank you."

"I'd do a better job if she would let me," Sam said as he stared at his wife.

"Go for it," Debo said as he patted Sam on the back. "We didn't see you at church this morning."

Sam raised an eyebrow. "I thought it was a deacon-only thing. I didn't want to crash your exclusive party."

"There's nothing special or exciting about hauling groceries. Last Sunday, Pastor was clear we needed all hands."

"I guess I must have tuned out that part of the church service," Sam said as he handed over his coat.

Debo wondered why his friend looked like something had ticked him off. "Next year, I'll be showing up bright and early at your door to drag you out."

Adele joined them in the foyer. She stood on tiptoe and kissed Moni and Sam on both cheeks. "Where's Shekinah?" she asked.

Moni and Sam exchanged a loaded look.

"She's outside," Moni said. "Taking her sweet time to come in."

Sam chuckled. "Text messages break your stride."

Adele shook her head. "Teenagers. They sure make life interesting."

Moni sighed. "I never thought I would be glad to have only one child. All I do these days is yell."

"Hey, no sad faces. We're counting our blessings today, remember? I'll get her. I'm sure Shekinah wouldn't say no to her favorite godfather."

"You're her only godfather," Sam said.

Debo shrugged. "Only, favorite. Same thing in my book."

He found Shekinah seated on the porch step. "Little Miss Glory."

"Hi, Uncle Dee. I'm not little anymore."

"You're up to my shoulder now." Debo sat beside her. "What are you doing out here?"

"I needed a break from them."

Debo frowned. "Your parents?"

"Yeah. All Mom and Dad do is yell at each other. The car ride here was awful." Shekinah took a deep breath. "It's quiet out here. And your garden is beautiful."

He resisted the urge to ask Shekinah for more details. "You can see the garden from the dining room. I think the boys are ready for their turkey. It's best we go in before they come out to get us."

As he had expected, Shekinah looked uneasy. She loved his boys, but as an only child, their enthusiastic physical affection was a bit too much for her. Number four usually covered her face with his wet kisses.

Shekinah stood and brushed the seat of her pants. "Yeah, that sounds like a good idea."

"Remember, you'll have to say one thing you're thankful for."

Shekinah shrugged. "*Meh.* Right now, everything sucks."

"Well, if you have nothing to be thankful for, today you can be thankful you're not an Ontario turkey."

Shekinah gave him a reluctant smile. "You say that every year."

"Only because it's the truth." Debo held out his hand. "Let's go in."

Shekinah took his hand, and they entered the house.

***

It was almost midnight by the time they made it to their bedroom. Any time they had guests, Adele would not leave the kitchen until it was spic and span clean.

"Everything you made was delicious. The turkey melted off the bones."

"Thank you. I could tell you loved it from the number of helpings you had."

Debo pulled up his pajama bottoms. "Did you get the sense that Sam and Moni are not on good terms?"

Adele plumped her pillow and sat on the king-sized bed. "Well, Moni did seem a little tense. I thought she was still upset about Shekinah's behavior."

His mind went back to Sam's comment. "It was more than that. They didn't speak to each other." He shared his conversation with Shekinah. "It looks like there's some serious trouble brewing in their home."

"If you're concerned about them, talk to your friend," Adele suggested. "You know Moni, and I are not that close."

His general rule was to stay out of marital conflicts unless invited. However, Moni and Sam meant a lot to him. "I'll do just that."

"I hope the boys sleep in tomorrow. Today was a long day."

Adele looked exhausted. "Maybe next year, instead of hosting, we can spend Thanksgiving in Montreal."

"My mother would love that. You know how much she misses the boys."

"It's a done deal." The happiness on Adele's face made his heart feel full. "Have I told you anytime I count my blessings, I always count you twice?"

"Every year. *Mon cher, moi aussi.*"

Debo held a hand to his chest. "I love it when you speak French to me. Repeat it."

Adele giggled as he switched off the bedside lamp.

Chapter Four

Sam emptied his half-eaten bowl of cereal into the trash can. The thought of dealing with a bunch of inattentive teens made him want to call in sick. He sometimes wondered how he'd gotten to this place in his career. Teaching was starting to feel like thankless servitude. Everything he did these days seemed to be that way.

Realizing there was no point in fantasizing about not going to Faith Academy; he washed his hands and retrieved his keys from the table. Tardiness was not an option.

Sam acknowledged it wasn't only his job that had him in a funk. Another early morning battle between Moni and Shekinah had left him feeling edgy. What he wanted to do was spend some quality time with a cold bottle of Molson Canadian. If he was honest with himself, he knew he would need to drink at least two bottles to take the edge off. He groaned. That amount of alcohol before nine in the morning could not be right for anyone.

Because his affair began after a visit to a hotel bar during a professional training trip, Moni had unilaterally decided he couldn't handle his alcohol and turned their house into a dry spot. He'd spared Moni's feelings with a half-truth. The flirting between him and Joy started long before the trip. The alcohol had only taken away their inhibitions.

Sam lifted his coat off the peg by the front door and pushed his arms into the sleeves as he exited the house. A rush of cold air made his eyes water as he hurried toward his car. A late October storm had left behind a foot of snow for them to shovel.

He slid behind the wheel of his car and did what he did every day which was to pray his ten-year-old Kia would start. Sam turned the key twice before it sputtered to life. The car might not make it to the following year. Another thing to worry about.

He attended church on a pretty regular basis, paid his tithes, wished most of his neighbors well, so why couldn't he catch a break from the Big Guy upstairs?

Sam reversed the car into the street. His body relaxed as he thought of his daughter. The nurse handed Shekinah to him, and he knew he would not be able to refuse her anything. On her good days, Shekinah's sweet laughter sounded like his mother's. Hearing it was one of the few things which still made him happy.

Not putting boundaries around Shekinah's demands was questionable parenting. But, to his disappointment, she was all he had. And it wasn't his fault they had one child. Moni owned the blame.

***

"Hey, buddy."

Sam raised his eyes from the workbench.

"I knew I would find you in here," Debo said as he walked into the wood shop room.

Sam's lips curled into his first smile of the day. "Stalker."

Debo smirked. "You like being stalked."

"Not by talkative giants sporting scrawny beards," he said. "I want stalkers who are easy on the eyes."

"Dream on. You're lucky Moni took pity and said yes despite your lack of a real beard."

Sam cracked his knuckles. "And you're lucky the school has a 'keep your hands to yourself' policy. Today, I can use a punching bag."

Debo's six-foot-five, two hundred and sixty-pound body, shook from his laughter. "Bring it, Bro. I can hold my own."

Sam grinned as he did some shadow boxing. "I'll sting you like a bee."

"You Ali wannabe." Shaking his head, Debo pulled up a stool and sat next to him.

Both sets of parents immigrated to Canada in 1970. Born within months of each other, he and Debo grew up in the Jane and Finch area of Toronto. Every year, they found themselves in the same class at school and became inseparable.

During those years, his parents worked two or three jobs at a time, which meant he and his younger sisters were latchkey kids. The Ajala's bigger apartment became their playground since they could not leave the apartment building.

Given their closeness, Sam wasn't surprised when their parents retired and moved back to Nigeria in the same year. His father and Debo's mother had never adjusted to the long winters.

"I didn't see you during the morning assembly. Where were you?" Sam asked.

"Number three had a doctor's appointment. Adele couldn't take him. Her kindergarten class had a field trip today."

It still amused him how Debo referred to his kids by their birth order. "I hope it's nothing serious?"

"He needed to get immunization shots." Debo pushed back his glasses. "I hear you, and one of the big boys got into a screaming match this morning."

Sam shrugged. He wasn't surprised the news had made the rounds.

"I heard whispering in the front office. Big Pete wasn't too happy about it," Debo said, referring to the principal. "You shouldn't let these kids get under your skin."

The front office women had way too much time on their hands. And, he didn't care about the principal's happiness. It wasn't like Big Pete cared about his well-being.

"The boy was texting who knows who, right in middle of my class. When I asked him to hand over his phone, he refused. You would have thought I'd asked him for an organ."

"So, you blew a gasket?"

Sam threw his hands up. "What was I supposed to do? Let him walk all over me in front of the whole class?"

"Bro, you're preaching to the choir. I know those cell phones mean way too much to them." Debo peered at him. "On a serious note, you've been a little off lately. Is there something we need to talk about?"

Debo had always been a 'let's hold hands and talk about everything' kind of man. Sam didn't share the inclination. "Your slip is showing. You know real brothers don't talk about everything."

Debo's smile dimmed. "I guess you'll let me know if you need my help."

The gentle words made Sam feel like a bonafide knucklehead. Regardless of how he felt, his friend didn't deserve the attitude. Life as a scrawny, asthmatic boy in their tough neighbourhood had made him an easy target for bullies. From an early age, Debo had stepped into the protector role. And he still watched out for him.

He gave Debo an apologetic grin. "I'm sorry."

Debo waved away the apology. "I know you have basketball practice after school. How about you guys come over for dinner tonight?" He grinned. "We can also go bowling. I need to remind you I'm still the boss."

Competitive to a fault, Debo's bowling name was Hulk Daddy. He gave his friend a grateful smile. Debo always knew what he needed. "Sounds like a date. Thanks a lot, man."

"Anytime." Stretching, Debo stood. "Time to get back to work. I'll call Adele to let her know you guys are joining us. Prepare your stomach. You know Friday's beef bourguignon night."

"And lemon soufflé for dessert?"

"I'm sure Adele can be persuaded to whip up some for you. The next time I visit your house, I'll expect some spicy *egusi* soup."

"Deal." The warmth radiating from the bottom of Sam's stomach rose to his smile. "I'm feeling better already."

Debo thumped him on the back before heading for the door. "Don't stay in here too long."

"I won't." The talk with Debo had helped calm him down. Sam decided he would not tell Moni about the dinner invitation. She attended choir practice on Friday nights, but if he told her, she might choose to honor the request. He wanted a fun evening. A night away from Moni's scowl.

Moni didn't like Shekinah being on her own at night. She would have to stay home or take Shekinah to church. Either way, she wasn't going to be happy. He didn't care. It was about time Moni stayed home and made peace with Shekinah. He no longer wanted to mediate their arguments. Sam pulled out his cell phone and dialed his wife's number.

Chapter Five

Moni didn't have to look at her watch to know she was running late for her mock sales presentation meeting. It took her boss Andy six months to land this potential client, and he needed their pitch to be top-notch.

She had tried to beat the traffic lights on the way to work. Brampton's morning rush hour's stop-and-go conditions had forced her into a crawl. She pulled into her company's parking lot at top speed. Moni acknowledged it was a miracle she hadn't rear-ended another car. She sent up a quick thank you for the lone parking spot, stepped out of her van and began a brisk walk toward the glass office building.

Moni chewed on her lower lip. Andy was particular about staff being punctual for meetings. On several occasions, she had been present as he berated her tardy colleagues. It had not been a pretty sight.

Andy stopped talking when Moni slunk into the board room. "I'm happy you decided it was worth your while to join us."

All the chairs in the room swiveled in her direction. Moni wanted to sink right through the carpeted floor. Mumbling her apologies, she took a seat in the nearest chair. None of her colleagues made eye contact.

"Are you ready?" Andy asked as Moni retrieved her USB flash drive from her suitcase.

"Yes."

She might be treading water in other areas of her life, but she was competent at her job. After several late nights of working on the presentation, she was ready for the challenge.

Moni exhaled. There were rumours of restructuring and layoffs going around the office. It wasn't the time to be the expendable link. If the deal fell through, Andy would be on the hunt for a scapegoat. Her lateness had slapped a bull's-eye on her forehead.

Unsteady on her three-inch heels, Moni made the long walk to the front of the boardroom. The sweat stains under her armpits widened as she clicked the pointer. If presentation impressed Andy, she couldn't tell. His face revealed nothing. He might as well be listening to a dull weather report.

When the presentation ended, for about a minute there was total silence. Andy stood to his feet and looked around the room. "Executives from DressCo will be here at about 10:00 a.m. I'm going to give them a tour of our offices. While they're here folks, please, no personal phone chats and no Facebooking. I'd like to give our clients the impression we're running a serious business." Andy picked up his hard copy of her presentation. "Okay team, let's get back to work."

At her desk, Moni went over the presentation several times. It had to be perfect. Ten minutes before the meeting, Moni escaped to the bathroom. She splashed water on her face and freshened her makeup. As Andy often told them during staff meetings, in advertising, creating the right illusion was key.

On her way to the boardroom, several colleagues gave Moni solemn nods. It had been a long time since she watched gladiator movies, but the phrase addressed to the Emperor, *We who are about to die salute you*, came to Moni's mind. Her heart raced as if she was about to face some hungry lions.

Her hand curved around the door handle. *Moni, snap out of it. You can do all things through Christ who strengthens you.*

It struck her that since her prayer and devotion times had become spotty at best, she wasn't sure if she had any business claiming biblical promises. She squashed down her doubts and walked in with a forced smile. From his seat, Andy gave her a terse nod.

Moni squared her shoulders as she picked up the pointer. Let the show begin.

***

If she had remembered how to, Moni would have done the moonwalk as she headed to her cubicle. The DressCo deal had gone through with minimal concessions on the agency's part.

Moni switched on her computer. There were still some loose ends to tie up. She was inputting her password when she felt her cell phone vibrate. She unclipped it from her belt and saw Sam's number flashing on the screen.

"Hey, you. How's it going?"

Given that morning's heated words, Sam's cheerful tone made her suspicious. "Is everything okay?"

"I wanted to let you know I'm hanging out with Debo tonight."

Moni pursed her lips. Just like Sam to make plans on a night she had to be at church. "But what about the movie date you promised Shekinah?"

"What movie date?"

Moni pursed her lips. "You promised her last night."

"Oh, I forgot. Why don't you take Shekinah? You ladies need some fun time together."

Dates with Shekinah were not her idea of fun. The child knew how to press every one of her hot buttons.

"Not going to happen. You know all Shekinah wants from me right now is permission to get a tongue piercing. I don't want to spend the evening listening to her whine about it."

Sam's laugh grated on her nerves. "Shekinah is your child. She knows what she wants and is not shy about letting people know it."

Moni kept scrolling through her work email. "Was there anything else you wanted to say?"

"I should be home around eleven." He paused a moment and then, "Debo sends his greetings."

A reluctant smile tugged at the side of Moni's mouth. Best man Debo. Over the years, she had grown to appreciate Debo's jovial personality. He knew how to make people feel better about themselves. Since Debo was a fine influence on his friend, he might help Sam get out of his sullen mood. "Please, tell him I said hello."

"Will do. Bye."

Moni returned the cell phone to her belt clip, turned her chair around and went back to work. Time flew by. She was picking up documents from the copy room when her cell phone rang again. Her heart skipped a beat when she saw the call was from Shekinah's school.

"Hello?"

She heard the principal's familiar voice. "Hello, Mrs. Badmus. Sorry to bother you at work. Unfortunately, there has been another situation. We need you to pick Shekinah up."

Moni swallowed hard. What had Shekinah done this time? She knew there was no point asking. It was policy to have these discussions in person. "I'm on the way."

The principal's voice brought tears to her eyes. "I know you'll need to get some things tied up first. I'll keep her in my office until you get here."

Moni gathered her pile of documents and hurried back to her desk. She decided it would be best if she called her mother to see if she could drop Shekinah at their place. She had no intention of rewarding Shekinah by letting her stay at home to do as she pleased. Mummy would find something constructive for her to do. *Lord, please, let Mummy be home.*

Her mother picked up the phone on the first ring. "My Moni." Mummy had a smile in her voice. "You're the true daughter of your father. I was thinking about you."

Tears came back to Moni's eyes. If she was anyone's girl, she was her mom's. She said her good afternoon in Yoruba. "*Ekaasan*, Ma."

"*Kaasan*, my dear," Mummy replied.

Moni's father had left Nigeria to lead Faith Assembly's Brampton parish when she was twelve and her brother, Gbade was ten. At home, Daddy had insisted on them only speaking their native Yoruba language. When she and her brother got married, and the grandchildren came, things changed. Gbade's wife, an Irish Nova Scotian, couldn't understand the language. And at age seven, Shekinah had told her grandfather she was Canadian and didn't want to speak Nigerian. Moni could still picture the stunned look on her father's face.

Moni lowered her voice. "I need help. Shekinah got suspended. Again." Her mother's voice remained calm. "What happened?"

"The principal didn't say. I'm on my way to pick her up."

Mummy made some sympathetic noises. "I'll be waiting. Please, drive safe."

Moni considered calling Sam. She dismissed the thought. He would probably go to the school, hold Shekinah's hand and tell her not to worry. Shekinah didn't need to hear that nonsense. She picked up her purse and headed out.

Chapter Six

The principal met her at the front desk. "Mrs. Badmus, thanks for coming."

His warm handshake and calm demeanor didn't make her feel less anxious. "I'm sorry it took me some time to get here."

"No worries." Mr. Scott ushered her into the vice-principal's empty office. "We should have a private discussion before joining Shekinah in my office."

Back rigid, Moni sat on the offered chair. "Please, what did she do?"

Mr. Scott cleared his throat. "Following the last bullying incident, things settled down. Shekinah was making the right choices and participating in class."

Dry-mouthed, Moni stared at his bushy moustache. *Give me the bad news.*

"Today, things took a nasty turn. Shekinah and some other girls were caught bullying another student in the bathroom."

Mr. Scott paused. "They had pushed the student's head into a flushing toilet bowl. This girl has an intellectual disability and has been an easy target since she joined us last year. From the interviews conducted, Shekinah didn't help in holding her down. But, she was present and knew what the other girls were going to do." Mr. Scott leaned against the desk. "We had a lengthy debate about contacting the police. The young woman's parents opposed police involvement."

Moni's voice came out as a croaked whisper. "I'm so sorry. How is the young woman doing?"

"Her parents took her home for the day." Mr. Scott shook his head. "Since this was not an isolated incident, I would have liked to see the police involved on some level. This group of girls needs a reality check. But the child's parents feel it would only escalate the bullying."

Moni took a deep breath. What had Shekinah been thinking?

"Shekinah is suspended for a week. During our talk, I made it clear if she continues down this path, we will transfer her to one of the board's alternative programs."

"An alternative program?"

"The board offers behavioral programs outside the regular school setting for students who need them. One of the things we decided is that when Shekinah returns from her suspension, the school psychologist will check in with her on a weekly basis. What do you think?"

Moni didn't know how putting Shekinah amongst the same kind of kids she should avoid would help. Still, she understood the other children needed protection.

Her cheeks burned from embarrassment. Shekinah was determined to send her to an early grave. She sighed and avoided the principal's eyes for a moment. When she couldn't avoid it anymore, she returned her gaze to his. "It sounds like a good plan."

"We are hopeful things will settle again. Shekinah has so much potential. It would be a shame to waste it."

Shekinah dragged her feet behind Moni as they left the school building. Moni was too ashamed to make eye contact with the office staff. They knew what Shekinah had done and most likely blamed the behaviors on her substandard parenting. Before Shekinah's misbehavior started, she would have thought the same of another parent.

All the way to her parents' home, Moni gave Shekinah a tongue lashing. "I don't know what else you want us to do," she said. Shekinah was silent. "All we ask is that you go to school, face your books and stay out of trouble. Is that too much to ask for?"

Through the rear-view mirror, she saw the glazed over look settle on Shekinah's face as she turned to face the window.

Seething, Moni wondered if anything she'd said sunk in. Why didn't children come with manuals?

Moni was glad her father was away on his annual mission trip to Nigeria. The last time Shekinah had been suspended, her father told her Shekinah struggled because she'd been sent off to full-time daycare as a baby and exposed to caregivers with different parenting styles. There were days when she wondered if there was some merit to his argument.

Mummy met them at the door. Shekinah ran into her grandmother's extended arms. "Good afternoon, grandma."

"Good afternoon, my child," Mummy said as she gave Shekinah a tight hug.

Moni followed them into the living room. The child didn't deserve any hugs. She knew Mummy sent Shekinah upstairs to help her sort her basket of knitting yarn so they could talk. She gave her a quick rundown of what had happened at school.

"Shekinah doesn't need any pampering right now. She needs to hear how unacceptable her behavior is."

"Trust me, Shekinah and I will have our talk. An angry face won't make her open up to me." She patted Moni on the arm. "I've told you, once you use the left hand to discipline a child, it's important you use the right hand to pull the child close. It's a balancing act."

Moni pursed her lips. The left hand, right hand thing was old school Nigerian parenting. Shekinah was a North American kid who questioned and challenged every directive. Her mother could not understand how difficult it was to deal with her. She stood. "I have to go back to work."

"Okay, my dear. We'll see you soon."

Back at the office, the rest of the day dragged. The buzz from her successful presentation had fizzled out. An extra-large cup of black coffee couldn't bring it back. The image of Shekinah's sullen face had taken over her mind.

Moni's head throbbed from a ruthless migraine as she drove back to parents' home. If the child knew what was good for her, she would get into the car without making a fuss.

Hearing laughter, she walked to the back of the house and found them harvesting tomatoes from the small vegetable garden her mother kept at the rear of the house.

When Shekinah saw her, she moved behind her grandmother. Moni smirked. *You're going home with me.*

"You closed a little early today," Mummy said.

"Yes, Ma. I didn't want to disturb your plans for the evening."

"My only plan was to catch up with the backlog of knitting for my babies at the hospital." Mummy drew Shekinah close. "My sweet child was a big help today. Her knitting is getting quite good."

Mummy handed the basket of tomatoes to Shekinah. "Please, go and wash them in the kitchen. Make sure to put half in a bag so you can take them home to make tomato sandwiches. A good laborer deserves her wages."

Moni watched as Shekinah hurried across the yard and went in through the back door.

"Come, let us talk," Mummy said as she pulled her toward the patio set. They sat.

"Did Shekinah say anything about the school incident?" Moni asked.

Mummy shook her head. "No. When I asked, she wouldn't stop crying."

Moni hissed in frustration. *How convenient.*

"Something is disturbing your daughter." Mummy had a thoughtful look. "Shekinah told me you don't love her."

"If tolerating her misbehavior would be a sign of my undying love, then, I guess I don't."

"Calm down. Moni, you're the adult. I know it's not true and I told Shekinah so. You have to be patient."

The pain in Moni's head made her grit her teeth. "Mummy, the time for patience is over. If Shekinah does not get her act together, the school is going to send her to a program for bad children." The tears she'd been fighting since she received Mr. Scott's call spilled over. "What am I doing wrong?"

"My dear, stop crying." Mummy's tone soothed her. "You know what your father says in times like these."

She clenched her jaw. "Yeah, my tears are a waste since God is not moved by them. It is my unwavering faith which matters. It's easy for Daddy to say. He's a pastor."

Mummy gave her a chiding look. "What your father is trying to tell you is that wallowing in self-pity will not help. Of course, God cares about our emotions. He gave them to us."

She reached across the glass table and linked their hands. "Moni, when the enemy of our soul is prancing and roaring, it is not the time to grovel before its paws. It's the time for us to raise our voices in prayer."

Moni closed her eyes. She had prayed nonstop for months. She had even fasted a couple of times. Nothing had changed. She couldn't tell Mummy she was at the stage when she doubted a change was on the way.

On their way home, Shekinah sat in the back of the car with the hood of her sweater pulled over her head. Exhausted, Moni didn't say a word to her. As soon as she unlocked the door to the house, Shekinah ran up the stairs.

Not so fast, missy. She caught up with Shekinah in front of her bedroom door. "You don't get to escape me. We still need to talk about the incident at school."

Sighing, Shekinah dropped her duffel bag on the carpet. "Mom, I'm tired.

Can we do the talking thing tomorrow morning? *Please.*"

"Not going to work for me. This needs to be settled now." Moni folded her arms. "Shekinah Ogooluwa Badmus, why did you stand there watching as your friends bullied a helpless girl?"

Eyes averted, Shekinah shrugged. "I just did."

Moni couldn't believe her ears. "You just did? Shekinah, why are you so angry?"

"I'm surprised you don't know." She lifted her chin. "Well, Mom, it's because we are all angry people in this house. You think 'cause I'm in my room, I can't hear you and Dad saying all kinds of mean things to each other?" She laughed, but there was no humor in the sound. "Some days, wearing ear plugs doesn't even help."

The words made Moni shrink under a dark cloud of shame. She held out a hand. "Sweetie—"

"And if you want to know why I stood there, I'll tell you. It's because if I hadn't gone along, it would have been my head in the toilet bowl." Shekinah threw up her hands. "I have to protect myself."

What had happened to her child? "Please, let us help you," she begged. "Tell me what they did to you."

Shekinah looked directly at her. She was taken aback by how tired, and old Shekinah's eyes looked. They weren't the eyes of a teenager.

"There's nothing you can do." Shekinah stepped away from her. "I think you and Dad should help yourselves first."

Shekinah's tone was soft, intended to be respectful enough to not lend itself to more punishment, but Moni wasn't fooled. She felt temper in the way her daughter closed the door and worse than the temper, Moni felt Shekinah's pain.

Moni's hand hovered above the door knob. The child was right. She had no response to her words. They were the same words Mummy spoke to her. Defeated, Moni turned away and took slow steps toward her bedroom.

Chapter Seven

Dressed in a neon green tracksuit, Sam stuck his head into the classroom. "Thought you had gone home. Are we still on for tonight?"

Glad for the distraction, Debo dropped the pen he had been using to grade essays. "Yes, we are. Unless you're afraid to face your imminent annihilation?"

"I come from a long line of fierce, African warriors," Sam said as he strolled into the classroom. "I knock down ten bowling pins with one puff of air."

He laughed. "I can't wait to see you try. It looks like the rest of your day went well?"

"Thank God, it did. My early morning rant scared them into shaping up. For those who refused to read the memo and fall into line, a slip for detention hall made a world of difference."

He doffed an imaginary hat to Sam. "Mr. B for Ballistic!"

"You better recognize." Sam grinned. "Keeping kids in check since 1995. Well, I'm off to the gym. I'll see you after practice."

"Later."

Alone, Debo struggled to stay focused on his tasks. From the pained look on his friend's face, he knew a night of bowling wasn't going to solve Sam and Moni's problems. He could have told Sam to pray about the matter, but on several occasions, Sam had made it clear his prayers were no longer working. He was having problems in that area, too.

Debo tapped the end of his pen on the desk. If Adele was open to the idea, there was a last resort option he could share. It would then be up to Sam to say yes or no.

Accepting he wasn't going to get much done, Debo decided to head home.

His sons' school had a half-day program which meant Adele was responsible for picking up the boys. When Debo arrived home, he found them doing homework at the kitchen table. Even Number Four had his plastic numbers and letters laid out before him. He gave each boy a rub on the head as he walked around the table.

Debo felt the day's tension drain away. The house was tidy, and Adele had dinner simmering in the crockpot. "You, my darling, are a force of nature." He gave her a kid-friendly peck on the plump lips he couldn't get enough of.

Adele shook her head. "You better recognize."

"Not from you, too. Sam is such a bad influence on you."

She laughed. "Leave Sam out of this. I can be bad without any encouragement."

Number One gave his mom a surprised look. Nothing got past his sharp ears. "I thought you said we couldn't be bad?" he asked in a puzzled voice.

"Oops," Debo said to Adele. "Can I see you in the living room, please? Boys, stay here until your mom comes back. And you better be on your best behavior."

"I was just kidding. You heard your dad," Adele said with a wag of her finger before she followed him. "What's the matter?"

"I invited Sam and Moni for dinner. Sorry for the short notice."

Her furrowed brow cleared. "That's fine. There's always extra food."

"I talked to Sam. There's some drama going on between them." He gave her a quick summary of the morning's conversation. "I'm thinking of taking him to Triple X."

Adele's eyes widened. "Are you sure they can handle that kind of intervention?"

It was the same question he had asked himself when Mr. Bassey, the head usher at their church, invited him and Adele to their house fellowship. The conversation during their visit had been a real shocker.

"Spicing things up helped our relationship."

"Moni is a bit uptight. She may not be willing to make the sacrifice."

Debo frowned. "*Sacrifice?*" He had thought their attendance was a consensual decision. "Is there something you want to tell me?"

Adele looked away. "You're happy, aren't you?"

"Yeah. But your happiness matters, too."

"If you think taking Debo to Triple X will help them, I trust your judgment." As she bit her lower lip, Adele searched his face.

He was confused by the vague, questioning look in her narrowed eyes. "Please talk to me."

Silent, she shuffled from one foot to the other.

"Adele."

"Not now," she said as she visibly pulled herself together. "We're having guests. I better go and make sure the boys finish their homework." His breath caught as her fingers grazed his left cheek.

Long after Adele left the living room, Debo stood there thinking. He didn't like to leave things unfinished. Up to that moment, he had not known Adele harbored any reservations about their marriage intervention method. What else had he missed?

He took a deep breath as he headed for the staircase. He and Adele needed to talk. But first, he had to help Sam and Moni. It sounded like they needed immediate assistance.

Chapter Eight

Sam battled envy as he drove through Debo's Gordon Woods neighborhood and surveyed the houses. It would be real nice to live in one of these brick, luxury residences instead of the aging townhome he and Moni owned. With the state of their finances, it would take a miracle for them to move.

Like everything else he touched, Debo had struck gold when he met his wife. He and Adele met at McGill University. Adele came from old Montreal money and from what he saw of Debo and Adele's lifestyle, her mother didn't mind sharing her wealth.

Adele came to the door. "I was beginning to wonder where you were." She ushered him into the foyer. "Where are Moni and Shekinah? Debo said they were coming, too."

"I forgot to tell him they had planned a mother-daughter night out."

"Aww, that is so sweet."

He didn't bother to dispel Adele's fantasies of having a daughter when she had only given birth to sons by telling her Moni didn't see it that way. "It sure is."

Debo waved him over. Sam walked a short flight of stairs into the sunken living room and sat beside him on the couch. "So, how was basketball practice?" Debo asked.

"It went well. We have a good chance at winning our next league game."

"That's great news," Debo said, patting him on the back. "You've done some good work."

Sam felt some of his envy dissipate. Debo made it hard for someone to harbor ill feelings toward him. They talked about a few other things going on at the school and then Adele summoned them to dinner. As chunks of beef and potato melted in his mouth, Sam listened to his hosts chat with their boys about their day.

A mouthful of chilled white wine washed down an acrid taste of regret. Sam couldn't remember the last time he and the people at his house sat down to enjoy a family meal. Most days Shekinah ate in her room while Moni had her meals at the kitchen table. Yes, he had messed up by cheating on Moni. But how were they going to get back to being a family again when she wouldn't meet him halfway?

When it was time for him and Debo to head out to the bowling alley, Adele walked them to the door. "Please, don't forget to tell Moni to call me. We need to make plans for a mamas' night out."

"I'll tell her to call you."

Adele gave her husband a pointed look. "You and your kids are running this mama ragged with your constant demands."

Debo wrapped an arm around Adele's waist. "It's because we adore you, *ma cherie.*"

Sam looked away as Debo and Adele exchanged a kiss. Moni wouldn't even let him hold her hand in public. He wouldn't be surprised if Debo and Adele were to make a baby number five announcement.

By the time Debo parked the car in front of the bowling alley, his excitement about the evening had waned. The brief time spent at his friend's home had only confirmed he needed something more in his life. One night out wasn't going to change anything.

Debo unclipped his seatbelt and faced him. "You've suddenly gone quiet on me."

He should have known Debo would pick up on his mood. "I don't think a bowling game is going to fix this."

"Fix what?"

"My life."

"Sam, it's time we have the talk you've been avoiding. What is going on? How are things between you and Moni?"

"Pretty bad. I know you think the world of Moni, but she has changed. She's making my life hell."

"What's happening?"

He swallowed hard. "Well, things started going downhill when I told Moni about Joy."

Debo shook his head. "That's why I said not to tell Moni about the affair. It wasn't your finest moment, but you broke it off at the right time. Most women can't handle that level of honesty. The knowledge eats them alive."

"I should have listened to your advice. Moni throws Joy's name in my face every chance she gets."

Debo gave him a sympathetic look. "You had the best intentions."

The euphoria of basking in the attention of a young, beautiful woman ended when guilt set in. His mind reeled with thoughts of adultery. Moni had not deserved his behavior. He had been hopeful about their future when Moni had agreed to attend marriage counseling. Six months down the road, it was evident Moni couldn't move past his affair. The disdain he saw in her eyes every day had reduced him to the mess he was. "I can't bear it anymore. If not for my princess, I would have asked Moni for a divorce."

Debo blinked. "You're thinking of getting a divorce?"

Sam nodded. The heavy word sat between them. Even though it had been floating around in his head for months, it was the first time he'd voiced it.

"Wow. I know you guys haven't been showing up for Wednesday Bible study. But I didn't think things were divorce bad."

"This will sound strange, but in the last couple of years, it's as if I went from living in a multicoloured world to this black-and-white nightmare. Everything drags, and I don't know why."

"How?"

"Well, it feels like I lost something and I'm not even sure what it is." Sam shifted in his seat. "Joy made me feel wanted."

His friend looked worried. "I thought you'd said you were over her?"

"I am. But, I need to do something new, something exciting."

"Please, tell me you've not told anyone at church?"

"Do I look stupid?" His father-in-law no longer pastored their church but Sam could bet the current pastor sought his wise counsel over matters about church members. He didn't think a son-in-law status made him exempt from such discussions.

"Please, let's keep it that way until we've figured things out," Debo said. "I know you guys love each other. If we all put our heads together, we can fix this."

Captain Debo to the rescue again. Sam shook his head. "I'm not even sure if I want it fixed."

"Is there someone else?"

It would have been easier for him to move on if he had a woman waiting in the wings. "If I had someone, I wouldn't need to beg my wife for sex."

"*Ouch.* There's a good reason why the Bible says couples shouldn't deprive each other."

"Moni has forgotten that part of her Bible," he said. "We're stuck in the 'an eye for an eye' section."

Debo looked stunned. "She's having an affair, too?"

"Moni's not that kind of woman. She's more interested in watching me suffer."

"What you guys need is a marriage intervention."

"A marriage intervention?"

"When Adele and I went through our stuff, spicing up things in the bedroom strengthened our relationship."

He and Debo talked about most things, and this was the first time Debo had mentioned marital problems. "When did you guys go through stuff? And what do you mean by spicing things up?"

"Every marriage goes through stuff," Debo said. His vagueness indicated he wasn't going to go into specifics. "You sound pretty desperate."

Sam nodded. "I don't know how much longer I can take Moni's indifference."

They stared at each other for several moments until Debo broke the silence. "If you're not ready to go home, there's somewhere I'd like to take you."

The words piqued his curiosity. "Feel free to lead the way."

Chapter Nine

His friend was quiet throughout the forty-minute drive to downtown Toronto. Sam couldn't figure out why a strange energy had settled in the car.

Debo parked in a cul-de-sac off Bloor Street and led the way. A brisk walk took them to the steps of a three-story brick building. Sam looked up. The awning over the entrance had the words "Triple X" written across it in splashes of white paint. It seemed like a nightclub. Neon lights flashed on either side of the building. Sam knew his friend was not a clubber or whatever people who frequented nightclubs were called these days.

He watched as the tight t-shirt wearing dudes manning the door ushered in a group of scantily dressed women. Surprised, he turned to his friend. "You brought me to a nightclub?"

"It's a different kind of club." Debo's response came quickly. "You did say you were looking for something new and exciting. Or, have you changed your mind?"

Undecided, Sam stared at the building. His curiosity got the best of him.

Since they were already there, he might as well see what Debo had to offer. "Let's do this."

"Here we go." Debo walked toward the building's entrance.

Sam followed. At the door, Debo exchanged greetings and handed over three twenty dollar bills.

One of the dudes held the door open, and they walked into a dimly-lit room. It was packed. With gleaming hardwood floors and several large screen televisions, Triple X looked like a sports bar. The sight of a woman curled around a shiny stripper pole at the other side of the room made Sam's steps falter. Things must have changed since the last time he visited a sports bar.

Debo knew his way around. Giving the bartenders a friendly nod, he led the way upstairs.

Half-way up the flight of stairs, Debo turned to him. "You're going to see some risqué things on these floors. But, I want you to keep an open mind."

Sam shrugged. In his days, he had been to a couple of nightclubs. "Sure."

Nothing could have prepared him for the sight of naked couples sprawled on leather beds partially shielded by red velvet curtains. Inside the rooms, patrons watched porn flicks.

Moans from bodies entangled in beds mounted against the wall made Sam's eyes bulge. The place was no sports bar.

Walking past a hot tub and folks wrapped in towels, Debo pointed out stands for condom boxes, disinfectant wipes, and pornographic magazines. "They're big on keeping things clean and safe here," he said, matter-of-factly. "You should see some other clubs in the city. Pretty disgusting places."

Sam stared at his friend. His body tingled from a sensory overload. He followed Debo as they made their way downstairs.

He was too rattled to protest when the bartender asked him to hand over three twenty dollar bills for one cocktail pitcher. Debo carried their tiny bowls of free peanuts.

After a couple of glasses, Sam finally found his voice. "What on earth brought you here?"

"Curiosity. When Adele and I decided to give swinging a try, I wanted to see what happens in a sex club."

Adele's girl-next-door face flashed before his eyes. "*Swinging?* As in wife swapping?"

Debo nodded.

"You're pulling my leg, right?"

"Nope. Like I told you before, Adele and I came to a place where we needed a marriage intervention. When someone first told me about swinging as intervention, I was convinced they had lost their mind. I haven't been here in years. I brought you here so you could see what worldly swinging looks like. I felt it was the only way you would appreciate the Christian alternative Adele and I have come to cherish."

Sam did a double take. He must have misunderstood Debo's words. "There is a Christian alternative to swinging? How is that possible?"

"It is," Debo insisted. "The alternative is for us Christians who believe we've been called to live an abundant life. And contrary to what the super religious folks say, it includes having an active sex life with our partners and others in a free and loving environment."

Debo sounded as if he was reciting a scripted sales pitch. Sam's confusion grew. It'd been some time since he opened his Bible. It laid gathering dust inside his nightstand. He didn't need to take it to church anymore since overhead screens displayed Scripture passages and they used devotionals at home.

He still had a hard time reconciling the abundant life Scripture Debo had described. "Are you telling me this swinging thing passes the Bible test?"

"Have you watched the news lately?" Debo asked. "The world is going to hell in a hand basket. Trust me. God has better things to worry about."

He agreed watching news was enough to plunge someone into depression. "I still don't get it. Isn't swinging adultery?"

"Since Adele and I had both agreed to do this, we're not cheating on each other. There's no creeping around behind each other's back. We get to enjoy the freedom of exploring our sexuality which has improved our relationship."

Sam's mind went back to Adele's hugs and kisses. Could it be that all along, she had been warming him up for a swinging session?

The thought made him avoid Debo's eyes. "What's this alternative thing?" he asked.

"Well, for the past four years, Adele and I have been part of an active group meeting in the safety of our homes. Since we're all Christians, I promise you, it's clean stuff. No pornographic materials. No voyeurism; nothing that would make you uncomfortable."

The thought of swinging was uncomfortable enough, Sam thought. He could see how different sexual partners could fulfill an uninhibited man's fantasies. However, most women had jealousy issues. "And the wives don't mind?"

"Nope. They too love the freedom it brings." Debo gave him a questioning look. "Since Moni was most likely a virgin when you guys married, I'm sure she would have developed some curiosity about another man."

As close as he was to Debo, they didn't talk about such things. "I doubt it," he said with an uneasy laugh. "Moni's pretty straight-laced." He peered at his friend's face. "How do you feel about sharing Adele?"

"I wouldn't share another human being. Adele agreed. We're all adults who know the rules. Believe me. There are no emotions involved."

Sam still had a hard time wrapping his mind around the idea. "Bro, how come you kept all this from me?"

"You weren't ready for it. And from the vibe I'm getting tonight, you're still not." Debo gave him a pointed look. "We both know that we church folks are quick to judge. So, let's keep this between us, okay?"

Sam reached for the cocktail pitcher and poured himself another glass. He should have gone to the bowling alley.

Chapter Ten

It was almost midnight when Sam entered his house. Debo had insisted on him spending some time at their home to make sure he was okay to drive. Walking by the living room, he saw Moni curled up on the couch. Sam shook his head. He'd told her several times not to wait up for him. But she wouldn't go to bed until everyone was back in the house.

Seeing the way her neck was positioned, he stopped. If she stayed that way, it would hurt in the morning. He moved closer to wake her. Before he could touch her shoulder, Moni spoke. "Your princess Shekinah was suspended today."

Sam sighed. He would have appreciated a "hello" or a "how was your day" greeting before hearing about more problems. He dropped in one of the chairs. "For how long?"

"A week."

He kicked off his shoes. "I guess Shekinah will be going to your parent's house?"

Moni rolled over to face him. "You don't want to know what she did?"

Despite attempts to distract himself, the sights and sounds of Triple X had put his mind on lockdown. He needed time alone with his thoughts.

He shrugged. "I figure you'll tell me when you're ready. Frankly, with the school staff out to get Shekinah, it could be anything."

"Oh Sam, your delusion is pathetic. Of course, the school is out to get your princess." She shook her head. "This morning, Shekinah was hypnotized and led into the girls' bathroom to watch her friends bully another child."

Jaw clenched, he stood. Moni's passive-aggressive personality thrived on sarcasm. It just made his blood boil. "This is going nowhere. I'm off to bed."

"And this is why I don't let you know when the school calls," Moni said to his back. "You've yet to have anything useful to add to the conversations."

When Shekinah's school challenges began, he had tried to work with Mr. Scott and her teacher. When they realized he wasn't going to do everything they recommended, their calls to him stopped. Moni became their contact person since she was ready to sacrifice Shekinah on the altar. "Before you start throwing stones, it's obvious your strictness is not yielding better results."

Moni looked like she was searching for an appropriate response when he walked away. Upstairs, he paused in front of Shekinah's bedroom door to listen. He couldn't hear any sounds. She was a lot like him. As a teenager, he had given his parents lots of gray hairs. But when he started going to church with Debo, he had straightened himself out. He was confident Shekinah would do well when given the space to breathe. The constant policing at home and school was not helping.

Moni was still downstairs by the time he got into bed and pulled the duvet over his head. On some days, she chose the couch over sleeping next to him. That was her choice. If she wanted a kink in her neck, so be it.

***

Sam tossed and turned. He tried, but he couldn't stop thinking about his visit to Triple X. For him, it felt like he was trying to un-ring a bell. It was impossible.

Without saying anything to each other, he and Debo pretended the evening had not taken place.

One thing his friend said during their visit to Triple X played over in his head. Debo had insisted there was no Scriptural evidence a swinging lifestyle was sinful. If it were written anywhere in the Bible, Debo would know. Before leaving for teacher's college, Debo had also spent two years at a theological seminary up in Northern Ontario. He still wasn't completely sure why Debo left the program three months before his graduation and returned home. Debo never offered to share, and Sam assumed his reasons were intensely personal. The departure from seminary did not affect his ability to obtain a position in leadership in the church.

In fact, shortly after he came home, Moni's father, who at the time pastored their church, selected Debo to serve as a deacon. When the position became vacant, Sam had hoped it would be his assignment. Even while he was at the university, he'd made himself available to the church. He had delivered meals to homebound members, worked with their prison ministry and pounded the streets as they shared the gospel with Brampton's homeless population.

Sam was disappointed, but he'd gotten over the slight and moved on. God was a rewarder of those faithful to him. That was teaching rammed into their heads. However, despite his patience, a promotion was elusive as his business ventures failed. He had done his part by showing up to do God's work when needed, but his reward, the prosperity which followed good works, had eluded him.

He glanced at Moni. With her alarm clock disabled for the weekend, she was sound asleep. Sam caught a glimpse of the young woman he had fallen in love with. As the pastor's daughter, their courtship took place under the church's giant microscope. Since he was not used to the level of scrutiny, it had been stressful watching what he said or did. But, he had also been proud to be the first person to break through Moni's ice princess exterior.

Sam wanted to touch her, but he was afraid she would wake up. Every time he saw the contempt in her eyes, it broke him down, further turning his guilt into indifference.

The more he thought about it, the more he wanted to give Debo's proposed marriage intervention a try. He doubted anything could worsen the pathetic condition of their relationship.

Sam rolled out of bed and made his way to his basement office. It was best he called Debo before he changed his mind.

An early riser, Debo picked up the call. "Good morning. Everything good?" Debo sounded worried.

"Yes. Can't stop thinking about our conversation."

"And?"

"You had mentioned you guys held meetings?"

"We call them play parties. Sounds better to me."

He guessed in a way Debo and the others were playing with fire amongst a host of things. "Can I attend one?"

"Well, we have one scheduled for this weekend. You can stay until the end of the meet and greet segment."

"Sounds good to me. Thanks, man."

"Anytime. I have to go. I can hear the boys."

"Later." Sam ended the call and placed his head on the desk. It was going to be a long week.

Chapter Eleven

Sam was stunned into silence when he showed up at the address Debo gave him and Mrs. Bassey, the head usher's wife, opened the door.

"Brother Sam! Welcome." She placed a hand on his arm. "Double D told us you were coming."

Sam almost choked on his saliva. *Double D?* He should have asked Debo for more information about the evening's hosts. Stuttering, he inclined his head. "Good afternoon."

Sam took off his shoes and placed them on the entryway shoe rack. He was silent as Mrs. Bassey carried on a monologue all the way to her living room. "When we meet here you must call me Ekaete," she insisted. "Have you heard?"

"Yes, Mrs. Bassey. I mean…Ekaete."

She gave him another pat on the arm. "You'll get used to this."

Before they left the school, Debo had assured him he and Adele would be present. "Is Debo here?"

"No," she said. "They're just running late."

Looking around, Sam experienced the second shock of the evening when he saw the Abegunde's. The previous Sunday, he and the congregation had pledged their support as a church family when the first-time parents dedicated their three-month-old baby.

Odosa and his wife, Ngozi gave him hugs. They were also long-time church members.

Sam declined Mrs. Bassey's offer of homemade meat pie and poured himself a cup of punch. He followed her when she insisted on introducing him to the strangers in the room.

"Brother, these are the Larkins, Leah and Harry." They exchanged handshakes. "The Larkins attend the church down the road from ours."

"We're all family," Sam said in a joking tone.

Harry winked. "I think the term kissing cousins would fit."

They laughed.

Hearing the doorbell, Mrs. Bassey excused herself. Minutes later, he heard Debo's laughter float down the hallway. Debo's face lit up when he stepped into the room and saw him. "You made it."

Sam returned the hug. "Glad you're here. I was going to leave in fifteen minutes."

He kept some space between them as Adele gave him her customary kiss on the cheek. He and Debo had agreed that if he were to join the group, their wives were off limits. It certainly would have made things awkward between them.

"Our babysitter was late," Debo explained. "Let me say hello to the rest of group before I walk you to the car."

When they stepped outside the house, Debo gave him a light punch on the arm. "So, what do you think?"

"Man, I almost had a heart attack when Mrs. Bassey opened the door. Aren't they grandparents?"

"They are. You're never too old to work on your marriage."

They stood beside his car. "Will Moni and I have to host, too?"

"We had decided the Bassey's would hold the parties since they don't have children still living at home. We do have a sign-up sheet for those weekends when they have guests or are out of town."

It made sense to him. "Cool."

Debo stopped at the end of the driveway. "Still have some reservations?"

Even though the warm welcome had made him feel less uneasy about the intervention, they might as well have gathered for Bible study.

"How do you guys go from sipping punch, talking about the kids, to...you know what?"

"During the meet and greet segment, you're expected to check out the other couples and initiate conversations to explore possibilities. Although, given the small size of our group, people tend to have regular partners. When we have new members or visitors, it's my job to make sure they don't get neglected."

"Sounds pretty organized. I like that."

"I can see you're warming up to the idea. What does Moni think?"

"My plan is for us to talk tonight." Knowing Moni there would be a fight, but he had a plan for helping her see things his way.

Debo glanced in the direction of the house. "I've got to go. They're probably waiting for me to get things rolling. Tell Moni I said hello."

"Sure. I'll see you at church on Sunday."

He watched as Debo hurried back to the house. He tried to imagine what it would be like to know Moni was having sex with another man while he held someone else in his arms in a nearby room. Sam turned away and opened the car door. The visit had left him with more questions than answers.

Chapter Twelve

To her surprise and delight, the movie date Sam had forced on her had gone well. During the drive home, Shekinah expressed some interest in learning how to make Nigerian meals.

She had learned by standing beside her mother and watching, but Shekinah wanted a recipe with actual measurements. A pinch of this and a dash of that didn't work for Generation Z. The YouTube channel they'd found had hundreds of Nigerian recipes, and they had agreed to try them out.

Shekinah stopped the video clip so she could write down the next step in the fried pastry ball recipe.

Moni smiled proudly. "I can't wait to tell your grandma you know how to make puff-puff."

Shekinah grinned. "Grandma would probably say it's not an authentic recipe." She mimicked her grandmother's voice. "What do you young cooks know?" She tapped her chest. "The measurements for ingredients have to come from your heart."

Shekinah's Canadian accent sounded nothing like her grandmother's.

Moni laughed. "Missy, your heart is on the other side. And I'm going to tell on you."

"Grandma wouldn't say anything. I'm her favorite grandchild."

"I've known her the longest," Moni pointed out. "I know the right things to say and do."

Shekinah shook her head. "That's not playing fair."

"You started it. Don't dish out anything you can't take. I think when you've mastered the Jollof rice recipe, we'll invite your grandparents over for dinner."

Shekinah nodded as she ended the YouTube clip. "The recipe is all written out."

"Good job." Moni opened her cupboard and brought out her mixing bowls. "Let's do this."

She read out the next steps while Shekinah measured out the flour, salt, sugar, water, and yeast. Even though the recipe had not listed nutmeg as an ingredient, she asked Shekinah to add some. Moni inhaled deeply as the aroma of the spice filled the room.

"Next, you have to knead the dough."

"What is that?"

She wiped off a streak of flour from Shekinah's face. "I'll show you what to do."

Shekinah giggled as she worked her fingers through the dough. "It feels like Play-Doh."

"It sure does. Put it back in a bowl. We have to let it rise."

Shekinah referred to her directions and frowned. "An hour's a long time to wait."

Everything had to happen now for this instant gratification generation. They were McDonalized. Moni remembered learning that term in some Sociology course in college.

"Just thank your stars you live where you don't have to go into the forest to hunt for an animal, kill it, and prepare the meat before cooking with firewood."

Shekinah gave her a skeptical look. "I'm sure you never had to hunt for your food."

"Just be glad you don't have to."

When they were ready, Moni closed her eyes as she bit into one of the fried pastry balls. The light brown puff-puff ball had the right crispy texture outside and a sweet, chewy inside. Moni licked her fingers. "They are so good. I'm not sure we'll be able to save some for your dad."

"Mom! We fried three-dozen balls. You can't eat them all."

"Oh, Missy. Trust me. I can eat them all. The real question is how would my hips handle it?" As Shekinah giggled, Moni narrowed her eyes. "I should have known you would fight for your father's interest."

For the umpteenth time that evening, she wondered where Sam was. In the past week, he had seemed preoccupied, and he had been vague with his destination when he left the house. Could he be cheating on her again? The thought made her mouth sour. *Moni, stop it.*

Shekinah walked over and wrapped her arms around Moni's waist. "That was fun, Mom. Thank you."

"You're welcome. Now, it's time to clean up."

Shekinah frowned. "This is the part I don't like. Can we load the dishwasher?"

Mimicking what she and her brother had named their father's 'no nonsense allowed at this address' voice, Moni shook her head. "My friend, before I open this eye, you had better move toward the sink."

Shekinah smiled. "Yes, ma'am."

***

Shekinah was in bed by the time Sam came home. They sat at the kitchen table, a plate of puff-puff in between them. "Your daughter saved these for you."

Sam ate two before speaking. "These are delicious. You guys had fun?"

"We did." She had prepared for some attitude and tears from Shekinah. "Not sure why, but our movie date helped. Thank you."

"I haven't heard those words from you in a long time." Sam's boyish grin took the sting from his words.

She felt a pang of guilt. "I've not been a very kind wife, have I?"

"My behavior led us here." Sam pushed aside his plate. "Moni, do you think you can find it in your heart to forgive me? Not the 'I forgive you, but I'm going to throw your sin in your face whenever I'm angry with you' version, but a genuine forgiveness."

Moni wrestled with her feelings. As far as she was concerned, if Sam can forget his wedding vows, nothing was stopping him from forgetting them again. If she didn't want her scarred heart to be crushed a second time, she had to stay behind her walls. "What you did is hard to forget."

"I guess the answer is no." Sam pushed back his chair. "Thanks for the puff-puff."

Moni opened her mouth to call him back. Perhaps they could find some common ground. Changing her mind, she stood to clear the table.

Chapter Thirteen

It was five minutes past eleven and Sam wasn't home. Tired of waiting for her father, Shekinah excused herself and went up to her bedroom.

Moni emptied her glass of water and placed it back on the coffee table. She was tired of worrying herself silly over someone who acted as if he wasn't accountable to anyone. Sam knew she found it hard to sleep when he or Shekinah were not home.

Relief coursed through her when Sam walked in shortly before midnight. Now that she knew he was okay, she was livid.

"You're still up?" Sam asked.

He moved close, and Moni wrinkled her nose at the smell the alcohol on his breath. "Where have you been?"

Sam flopped beside her on the couch. "We need to talk."

The serious tone of his voice brought a déjà vu moment.

Her hand shook as she picked up the television remote control. Shekinah's bedroom was right above their living room; she didn't want her to hear any part of the conversation.

She forced herself to take deep breaths as she searched for an infomercial channel. She had known it was only a matter of time before Sam cheated again.

Moni increased the volume and dropped the remote in her lap. "I'm listening."

"This past year, all we've done is fight each other." He cleared his throat. "I've done a lot of thinking. It would be best for us to get a divorce."

A burning sensation radiated across her chest. "*A divorce?*"

"Yes. I'm not happy. If you're honest, neither are you. What's the point of staying together 'til we're old and gray when we can cut our losses now and start all over?"

Confused, Moni stared at him. She had been expecting the news of an affair. Not a request for a divorce. "Let me get this straight," she said after gathering her thoughts. "You want a divorce because you're not happy?"

Sam stood from the couch and began pacing. "You make it sound like happiness should not be a valid expectation in a marriage?"

"I agree happiness is important." Moni's mind went to the child upstairs. "But, this marriage is not only about *our* happiness. Have you thought about what a divorce would do to Shekinah?"

Sam shook his head. "Shekinah's old enough to understand parents are human and have lives, too. And contrary to what you think, divorce is not new to her. Even at our school, a sizeable population of the students is from single or blended families."

Sam sounded as if he had given his request much thought. Moni moved to the edge of her seat. "We can go back to counseling," she offered. "We're in a different spot now."

He snorted. "Moni, I never moved. I still remember what happened the last time we tried. *You* decided you no longer wanted to attend."

The need to defend herself brought Moni to her feet. "I was tired of listening to you rave about how that woman made you feel good about yourself. Like it was my fault when the truth is you couldn't keep your pants zipped."

Sam threw up his hands. "I knew you were going to bring that old matter up. Moni Badmus, just let it go."

Moni took in his frustration and tried to force the sarcasm out of her voice. "Well, if you've forgotten your marriage vows, I haven't. As bad as things are, I don't want a divorce. God hates divorce."

Sam's snicker made her glare at him. "*Please.* I know what God hates. And dishonest people are amongst them. You're tired of this marriage, just as much as I am."

Their eyes caught for several moments.

Sam continued, "Moni, look at us. We treat each other like we're enemies."

Moni acknowledged that he had a point. Things were horrible, but she wasn't ready to give up. "All marriages go through ups and downs. We just need to figure out how to get out of this down valley we're in."

"If you're bent on working things out, I sure hope regular sex is part of your plan."

"Is that all you think about?"

Sam glared at her. "What's the point of having a wife?"

"You know what happens on some of the days I do try. There is a medication for the kind of problem you have."

"I don't have any problem in that department," Sam declared. "It is just hard to stay in a romantic mood when your wife's body turns to wood as soon as you touch her."

Moni, the words of the reckless pierce like swords, but the tongue of the wise brings healing.

She snarled a retort. "I guess Joy had a more accommodating body?"

Sam threw up his hands. "Here we go again. When will you leave the poor woman alone and admit this relationship has always been about what Madam Moni wants, Madam Moni gets?"

She didn't have any sympathies for Joy. "That's not true. Well, not entirely," she added. "I try my best to ask for your input before making decisions."

Sam's mocking laugh grated on her nerves. "Remember, it's your fault we have only one child. All because of a lousy career opportunity."

Her infertility problems came as a shock. "It was a stupid mistake. I'd thought there would be plenty of time for us to expand our family. Sam, I'm sorry. And I've told you so several times."

"Just like I've told you I'm sorry for the affair," he pointed out. "Have my apologies meant anything to you?"

Faint, she sat on the couch. How did they get to this point? Moni wondered as tears flooded her eyes. She blinked them back. It wasn't the time for her to show weakness. "Getting a divorce can't be our only option."

Sam ran a hand over his head. "I don't understand you. You're not prepared to change anything. You won't let me go. You just want to see me suffer."

She had known he was frustrated by her detachment in bed. Sam had a high libido. The truth was she'd been punishing him by withholding sex. She knew it was wrong but wasn't that what all cheaters said when they got caught? "Yes, I had wanted you to suffer. Not anymore."

Sam froze. "Come again?"

She would have to dig down for some forgiveness. "I don't want a divorce."

Sam sat and reached for Moni's hand. His palm was as sweaty as hers.

"For us to forge ahead, I need to know if you're ready to work on our relationship."

Moni squared her shoulders. "I am."

"You'll be open to the things I think are important?" Sam asked.

"Yes."

"Then, there's something else we need to talk about."

Her heart raced as Sam told her about his visit to Triple X and the swinging group. Repulsed, she snatched her hand away. "Sam, you can't be serious."

His soft response chilled her. "I am."

Moni's hand went to her mouth.

Sam stood. "If divorce becomes our only option, remember Shekinah is old enough to have a say about where she wants to live. We both know what her preference would be. Good night."

Chapter Fourteen

Moni's eyes scanned the letter she had found in her work mailbox. The letter, signed by the company's human resource manager, advised her that effective from the next pay period, she would receive a substantial raise.

Instead of doing a victory fist pump, she flung the letter on her desk before covering her face. Anxiety muddled her mind and held her stomach in a vicious grip. There was no room for joy.

Moni dropped her hands. She was not being paid to focus on personal problems during company time. She switched on her computer and re-opened the document she'd been working on. Moni rubbed the base of her thumbs over her eyes, wondering how she was going to meet her looming deadline. The smiles she'd been getting from management since the DressCo deal went through were sure to disappear if she messed up this assigned sales pitch.

Shoulders hunched, Moni willed herself to focus as she tried reading the document from the beginning. Despite her resolve, nothing was sinking in.

The words blurred and her mind wandered off again. Her thoughts traveled back to the first time she'd met Sam. He was twenty, and she had just turned eighteen. He was a new member of their church. He and Debo were serving as members of her father's select group of armour bearers.

As a little girl, she'd thought the young men carried real armours. But their role was more like the pastor's helper. They carried her father's Bible, bottles of water and other necessary chores. Because the group of young men visited their home for meals, Moni grew to know them. Her parents' undisguised acceptance of Sam and those warm childhood memories made it easy to love him. With her parents against dating just for the fun of it, Sam had been her first and last serious boyfriend.

Through their one year courtship and twenty-year marriage, her parents had continued to be his champions. Moni imagined how shocked they would be if she told them what he wanted her to do.

Moni thought that Sam would come back to say he was mistaken. Instead, he bounced around the house looking as if he had rediscovered his life's purpose.

Yes, she struggled with staying committed to God. Still, Moni found it hard to accept that swinging was the right thing for them to do. Even if a husband and wife agreed to swing, she doubted it made it good for them to commit what she saw as a sin.

Her tired eyes landed on the picture frame propped up on her desk. Shekinah's round face smiled at Moni from the grade eight graduation picture. Her fingers reached out and caressed the glass.

After he'd told her about the play parties, Sam had declared that Shekinah's behavioral problems were linked to the sorry state of their marriage. Like she didn't know this already.

Things were much better than they had been in months, but Shekinah was still her father's daughter. In the event of a divorce, Shekinah may decide to live at Sam's house. He wouldn't discourage her. And if she did, Moni knew that she would lose her daughter. Sam couldn't grasp that this wasn't the time for them to be Shekinah's friend.

Contrary to what Shekinah must think when she said no to her requests, she loved her. How could she not? The thought of losing her only child had stripped ten pounds off her body in just two weeks.

Conscious of the thin walls of her office cubicle, Moni placed her hand over her mouth to muffle a cry. She didn't know what to do.

Beloved, trust Me.

Tears filled her eyes as fear's roar continued to build inside her mind.

Chapter Fifteen

Debo went around and welcomed everyone. He then sat on the chair facing the Bassey's front door. He had announced to the group that Sam and Moni were joining them for the evening and he wanted them to see a friendly face when they walked in.

"Double D, can I get you something to eat or drink?"

Mrs. Bassey was always trying to feed him.

"I just finished the lovely meat pie you made," he said. I'll have something else to eat later."

"I'll make sure you do," Mrs. Bassey promised.

Adele came to sit beside him. "People are getting restless. Are you sure they're coming?"

From what he could see, people were still having lively conversations. "Are *you* getting restless?"

Adele frowned. "What do you mean by that?"

"I've been watching you and Mr. Bassey. You don't have to look so eager to leave the room."

Adele raised an eyebrow. "Don't tell me you're jealous?"

Debo snickered. "Of him? A potbellied grandpa is no competition for me."

"Then, what's your problem?"

Adele's laughter in Mr. Bassey's presence was a little too loud. The look on Mr. Bassey's face was proprietary. "Show some decorum, will you?"

Adele raised an eyebrow. "Decorum at a swinging party?"

"Why not? I didn't think your self-respect was situational."

Adele's face flushed. "You wanted this, remember?"

He was beginning to regret it. "We can stop coming."

Adele shrugged. "Fine. Let's go home."

He had not expected her to call his bluff. Debo opened and closed his mouth.

She gave him a smug smile. "We both know you aren't going anywhere."

He was relieved when the doorbell rang. Mr. Bassey opened the door for Sam and Moni. Moving as if she had wooden stumps for legs, Moni looked as if she was on the verge of tears.

Debo watched as Sam placed a hand on the small of Moni's back and nudged her forward. When Moni only took two steps, he glared at her before marching ahead.

He felt somewhat responsible for Moni's obvious discomfort. Sam shouldn't have forced her to attend since it defeated the whole purpose of strengthening their relationship.

"It looks like Moni's having a hard time," he said to Adele. "Perhaps you can talk to her about your experience? You'll have a female perspective to offer."

"I don't want to get involved in their problems." Standing, Adele gave him a chaste kiss on the cheek. "See you later."

He stood as Sam hurried toward him. "Hey. We made it."

"We?" In Sam's eagerness, he hadn't noticed when his wife turned and hightailed out of the house. "Where's Moni?"

"Moni is right…" Sam's jaw dropped when he looked back and saw that she was gone. "But she had agreed to come."

"Do you have the car keys?"

Sam jiggled the bunch in his pocket.

"Then she's probably just sitting outside. Is it okay for me to talk to her?"

Sam looked relieved. "Please. I don't know what else to do."

He gave the go ahead for the party to start before leaving the house. He found Moni seated on the hood of their car. The crunch of his footsteps on the landscaping rocks must have startled her. She jumped with her hands held in a karate pose. He'd forgotten that she ran the self-defense classes for women at their church.

"Moni, it's me."

She didn't look happy to see him. "It can be dangerous to sneak up on people."

"I was just checking up on you."

Her arms fell to her side. "I needed to breathe in some clean air." She wrinkled her nose. "There was a funky human smell in there."

He ignored her nastiness. Sam had not gotten her on board as he thought. Debo leaned against the car. "Your husband was wondering where you were."

Moni snickered. "I guess he wasn't concerned enough to come out and look for me?"

"Sam didn't think you would want to talk to him."

"So as always, he sends his bestie to do his dirty work. Debo, how long are you going to keep on cleaning up after him?"

In his big brother role, he had spent hours pleading on Sam's behalf. "I guess you're still mad about Joy?"

"That's old news," she said. "Right now, as far as I'm concerned, you're the evil serpent who wandered into my garden and twisted Sam's gullible mind."

She gave him more credit than he deserved. Shaking his head, he sat beside her. "I understand you don't want to attend our parties."

"You mean your orgies?"

Debo pressed his lips together to keep from chuckling. "It isn't like that, Moni." He paused for a moment. "I thought Sam had explained how things work. The only reason I told him about our little group was to help you guys work on your marriage. I know it all sounds a bit scary and different, but the first time is the hardest."

"Debo, we've known each other for ages. I've always seen you as a man of integrity." She shook her head. "You're one good actor. I'm sure if you were to take up acting, you would land a movie role in no time."

His smile faded at the insult. "Was I wrong to come out here to check on you?"

"We both know why you came. We've already discussed that. What I want to know is how can you, a deacon, a Bible teacher, think this is the way for us to go? That this is right for any married couple?" Her voice broke. Debo could hear the pain, and he could see her frustration as she twisted the strap of her handbag into a knot. She continued, "I know that Sam listens to you. He wouldn't have considered this nonsense if you had not given him your approval."

"Moni, your husband is a full-grown man. I just gave him an option. It is still his choice to make." He straightened his body. "Here's some free advice.

If you want to keep your home, you had better figure out what you're going to do, because long before any serpent wandered in your perfect little garden, you had both let the weeds grow untamed. Good night."

He could feel Moni's eyes boring into his back as he walked away. Moni was right about one thing. It was time he stopped cleaning up Sam's messes. He had not enjoyed being the subject of the scorn in Moni's eyes.

Chapter Sixteen

Sam clenched his hands at the sight of Debo's grim face. Debo nodded for him to come over. Sam hurried to his side. "What did she say?"

"We need some privacy." Debo led the way to the kitchen. He closed the door behind them. "Moni is not ready for this."

He couldn't mask his disappointment. "I can't stay tonight?"

Debo gave him a sympathetic look, "We won't have an even number."

"I was looking forward to this," he said, hoping Debo would offer to sit out on the party. He was out of luck because Debo's next words did not include that option.

"You may have to give this intervention method some more thought," Debo said.

Sam nodded agreement. "Thanks for trying."

Debo patted him on the shoulder. "I'll see you on Monday."

Moni was missing when he went to their car. Sam swung his head around. Where could she have gone? Half an hour later, he concluded she must have taken a cab home.

Prepared for battle, Sam was surprised to walk into a dark house. He switched on the entry light and called out, "Moni. Shekinah."

When silence returned to him, he began to wonder where they could have gone.

Looking around, he saw a piece of folded paper on the kitchen island. The note addressed to him said Moni and Shekinah were at her parents. They would be back the next day. He left the note on the island. Moni was only delaying the inevitable.

His mind went back to Debo and to what he was missing that night. He squeezed his eyes shut, but the vivid images of what he could have been doing with Ngozi kept scrolling through his mind. Clips from the things he had seen at Triple X followed.

He cradled his head and groaned.

Debo didn't know that Sam had been going back to the club on his own. All he had done during visits was watch. He had hoped Moni would change her mind.

He took a deep breath. With the stunt Moni had pulled on him, he deserved a good time. And he was going to Triple X to get it.

Sam switched off the light and walked out of the house.

***

Moni gave him a wary look when she stepped into their home office. "Are you still mad at me?"

He was too relaxed to be mad at anyone. "I was. You made me look foolish."

Arms crossed, Moni leaned her back against his desk. "That wasn't my intention. When I heard Odosa's voice, I had to get out of there. I couldn't believe he and Ngozi were there. We had just been in choir practice together."

"The bottom line is…are you coming back?"

"I don't know. I don't want to." She gave him a guilty look. "I'm sure Debo told you I was rude to him."

Sam sat back in his seat. "No, he didn't."

"Well, I more or less called him Satan," she whispered.

"Debo is not the problem."

"I know. All night, I thought about our conversation. Debo was right that we had allowed external things to affect our relationship. We do need a marriage intervention. Just not this one."

"I'm sorry you feel that way. It's either we do this or we file for a divorce. Your decision."

"Sam, what's come over you? You just want to throw everything we've worked for away?"

"You know what? I'm done having these pointless conversations. I don't need your permission to file the papers."

Running fingers through her braids, Moni took a deep breath. "I need more time."

His mind went back to Ngozi's enchanting figure. "Moni, I already gave you time."

Tears filled her eyes and spilled onto her cheeks. "Getting a divorce can't be our only option. Please, don't do this to us."

Sam took in her pitiful appearance. Guilt nagged at him a bit. While they were courting, Moni had told him she'd been planning her wedding since she was ten years old. A family meant everything to her. There had to be a part of her that would fight to keep her dream. He straightened in his chair. "Okay, you have twenty-one days to figure things out."

"Twenty-one days?"

Sam nodded. "Yes. One day for each year we've been spent together."

"Well, miracles still happen," Moni said as she headed for the door.

"I believe in miracles, too."

She didn't respond.

***

"So, how was your weekend?" Debo asked as they made their way across the school parking lot.

He gave Debo a smug grin. "Triple X delivered the goods."

Debo's eyes bugged. "You went back?"

He decided not to tell Debo it wasn't his first time. He was entitled to some secrets. "It was the best decision I've made in a very long time."

"You be careful out there. It's a rough kind of world."

Sam pushed out his chest. "I can handle it."

"Mhmm."

He could sense that Debo wanted to say more, but he didn't.

"What did Moni say about the play parties?" Debo asked when they stopped beside his car.

"She said she needs some more time."

"And?"

"She has twenty-one days starting from Saturday."

Debo shook his head. "That's cold. An ultimatum isn't the way to go about things."

"That's easy for you to say. Adele is on board."

"I didn't have to threaten her."

"People need different levels of incentive."

"What happens if Moni comes back and says no?"

"I'm moving out, and we're getting a divorce."

Debo paused before speaking again. Sam could tell he still didn't agree with his strong-arm tactic. "That decision is a big one. I guess you can start going to a different church. But, what about your job?"

Faith Christian Academy's policy on separation and divorce meant his employment at the school would be subject to review by the board of directors. An interview was part of the process, and he wasn't prepared to talk to anyone about his business.

He couldn't shake the feeling that there was something bigger and better waiting for him. All he needed to do was step out on faith and find it. "I know what the policy says. There are other teaching jobs out there you know. And frankly, if I don't get a teaching job, it wouldn't be a loss. It might be the time to start something new."

"Whatever ever you decide, I'll support you."

Debo's approval mattered to him. "Thank you."

"I've got to run," Debo said after a glance at his watch. "Love to your ladies."

"Say hello to Adele and the boys."

Chapter Seventeen

It was day fifteen. When Sam had given her twenty-one days, her first thought was: *"Enough time to fast and pray. Perhaps this time, I will get a response."* But now the days were ticking away. Despite her many petitions, there was no miracle in sight. Moni was beginning to think God had forgotten about her.

In her forty-four years, she had never felt the level of anguish Sam's request had brought to her life. It haunted her dreams and made her days spin.

Flexing tight shoulder muscles, she walked into their home to find Shekinah looking as if her world had ended. "Is everything alright?"

"You said you would be home early to help me make some puff-puff for my dance group." Tears filled Shekinah's eyes. "I called, and you didn't pick up your phone."

The promise had slipped her mind. To avoid coming home, she had voluntarily accepted a project at work. She gave Shekinah an apologetic smile. "Some things came up."

"Sure, Mom, things always do."

Moni dropped her briefcase on the couch. "When do you have to leave? We can still make some."

"No, we can't." Shekinah wrapped arms around herself. "Marcy's mom is picking me up in twenty minutes. I guess I will just have to tell the other girls I forgot it was my turn to bring snacks."

"I don't want you to lie. I can ask Marcy's mom to stop so you can pick up some snacks on your way to practice."

"Mrs. Watson is not my mom. You are. And I must let you know you're doing an excellent job."

Moni winced. Where did the child learn such cruelty? "Shekinah, I said I forgot! Since you want to be rude about it, please yourself."

"You forgot because the things I want are not important to you." Shekinah's tone was accusatory.

"You're just like your father. You both think the world should revolve around you." Moni's temper rose with her voice. "It doesn't."

It was a good thing she couldn't hear what Shekinah was mumbling under her breath because she was very close to losing it. She turned away from her.

"I don't need this. Just go to your room. Now. And you had better stay there till you have to leave for your dance practice."

"Fine. I don't need you, either." Shekinah stomped up the stairs. The house rattled when she slammed her bedroom door.

Moni bit hard on her lip. The walls were closing in on her. She needed to see her mother.

***

Mummy took one look at her face and insisted on making tea. When it came to tea, their mother was more British than the Brits. Mummy often joked it was a taste she had acquired while in her mother's womb. Their grandmother reportedly drank copious amounts of tea from a treasured Pyrex dish.

Moni didn't believe the beverage could cure as many things as Mummy thought, but the familiarity of watching her mother brew their tea gave her some comfort.

Mummy placed a cup in front of her and Moni thanked her. She took a sip, letting the beverage soothe her body until her taut nerves began to relax. Then she determined it was time to work on her spirit. "How do you know when something is God's will?"

As always, Mummy was quick with her answer. "His will never contradicts His Word." She placed a mug on the table and took a seat in front of Moni. "I test it against the Word of God."

"How you do know in here?" Moni placed a hand on her racing heart.

Her mother's conviction was evident. "You will feel His peace."

She exhaled. Mummy made it sound simple. "But, what if His peace doesn't come? What if His miracle is elusive and your time is running out?"

Seek Me first.

Moni fanned her legs under the table. She gave her life to Jesus at the tender age of ten. What other seeking did she have to do?

Wherefore let him that thinketh he standeth take heed lest he fall.

Scriptures were flooding her mind, but still, the days ticked by. Moni put down the mug and burst into tears. The contents of the mug that had given her a moment of solace now offended her. There was no comfort in a cup. Her problems were bigger than tea.

Mummy looked concerned. "Child, what is the matter?"

Everything. "Nothing."

"Moni, He makes everything beautiful in His time."

"I'm supposed to wait?"

"Yes."

She had thought her mother would have something new to offer. Moni pushed back her chair. "I have to go."

"Moni, please, sit down."

Broken in many places, she couldn't be gracious. "I'll see you later."

***

Sam sat across from her at the kitchen table. "Moni, you've had your twenty-one days. So, what's your decision?" His frown deepened as her silence grew. "Why are you making this harder than it has to be?"

"I can't do it. Please. It will destroy us."

"Don't you get it? Moni, at this point there is no *us*. We're just two people sharing a house because it's convenient."

He reached inside the messenger bag slung over the back of the chair, pulled out a large manila envelope and pushed it across to her.

"I went to the courthouse and picked up a divorce application packet. I'm hoping you will be reasonable and agree to an uncontested, no-fault divorce. That way, we can apply without the services of a lawyer. You know we can't afford the legal fees."

Moni's eyes flickered from his face to the envelope. The divorce was becoming a reality. "Sam—"

He interrupted her. "Since we have Shekinah, we'll have to include an outline of our child custody and support arrangements. You already know how I feel about my daughter. It's my understanding that she's old enough to choose which parent she'd prefer to live with."

Moni gripped the edge of the kitchen table. "Sam, I—"

He held up a finger. "Please, let me finish. Another thing, a no-fault divorce requires a completion of a one year separation period. That's fine by me. But if you're in a hurry to start your new life, we can file a fault divorce under the grounds of adultery." A smirk tugged at a corner of his mouth. "You'll finally be able to let folks know I was a lousy husband." He stood. "Let me know if you have any questions."

Under Moni's gaze, the envelope size expanded until it was all she could see. She glanced at the stove. If she burned it, then she wouldn't have to look at the documents. But she knew that would be a waste of time. She could just hear Sam's response to it. *There were more papers where those came from.*

Tears welled up in her eyes, and she began to shake.

Beloved, wait. Resist the devil, and he will flee from you.

For the first time, Moni spoke to the voice. "Wait for what? Sam has won. He won."

Of course, there was no response. Teeth bared, Moni picked up the envelope and flung it across the room.

Chapter Eighteen

Moni wore her new underwear. She walked across the room and opened her closet.

Given the nature of the event, she had two options: demure or provocative. The only item of clothing she had in the latter category was a white, see-through, chiffon blouse. Deciding on the demure option, she settled on a ruffled pink blouse and a pair of black pants.

Her lips curled at the irony of stressing over what to wear when she was on her way to commit adultery. She should have given Sam what he wanted and kept Joy's name off of her lips. It may have been enough for Sam. She would never know. Should have wasn't going to change anything tonight. Moni took a deep breath and steeled her nerves.

Moni's legs felt wobbly. She wasn't sure she would make it down the stairs, so she took a minute and sat on the bed. Before she could reclaim her resolve, a loud knock on the door startled her. She nearly jumped through the ceiling.

"Mom, Dad says it's time for you guys to leave," Shekinah yelled.

Shekinah's rude tone made her want to kick off her shoes and crawl into bed. This was the child she was making a huge sacrifice for? Moni took a deep breath and counted to ten before yelling, "Tell him I'm coming."

Boots zipped up, purse placed in the crook of her arm, Moni stood in front of the closed bedroom door. It blurred before her eyes. She knew that once she passed through it and made her way down the stairs, her life would never be the same. Still, she stepped forward and turned the handle.

***

They drove to Ngozi and Odosa's house in silence. Sam had told her the Bassey's had traveled for the weekend.

Ngozi hugged her before pointing in the direction of the dining room. "The rest of the gang is in there."

Not trusting herself to be civil toward Debo, she stayed away from him and Adele. They, too, kept their distance.

Moni headed straight for the dining table. She ignored Sam's raised eyebrow and picked up a bottle of wine and filled her goblet to the brim. She needed some fortification to make it through the evening. And given what was about to happen, hypocrisy no longer seemed like such a big deal.

By her third glass of wine on an empty stomach, things were hazy, which suited Moni just fine. From her spot on the couch, she watched Sam and Ngozi's animated conversation.

Looking bored, her husband, Odosa, paced nearby. Earlier in the evening, Odosa had sat next to Moni on the couch. He left when she didn't say a word to him.

She was halfway through glass number four when Sam waved her over. Ngozi was talking to her husband.

Sam's excitement shone through his bright eyes. "The meet and greet segment is over. What do you think of going with Odosa?"

The alcohol had slowed Moni's thumping heart. She peered at him through hazy eyes. "To where?"

Sam gave her an impatient look. "Moni, it's time to split up."

"Oh." She glanced at their hosts. Sam was itching to leave. Did he always have a thing for the other woman?

She shrugged. "Sure."

Odosa held on to her arm as she stumbled up the stairs. "Where are we going?" she asked.

"Ifueko's room." He gave her a gentle squeeze. "I am happy you came."

Moni blinked at him, wondering how she had never noticed Odosa's crooked front tooth. It was a good thing she didn't have to kiss him. According to Sam, one of the rules at these play parties was no kissing.

Ifueko's pink bedroom was a Disney princess' dream. Moni took her clothes off and sprawled on the airbed placed in the corner of the room. The glow in the dark stars winked from the ceiling.

Ifueko was in her Sunday School class. Moni could almost hear her voice as she sang "Twinkle, Twinkle, Little Star" while being tucked into bed.

Oh, God. I'm desecrating a little girl's sanctuary.

A sudden wave of nausea came over her. She began to cry.

Odosa who'd been busy putting on protection flopped beside her on the air bed. "Moni, what's wrong?"

The concern in his voice turned her tears into sobs.

"Please, don't cry," Odosa whispered. "I know all this is new to you. Listen, we don't have to do anything tonight."

Moni shook her head. "Let's get 'er done," she said in a strangled voice. All she had to do was close her eyes.

Odosa leaned over and wrapped his arms around her. "No," he insisted. "Not tonight."

She laid her head on his chest, sobbing, as Odosa stroked her head.

By the time she went back downstairs, she had decided she wasn't telling Sam what had taken place between her and Odosa. It had felt like a special moment.

"Hey, beautiful," Sam said to her when she walked into the living room.

She ignored him. From the glow on his face, his time with Ngozi had not been a hand holding session. The evening had been perfect for her as well. It had been the first time in a long time that her feelings mattered.

***

The following weekend, it was Moni's turn to teach at Sunday School. Odosa's awkward look when he came for his daughter at the end of the service must have mirrored hers. She wasn't sure where to look. "Hey, you."

She moistened her lips. "Hey." Odosa moved close, and Moni caught a whiff of his cologne. The scent took her back to Ifeuko's bedroom. She wondered what was on Odosa's mind.

"Your outfit looks lovely," Odosa said as she handed over the coloring pages Ifueko had worked on during the service.

"Thank you. Ifeuko had a great time."

When his daughter went to get her backpack, Odosa whispered, "I didn't say anything to her."

Moni knew what he meant. She whispered in response, "Me, either."

He gave Moni a questioning look. "I guess I'll be seeing you at the next house fellowship?"

"Well, I don't know if—"

His daughter walked toward them. "Please come," Odosa begged with his eyes and his tone. "It won't be the same." Then he smiled. Odosa's big smile made her feel warm all over. It had been a long time since her husband's smile made her feel that way.

Even though she had told herself she wasn't going back, Moni nodded. "I'll be there."

"I'll be counting the days." Odosa reached for Ifueko's hand, and they left the classroom. Moni wanted to fight the feeling, but she couldn't help being happy someone was looking forward to her company.

Chapter Nineteen

Pastor Iginla tapped Debo on the shoulder at the end of the deacon's meeting. "I'd like to see you before you leave."

"Yes, Pastor."

Minutes later, he ended his conversation with the church secretary and headed to the church office. The pastor invited him in after a knock.

"Please, have a seat," Pastor Iginla said.

He sat across from the pastor. Nervous, he folded his hands and placed them on his lap. Their meetings always reminded him of his countless trips to the principal's office when he was in grade school.

Pastor Iginla cleared his throat. "What I'm about to share is a sensitive matter. I'd prefer it stays confidential."

"Of course."

"I received a shocking letter today," Pastor said as he tapped a finger on his oak desk. "I wanted your input on it."

Debo nodded. "Yes, sir." To his shock, the typed letter handed to him was more or less an *exposé* on their swinging group. "Such depravity in our church? Sir, this is disturbing."

Pastor Iginla clasped his hands under his chin and leaned forward. "Very. But who can these people be?"

He wondered if the pastor knew and was just giving him an opportunity to confess. Debo cleared his throat. "Sir, we have a congregation of almost one thousand people. It's hard to tell."

"Indeed. I know you're one of the favourite deacons in the church. You're approachable. People trust you. I'm hoping that you would come to me if you hear anything about this group. They will be exposed before they lead more people astray. Mark my words. God will not be mocked."

Debo took a deep breath as he imagined the roof scrolling open and a hand coming through the ceiling holding a list of names. His would be the first. Who could have been so stupid to put them all at risk? His mind went to

Moni. Could she be trying to get back at him? Didn't she know she would be affected, too?

Pastor Iginla took the letter back. "There's something else we need to discuss."

Debo squirmed in his seat. His sense of relief had been premature. The pastor knew about his involvement. And he had not confessed as expected. Debo held on to the chair arms as his heart raced. "Yes, sir."

"Last week, our parish in Moose Jaw, Saskatchewan made a request. They need someone to fill in for the current assistant pastor. His wife had quadruplets, so they're moving back to Nigeria for a year or two. Taking care of six children under the age of seven is more than they can handle on their own."

"Children need a lot of attention," Debo said as he relaxed his grip and tried to slow his breathing.

"They do." Pastor Iginla paused like he was still considering his words. "I know you have attended a theological seminary."

"Yes, sir." Once upon a time, he had thought of being a pastor. Being around Moni's father had been such an inspiration. But he had begun to doubt his journey, to question if God had called him or if he had called himself, so he had left the seminary.

"I wanted to know if you would consider going to serve in Moose Jaw. We need a family man, a mature Christian." Pastor Iginla paused again, but this time his words were more certain. "The move will not affect your job here. You would get the same salary."

At first, Debo was speechless. Then, he gave a nervous laugh. "I didn't graduate from the seminary."

"I am aware of that. There's nowhere in the Bible that says an individual must have a seminary degree to pastor a church," Pastor Iginla continued. "During the posting, the church will also subsidize your living expenses since Sister Adele may not be able to find comparable employment in Moose Jaw. So, what do you say?"

"I will have to pray about this, sir. And of course, talk to Adele."

Pastor Iginla looked pleased by his response. "It is important that you are both in agreement. I'll pray along. If Sister Adele has any questions about the responsibilities of a pastor's wife, please tell her my wife will be happy to meet with her."

"Yes, sir." Debo stood. "Thank you, sir."

"My greetings to the family."

They shook hands, and Debo left his office.

***

When he told Adele about the pastor's request, her response was a resounding no. He tried to reason with her. "Adele, this is God's work."

She snorted. "Please, don't even go there, holy man of God."

He was taken aback by her hostile tone. "Is there something I'm missing?"

"Debo, you only see what fits into your agenda. Did you think about the impact on me, on my job?"

"We're just putting our life here on pause for a while. It would be a great opportunity for the children to see another part of Canada."

"I'm not moving to Saskatchewan."

"You and I have had several discussions about working in the mission field. Perhaps this is God's answer."

"Debo, that was before we had four children back to back. I'm too settled in my life."

"I thought this was *our* life."

"Stop splitting hairs. If you want to go, fine. The kids and I will stay here."

Given his suspicions about Adele and their swinging partner, Mr. Bassey, he had expected some resistance. "I guess you can't leave your boyfriend?"

"My boyfriend?"

"You know who I'm talking about." He remembered the anonymous letter sent to the church. "Anyway, the group will be folding up soon."

Adele stopped pacing. "What?"

"Pastor knows about the group and the play parties. The church received a letter."

She went pale. "They have our names?"

"No. But this would be a good time to get out." He moved closer to her. "Up till now, we've done things our way. Perhaps this is the sign that we need to get right with God."

Still pale, Adele looked confused. "I have to think about this."

"What is there to think about?"

"Us. The direction of this marriage."

"This marriage is doing just fine."

Adele gave him a frustrated look. "Debo, open your eyes!"

He would not let Mr. Bassey ruin his life. "All I want to see is you, my love, our boys and this beautiful life we've built for ourselves. Nothing else."

"This our so-called beautiful life is a mirage."

"It boils down to choice. I chose you to be my wife. Today, I still choose you for the rest of my life. What do you say?"

Shaking her head, she backed away from him. "I need to go for a walk."

"Adele, I—"

She held up her hand. "Just stop! Badgering me is not going to help me think."

The distant look in her eyes scared him. "I love you. Please, *ma cherie*, choose us."

Red-faced, Adele fled from the room.

Chapter Twenty

Moni thought she was still dreaming of Odosa when Sam's toe curling kiss woke her.

"Good morning," Sam said when she opened her eyes.

She covered a yawn. "Wow. What did I do to deserve that?"

"You look so beautiful when you're asleep."

"Were you staring at me?"

Sam peered. "And me likey what I see."

How things change, Moni thought. A couple of weeks back, they were barely speaking to each other.

Sam's expression became serious. "There's something we have to talk about."

She sat up. "What?"

"We need a family meeting."

They'd never had one of those. "Why?"

"We need a talk with Shekinah. Things have been chaotic to say the least and you know how much that has affected her."

Moni sighed. "Sam, she's been so rude to me. I don't know what came over her."

"But we haven't been nice to each other," he pointed out. "Shekinah sees all that."

"Still."

He held out his hand. "I agree she owes you an apology. Let's go to her room and iron this out."

Shekinah gave them a suspicious look when they walked hand-in-hand through her bedroom doorway. "Hello, Princess."

"Good morning Dad, Mom," Shekinah said, looking up from her magazine "Am I safe?"

Moni sat at the foot of her bed. "We just wanted to chat."

"Should I be scared?" Shekinah asked as she placed the magazine down.

"No." Sam sat on the bed beside her. "You've always complained about us not listening to you. This is your opportunity to tell us why you've been out of sorts."

Shekinah's head swung between them. "You want to know?"

"Yes," Sam said.

Shekinah hesitated for a moment before asking, "I can say what's on my mind?"

He nodded. "Yes. No fear."

Shekinah sighed. "Well, it's all good that you guys are all lovely-dovey now. But this isn't new behavior. When I see you talking instead of yelling at each other, I get all excited and then…" She clapped her hands. "Bam, the other shoe drops and we're all back on the Badmus House merry-go-round."

Disputing Shekinah's words was hard. She and Sam exchanged a look. "That's a fair statement to make," Moni said. "We are truly sorry. This time, we're going to work hard at things."

Shekinah rolled her eyes. "Are you kidding me?"

Moni spoke up. "What do you think?"

Shekinah folded her arms in front of her chest. "That somehow, I slept through March, and it's April Fools' Day."

Shekinah wasn't going to make things easy for them, Moni thought. She had not expected anything less. As their child, Shekinah's stubbornness was almost a given.

"Things are going to be different around here," Sam said. "I promise." His expression became stern. "But, regardless of what has been happening, you owe your mom an apology for the way you've treated her."

"Yeah." Shekinah looked shame faced. "I'm sorry, Mom."

Moni stood and walked over to give Shekinah a tight hug. "I love you so much," she whispered in her ear.

"Don't suffocate the child," Sam chuckled.

Laughing, she let Shekinah go.

"Thanks for saving me, Dad." Shekinah grinned.

The happy look on her daughter's face made Moni feel thankful. She wasn't going to lose her child.

"So, what do my ladies want me to make them for breakfast?" Sam asked.

"I think I need someone to pinch me." Moni folded her arms across her chest. "This can't be real."

A mischievous look on her face, Shekinah flexed her fingers. "I can help out."

"Don't you dare," Moni said, as she picked up one of Shekinah's many pillows and threw it at her.

Sam picked up another pillow and threw it at Moni. Shekinah giggled as she tossed two pillows at him.

***

Downstairs, Sam held open the refrigerator door. "So how do you ladies want your eggs?" he asked, glancing over his shoulder.

"I'll take mine scrambled, please," Shekinah replied as she brought out the frying pan without being asked.

"I want a super-sized omelet," Moni replied. "Cheese, tomato, onion, mushroom and green pepper. It's not every day we get to eat one of your breakfast creations."

"Well, it wouldn't be a special treat if I made them all the time," Sam pointed out.

Bringing out the tray of eggs, he asked Shekinah to dice a bulb of red onion. She happily left the kitchen table and got the onion from the pantry before standing next to her father.

Watching them carry on an animated conversation as they worked, again, Moni marvelled at how things had changed in their home since they had started attending the play parties.

Over a period of two months, they had gone to six parties. She wouldn't admit it, especially not to Debo, but he was right about the first time being the hardest.

Odosa's willingness to listen to whatever she had to say also made the evenings special. It was his gentleness she valued the most. It had made her able to ignore lingering guilt feelings over what they were doing.

"Dad, stop it!"

Sam, who was also making waffles, had flicked some of the flour on his fingers in Shekinah's face. Laughing, Shekinah stepped away from him.

Moni stood from the kitchen table. "Since you guys are working on the eggs and waffles, how about I make us some bacon?"

"Mom, you go and relax. I'll come and get you when we're done."

"Yes, you go up and relax," Sam echoed. "Remember, we're going bowling with Debo and his gang later today."

Moni held up her hands. "I'm going. I know when I'm not wanted." She narrowed her eyes at Shekinah. "Missy, don't eat all the bacon as you fry it."

"Dad sneaks up and eats it when I'm not looking."

Sam smirked. "I'm just doing a taste test."

"You know I treasure my bacon." Moni wagged her finger. "You've both been warned. I don't want to hear a 'how the bacon got lost' story."

Their laughter followed her upstairs. In their room, she picked up the neglected novel on her night stand, snuggled under the duvet and removed her butterfly bookmark. She could easily get used to days like this.

Chapter Twenty-One

Her father opened the door when they arrived at her parents' home. "*Ekaabo*," he greeted as the three of them trooped into the house. "Your mother has been looking out of the window."

Moni smiled. The consummate hostess, Mummy, would have been tidying the house since she woke up. Not that the house was anything but spotless.

Moni waited for Sam and Shekinah to hug her father before she did. On a scale of one to ten, her father's hugs were an easy twelve. "Welcome back, Dad. We missed you."

He smiled. "It's always good to be back home. Your mother told me you were checking up on her. Well done. I know she doesn't sleep well while I'm away."

Even though Mummy had told her the house rattled when she was alone, she wouldn't spend nights at their house. "I think you should take her next time you go."

Daddy nodded. "That is a good idea. If she will go."

Her mother loved the comfort and familiarity of her home. "I'm sure you can persuade her." Moni noted that as usual, her father had grown lean from his five-month stay in Nigeria. Traveling around the country by road to conduct open air crusades in remote villages was hard on a seventy-three-year-old body.

Moni handed the bag of baking supplies she brought to Shekinah who took it to the kitchen. She and Sam sat across from her father.

"Sir, was everything successful?" Sam asked.

Daddy beamed. "To the glory of God, many souls were won for the kingdom."

Moni only had a faint recollection of Nigeria. She had not been back since they moved to Canada. "Did you visit the family house at Iwo?" she asked referring to the town where her father was born.

"I did. Every time I go to Nigeria, everywhere looks different. I come back to hear of family and friends who have passed on. This time as I left, I wondered if it would be my last time walking on that soil. But, whatever happens to me, I know God's work will go on."

They often worried about something happening to her father while he was in Nigeria. He had cardiac disease, and his evangelism team was often in villages far away from good medical care. "Perhaps, it's time to stay close to home," Moni said.

"Did your mother put you up to this?" he asked. "There's nothing to worry about. I live ready for heaven."

The words struck her spirit. Moni knew she couldn't make the same claim.

Daddy turned to Sam. "Pastor Iginla visited yesterday. He told me you have not been coming to church. Is everything okay?"

Moni felt Sam freeze beside her. Since the swinging began, Sam's church attendance had become sporadic. Even though her parents now attended the Faith Assembly parish closer to their home, as the retired pastor, Daddy maintained a close relationship with the leadership of their parish. It was why she forced herself to church.

As Sam sputtered his words, Daddy turned to her. "Perhaps *you* can give me an explanation?"

Moni squirmed under her father's steady gaze. Somehow, her father could tell when she was untruthful. "I've been attending," she said as Sam gave her a dark look.

Daddy faced Sam. "Son, have you discovered your tongue?"

Moni stood. "I'm sure Mummy will need my help in the kitchen." She'd let Sam explain since he was the head of their spiritually depleted home.

She hurried from the room.

"*Ekaasan*," Moni greeted, interrupting an animated conversation between her mother and Shekinah.

"My child just told me she's going to be in charge of making puff-puff," Mummy said to her as she pointed to the pastry ingredients arranged on the kitchen counter.

"Shekinah has been learning how to cook Nigerian dishes by watching YouTube videos."

Her mother's eyebrows furrowed. "What is that?" she asked.

Moni listened as Shekinah explained what people did on the website.

Mummy waved a dismissive hand. "No video woman can teach you to cook the proper way. Shekinah, why didn't you tell me you were interested in learning?"

"I'll tell you why." Shaking her head, Shekinah tightened an imaginary piece of cloth around her waist as she mimicked her grandmother's accent. "Forget recipes. Child, all you need is a little dash of this and a little dash of that. You must gauge the amount of the ingredient with one eye."

Mummy's jaw dropped. "Shekinah, are you mocking me?"

"No, Grandma." Shekinah giggled as she hid behind Moni. "I just don't know how to do eye measurements."

"You children of nowadays. I guess your video woman knows better than your grandmother."

Shekinah walked over and wrapped her arms around her grandmother's neck. "You know I love you."

"Leave me alone," Mummy said in a gruff voice as she snuggled against Shekinah.

Remembering the pleading look Sam gave her as she left the living room, Moni decided to send Shekinah out as a distraction. "I'm sure grandfather will enjoy your company."

"He brought back the Lagos edition of the Monopoly game." Mummy untangled herself from Shekinah's embrace. "Instead of go to jail, this one says go to Kirikiri."

Moni knew Kirikiri was the maximum-security prison in Lagos.

"Where is Kirikiri?" Shekinah asked.

Mummy shuddered. "A very horrible place my child. My descendants will never be found there."

"I'll be back to make my puff-puff," Shekinah said as she made her way to the kitchen door.

Mummy shook her head. "We have heard you. Madam You Tubing."

"Grandma, it's YouTube."

Mummy gave a comical shake of her head. "I know things about your Internet."

"Indeed you do," Moni said.

"*Oya*, let's start cooking. Your father needs to eat early."

Moni watched as her mother walked over to the stove and lifted the cover of her pot. The aroma of spicy *egusi* soup and smoked catfish filled the kitchen. "It's ready. I'm sure the men are ready to eat."

She loved to eat Nigerian food. The spicier, the better. "I don't know about the men," she said. "My stomach is rumbling. I'm seriously praying there'll be enough left over for me to take home."

Mummy laughed. "I will save some soup for you."

"Thank you." Moni began washing up. The large window above the sink presented a clear view of the fenced-in back yard. Shekinah and her grandfather were outside, playing Monopoly on the picnic table. Shekinah's earphones were tucked away, and she looked like she was having a relaxing time. But then, she was happiest at her grandparents' home.

Mummy's voice made her turn around. "Why the deep sigh?"

"I was thinking about Shekinah."

"Did something happen at school this week?"

"No, things have been good." Too good, which was why she was on edge. Placing the last pot in the dish rack, Moni tore off a sheet of paper towel and dried her hands. "I guess I'm so used to the school calling us."

Moving away from the stove, Mummy sat at the kitchen table. She motioned for Moni to sit.

She did.

"Child, you should be thankful for all the positive changes, not worried. Shekinah told me things have been good at home since you and Sam started going on date nights."

It was how she had explained their absence on play nights. Moni picked at imaginary lint on her blouse. "The child talks too much."

"Shekinah was beaming when she told me. Is she not allowed to tell me things?"

Moni gave her a placating smile. "Of course she is. And it is true Sam and I have been working hard on our relationship. In fact, we're planning a weekend away, possibly to Niagara Falls."

Mummy's face lit up. "Good. As I've always told you, God answers prayers." She stood. "Please, go and tell them dinner is ready."

"Yes, Ma."

***

"Can I see you outside for a second?" Sam asked.

From his somber look, she could tell he was still sulking over Daddy's rebuke. She would rather not be alone with him until he had calmed down. "The food is ready to serve," she said. "Can't it wait?"

"It will only take a couple of minutes."

Conscious of her father's presence, she decided not to make a scene. "Sure, let's go."

"You couldn't even defend me?" Sam said to her as they walked out of the side gate.

She looked around. There were people seated out on their porches. "Can we wait until we get home to have this conversation?"

"I didn't want to come in the first place," Sam said as she followed him to the car. "I respect your father, but I'm a grown man. I shouldn't have to discuss my church attendance record with anyone." Sam took his keys out of his pocket. "I'm not going back in there."

"What? How are we supposed to get home?" Most importantly, what was she going to tell her parents had happened to him?

"Get a cab." He unlocked the door, reached for the purse stowed under the car seat and held it out.

Confused, Moni took it. "What did you want me to say?"

"I shouldn't have to tell you how to defend your husband," Sam said before driving away.

Moni glanced at the house. She couldn't keep them waiting. She just had to come up with the right excuse.

They were waiting at the table when she walked back into the house.

"Where's Sam?" Mummy asked as she pulled out her chair and sat.

"One of his friends called for assistance. He had to leave."

"And he couldn't come in to say goodbye?" Daddy asked.

"His friend said it was urgent."

As Daddy opened his mouth, Shekinah began coughing. Mummy passed her a cup of water. "Sweetie, are you okay?" she asked.

Under the table, Shekinah stepped on her foot. Moni realized Shekinah had been trying to protect her. She felt a deep sadness. What were they doing to their child?

Daddy cleared his throat. "Let us say grace."

She reached for Shekinah's hand and gave it a gentle squeeze. Shekinah's heavy sigh made Moni's head hang low.

Chapter Twenty-Two

Catchy calypso beats from the steel drums had people on their feet. Moni tightened the yellow beach towel around her one-piece swimsuit as she swayed her hips to the music. The annual Faith Assembly church picnic at Brampton's Professor's Lake was one of Moni's favorite "end of summer" events. Despite an earlier forecast of rain, it had turned out to be a beautiful day with mild weather and blue skies.

She covered her face when one of the drummers, a member of her youth group, began chanting: "Go, Mrs. Badmus."

Moni bowed to scattered applause. She decided to sit for a while before joining Shekinah in the water.

"Moni!"

She turned at the sound of her mother's voice. Mummy soon caught up, held her arm, and walked her to a private spot. "Your husband needs your help," she said through clenched teeth.

The last time she saw Sam, he and a group were playing volleyball. Moni frowned. "What happened?"

"His behavior is hurting your reputation. He and Ngozi seem to have forgotten they're married to other people."

Moni scanned the beach area until she saw them at the edge of the picnic site. Her heart almost stopped.

Sam, dressed in swim shorts, had his arms wrapped around Ngozi's waist while her face was buried in his chest.

Moni's stomach clenched from waves of anger and humiliation. The only explanation for the behavior was that Sam had lost his mind.

Mummy nudged her on the arm. "*Oya*, go and separate them!"

Conscious of staring eyes, she held a smile as she walked toward the hugging couple. It was a good thing her father had left the picnic for another engagement. His hearing about Sam's behavior would be less traumatic than seeing it.

Sam's arms dropped to his sides when he looked up and saw her marching toward them. Wide-eyed, he stepped away from Ngozi. "Moni—"

She would have gladly smashed one of the picnic chairs on his coconut head. "Save it."

Ngozi stepped away from Sam, whispering, "Moni, I'm so sorry."

Sorry wasn't going to cut it. "Mr. Romeo and Mrs. Juliet," she whispered through clenched teeth, "you've put on quite a show for the whole church."

Moni placed a hand on Ngozi's shoulder and applied some pressure. Ngozi winced. "Listen, if you don't want a scarlet woman label, you'd better let me hug you. Real tight."

She turned to Sam. "Then, we'll bend our heads, and I'll say a prayer of thanks your husband isn't here to see this crazy behavior. When we're done, Ngozi, you will get your things, and I'll walk you to the car. Are we all in agreement?"

Sam and Ngozi nodded and held out their hands.

Moni fought back tears as Ngozi drove away. Sam had ruined a perfect day. Even though all she wanted to do was leave, she knew they both had to stay until the end. It was what they did every year.

On her way back from the parking lot, she found Sam still standing in the same spot. "You had to do that here?"

"Can we continue this discussion at home?" he asked.

Now he wants to continue a discussion at home, Moni thought. "Oh, we will. Right now, we're going to join our daughter in the water and show everyone how happy we are."

Sam gave her a dirty look. "Yes, ma'am."

Oblivious to what had happened, Shekinah was happy to see them. She tossed a beach ball in their direction. For the rest of the picnic, they stayed in the water. About every other minute, Sam's loud laughter rang out. Moni smirked to herself. He, too, knew it was all about creating the right illusion, but she hated herself for being caught in this situation. Pretending was hard. Hard on her psyche, hard on her heart and hard on her soul.

Shekinah decided to spend the night with her grandparents. Moni could tell from the looks Mummy sent Sam as they walked toward the parking lot that she wanted to give him a piece of her mind.

Moni flung her handbag in the back seat of the car and climbed in. "You're falling for Ngozi."

Even though he must have heard her, Sam appeared to be distracted and confirmed it when he said, "Pardon me?"

She snickered. "Sam Badmus, you're falling head over heels for Ngozi Osayi."

He gave a dismissive wave. "Don't be silly. My emotions are not involved."

His nonchalant tone irked her. "*Really?* You think I don't see how you perk up when she walks into the room? Huh? On the days she and Odosa don't show up at the parties, you suddenly get a headache and ask to go home. Newsflash. Your emotions are involved."

Sam raised an eyebrow. "Are telling me you've developed feelings for Odosa?"

Moni's heart skipped at the sound of the name. "Don't even try and make this about me. You know what, maybe it's time to switch couples."

Sam shrugged. "Sounds fine to me."

She almost took the words back since she was going to miss seeing Odosa. Sam owed her for the stunt he'd pulled with Ngozi, and she knew it was the perfect way to punish him. "I'm sure we'll all have fun," Moni said as she slammed the car door shut.

Chapter Twenty-Three

Debo reached for the bottle of shampoo, rubbed some in his hair and stepped under the shower. As the lather ran over his closed eyes, he could picture the look on Moni's mother's face when she saw Sam and Ngozi. It was a miracle Sam had not burst into flames from the fiery look his mother-in-law sent his way. To avoid being dragged into the messy situation, he had found refuge under a beach umbrella.

He gave his hair and body a good rinse. Moni's performance had cracked him up. He was sure compassion was the furthest thing from her mind as she held Ngozi's hand. He would have loved to hear her prayer. And she had the gall to call him an actor.

As he turned off the water, his mouth soured. It was only a matter of time before the pastor began connecting the dots. Since everyone at church knew he and Sam were best friends, there was no way he wouldn't get pulled in for a discussion. Debo sighed. He didn't need anything extra to worry about.

Adele was making their bed when he returned to their bedroom. He still couldn't understand why she needed to make it before getting in.

"I'm beginning to regret telling Sam about the group," he said to her. "I had thought Moni was the letter writer. Now, I think it's Odosa."

Adele was silent as he opened his dresser drawer for a clean pair of sleep shorts.

"You would think everyone would be on their best behavior."

Adele shrugged as she plumped up the pillows. "Sam and Ngozi probably can't help themselves. I know you find it hard to accept, but sometimes, the heart wants what the heart wants."

He slammed the drawer shut. "That's a pretty selfish heart. They're not love-struck teenagers. If Moni hadn't handled things like a pro, things could have turned ugly. I'm disappointed in Ngozi. Her daughter and other kids were present for crying out loud. You women are meant to be more sensible in these kinds of situations."

Adele kept her eyes averted. "Well, sometimes, sensibility is the last thing one thinks about. Who says men are the only ones allowed to care less about the consequences?"

"These are societal rules. I didn't make them."

Hands folded across her chest, Adele sat at the edge of the bed. He walked over and sat next to her. Sam and Moni's relationship was their problem. He was more concerned about the state of his marriage. "You promised to think about the Saskatchewan move. Have you decided?"

Adele moved away from him. "No. I'm still thinking."

"Pastor needs an answer before the end of the month."

"You'll have your answer soon."

He searched her face. The somber expression didn't offer him any hope. "Should I be worried?"

"Debo, it's been a long day. Please, let's go to sleep."

Frustrated, he stood. How was he going to fix things when she wouldn't even speak to him?

Debo went over to his side of the bed and pulled back the comforter. What had happened to his beautiful life?

✳✳✳

The next day, Debo was surprised when Sam and Moni came to church. Odosa and Ngozi sat in the pew behind them.

At the sight of Odosa's stoic face, he wondered if Odosa had been briefed about his wife's behavior by a concerned church member. He wasn't sure if the electricity in the air was his imagination, but he had intercepted a few stares and whispers.

During offering collection, he noticed Sam leaving the sanctuary. Debo waited for a few minutes before following him. He found Sam in the restroom washing his hands.

Sam's face lit up when he saw him. "Hey."

Debo ignored the greeting. A quick glance under the doors confirmed that the stalls were empty. He turned to Sam. "I'm disappointed."

Sam rubbed his head. "I know I messed up."

"On a colossal level. You know the rules. And with the current situation, you're making things very unsafe for everyone."

Sam turned off the faucet. "You think I want my name dragged through the mud?"

"It appears you're letting another part of your anatomy think for you."

Their eyes locked in battle until Sam sighed. "You're right. I can't help myself."

He wasn't in the mood to hear another 'the heart wants what the heart wants' speech. "Maybe you need to sit out a couple of parties. Give each other a break."

"It won't help. I can't stay away from Ngozi."

It was worse than he had thought. "You've been seeing Ngozi outside our meetings?"

Sam looked away.

Was everyone around him losing their mind? "Listen to yourself! You're not in a relationship with Ngozi. She's married to someone else. And unless that ring on your finger is a prop, so are you."

Sam gave him an accusatory look. "I thought you were sure this swinging intervention would just be a physical thing? That our emotions wouldn't be affected."

Now it was Debo who looked at Sam like he was crazy. How did it end up being his fault? "Sam, this is what you've always done. I go out of my way to save you, and you come back to throw my kindness in my face."

"It's not my fault you always want to play the role of rescuer."

He threw up his hands. "You know what? I'm done. From this moment on, you're on your own."

Sam lifted his chin. "Fine. I'm very much capable of—"

Debo held a finger to his lips when he heard footsteps. Before the door opened, he scurried into a stall while Sam washed his hands for the second time.

He waited until he heard Sam leave before coming out to splash water on his face. Sam was no longer thinking with his head. He had to put more pressure on Adele. The sooner they left for Moose Jaw, the better.

Chapter Twenty-Four

Lost in thought, the shrill ring of the phone made Moni jump.

Her mother's voice greeted her on the other end of the line. "Are you home this evening?"

From the tone of her mother's voice, she knew they were going to be having a serious conversation. She wasn't in the mood for one. "I was thinking of going out to run some errands."

"Is it something urgent?"

She hesitated. One more lie wasn't going to increase her indisputable need for prayers. "Well—"

Mummy interrupted. "What I have to say can't wait. I will be at your place before seven tonight. Bye."

She placed the phone back on the charger, wishing she could leave the house before her mother arrived.

Mummy bought a bag of fresh tomatoes for Shekinah. "Thank you, Ma."

"Please put them away and join me," Mummy said.

"Yes, Ma."

"Are you sure you don't want anything to drink or eat?" Moni asked for a second time as she stood before her mother.

"I'm fine." Mummy patted the couch. "Sit down."

She sat on the other end of the couch and waited for Mummy to speak.

"I'm worried about you and Sam," Mummy finally said. "I can't shake the feeling something is seriously wrong in this home."

She averted her eyes. "We're doing fine."

"Look at me!"

Moni swung her head back.

"Child, you are not doing fine," Mummy said. "First, your husband leaves our house without bothering to say goodbye. Then, he wraps himself around a woman in your presence."

She tried to smile. "Mummy, what you saw at the church picnic was innocent. Sam and Ngozi are just friends. She had some problems. Sam was just comforting her."

"Friends?" Mummy raised an eyebrow. "The kind with benefits?"

She was shocked her conservative mother even knew the term. "Mummy!"

"Don't 'Mummy' me. Moni, the Bible says we should abstain from all appearance of evil. Sam's behavior at the picnic was concerning." She shook her head. "There are few things as dangerous as self-deception. We didn't believe your happy family of three frolicking in the water show."

Her heart sank at the sight of unshed tears in her mother's eyes. "Mummy, please don't cry."

The plea only made the tears fall. Sniffling, Mummy wiped her eyes with the back of her hand. Moni picked up the box of tissue and passed it to her.

Mummy dabbed at her eyes. "Do you remember our conversation after you told me Sam had asked you to marry him?"

She nodded.

"What did I ask you?"

Her mind went back to their conversation. "You asked if I had prayed about it."

"I did. I had also asked how you knew Sam was the best man for you. What did you tell me?"

Moni searched her memory, but she didn't have to look far. She knew the reason she married Sam. "I said he was my best friend." The words tasted like charcoal bits in her mouth.

"Is Sam still your best friend?" Mummy's mournful look was her undoing. Fighting tears, Moni hung her head.

Moving closer, Mummy lifted her chin. "Moni, are you ready to rebuild your friendship with your husband?"

If only Mummy knew how far apart she and Sam had grown. It would have been easy for her to say yes. But she couldn't force out another bold-faced lie. "I don't know. Sometimes, I think it's too late for us. I'm tired of fighting."

"Who told you battles were easy to win?" Mummy shook her head. "I know I did not."

"Mummy, at this point, I just want a ceasefire."

"Moni, you are trying to fight God's battle," Mummy said. "Ever since you were a little girl, you've always needed to control everything around you. My dear, your power is limited. You can either worry about the challenges in your life or you can trust God to handle them. You cannot do both."

Mummy pulled her close for a tight hug. "Know your father, and I are praying for you and Sam. We love you both, and we are here if you need us."

It was a good thing someone was praying, Moni thought. She couldn't wait anymore. Her prayers had turned into scripted conversations that bounced back to her. It was a good thing someone was praying, Moni thought. She couldn't anymore. Her prayers had turned into scripted conversations that bounced back to her.

Rejoicing in hope; patient in tribulation; continuing instant in prayer.

The familiar quiet voice took Moni by surprise. It had been a while since she'd heard it.

Mummy stood. "I told your father I would be back early."

"Thank you for the advice."

"Thank God, my child, and trust Him."

***

Drained after her mother's visit, Moni sat in front of the computer to fulfill the promise she made. She had admitted to lying about the weekend away, so her mother had begged her to book one.

The romantic couple's getaway package deal she had selected included a candlelit dinner and a massage session for two. She figured if they had to go away to rekindle the fire in their relationship, they might as well do it right.

She waited until they were in bed before she told him about her mother's visit. He was silent until she mentioned the trip. "A romantic getaway to Niagara Falls? You're kidding, right?"

"No, I'm not. Sam, my mother was crying. I couldn't let her leave here in that state."

Sam propped himself up. "Moni, I don't want to go."

"Why?"

"What's the point?"

The question made her take a hard look at him. Sam cared so little about her that he wasn't even willing to try?

"I guess we'll forfeit the money I paid." She had booked a non-refundable package knowing Sam hated to waste even a cent.

His scowl was identical to his daughter's. "Moni, you're trying to manipulate me again."

"In the spirit of reconciliation, I won't say it's how I felt when you came up with this swinging thing. You started this by throwing divorce papers in my face."

Sam glared at her. "It's is not as if I had to drag you into the car."

"Remember you said the swinging would make our marriage better? Thanks to your obsession with Ngozi, the good times certainly didn't last long," she said. "So, maybe a change of scenery will help reboot the change process. What do you think?"

"Congratulations. You win, again," Sam said as he turned away from her.

A weariness came over her. "This isn't about a winner or a loser."

Sam snickered. "I thought I was the deluded one?"

Moni closed her eyes. Some questions didn't have easy answers.

***

The following Friday, they left Shekinah at her grandparents' and left for Niagara Falls. Driving against rush hour traffic on the QEW highway, they arrived in time to change for their reservation for dinner.

Surprisingly, dinner at the hotel's rooftop restaurant went well. To Sam's credit, he stopped brooding when they arrived in Niagara Falls. They ended up having a lovely evening. He pulled out her chair, remembered her favorite dessert and even paid the roaming restaurant musician to play a medley of her jazz favorites.

On their way up, they stopped and picked up some sightseeing brochures for the next day. They were holding hands when they returned to their hotel room.

Moni was pleased to see the box of chocolate truffles and bottle of wine waiting for them. So far, the hotel had delivered the package advertised online. She was looking forward to the next day's couples massage session.

At the sight of the turned down bed, her heart began to pound. She wasn't looking forward to that part of the evening as it now left them both unsatisfied.

She excused herself to freshen up. By the time she came out of the bathroom, Sam was ready for her. Apprehensive, Moni took measured steps toward the bed. It would be great if things worked out.

They didn't. Half an hour later, it was clear Sam's mounting frustration only made her body unyielding.

"I'm sorry," she whispered as Sam rolled away.

Sam looked as if he was close to tears. "Me, too."

Moni wasn't surprised when he headed straight for the ice bucket. She stood from the bed, pulled on her robe and walked toward the floor-to-ceiling window.

The hotel room had a perfect view of Niagara's Horseshoe Falls. Illuminated by huge spotlights, the gushing waters were transformed by the vibrant colors of the rainbow. The sight soothed her. At that moment, she could push all her problems out of her mind.

Behind her, she could hear the steady slosh of ice and liquid as Sam filled his cocktail glass. He was snoring when the light show ended at midnight.

She knew part of why things had gone downhill was because like on many other nights, Odosa and Ngozi were in their bed. Achieving intimacy between four people had its challenges.

Moni wrapped her arms around herself. She was also no longer sure about what she felt for her husband. Or exactly what she felt for Odosa. Mummy had talked about rebuilding. But, where was she supposed to start?

Beloved, many waters cannot quench love, neither can the floods drown it.

Theirs wasn't a flood situation, Moni thought. They were trapped under giant tsunami waves. Sighing, she walked over to the bed and curled into a ball beside Sam.

The following morning, Sam didn't say a word when she packed up her suitcase and went down to the lobby. He joined her half an hour later. They both knew their romantic getaway had ended the night before.

Sam drove straight home since he didn't want them to pick up Shekinah until late the next day. To avoid being seen in town by her parents, they didn't leave the house. Sam spent the rest of the weekend in the basement while she stayed upstairs.

Late Sunday evening, she drove to her parents' home to pick up Shekinah. Mummy opened the door. "My Moni," she said as they hugged. "So, how did your trip go?"

Nervous, she launched into an overdrawn recount of the candlelit dinner. "Mummy, it was so beautiful. We should all go there sometime."

Mummy gave her a pleased look. "I'm glad you enjoyed yourselves. You'll see. Things will get better. You continue to do your part in rebuilding your home. God will take care of everything."

Throughout her visit, she made an extra effort to laugh. It was good that her parents couldn't see that inside, everything was shriveling.

Chapter Twenty-Five

Moni concluded it was a good thing her mother was not in charge of making any forecasts because her prediction of change did not come true.

She and Sam now tiptoed around each other. The silence between them meant she didn't have to worry about Shekinah overhearing any arguments.

On the other hand, there were hardly any confrontations between her and Shekinah as she began spending most of her after-school time outside the house.

A standing house rule banned Shekinah from visiting her friends at home until Moni had met the child's parents and at least, seen their homes. Moni was particular about visiting the homes of Shekinah's friends if older boys lived there. Of course, Sam thought she was paranoid. She didn't think any parent could be too careful.

However, with Shekinah's new friend, Allie, she'd let the rule slide. Allie's respectful behavior during her visits had impressed her. Shekinah's other friends didn't help her do chores. All they did was rummage through Moni's refrigerator and pantry as if they were in their own homes.

The few times she had eavesdropped on their conversations, all Shekinah and Allie talked about were stories about the good-looking boys in their class, movies they wanted to see and cool clothes. Normal teenage stuff.

Given the positive changes in Shekinah's behavior, the school principal's phone call was unexpected.

"Mrs. Badmus, I'd been hoping our next conversation would be a much more pleasant one," Mr. Scott said in a measured tone. "Unfortunately, earlier today, a teacher found Shekinah and her friend with Molly."

Moni ran the names of Shekinah's friends through her mind. She couldn't recall any of them with the name Molly. "Were they hurting her?"

Mr. Scott paused, and then Moni heard the irritation in his voice when he spoke. "Molly isn't a person. It's the new street name for the drug Ecstasy."

Moni's heart dropped. She knew that name. What on earth was Shekinah doing with illegal drugs?

"A classmate saw the yellow pills and reported it to a teacher. We've been talking to our students about the dangers of street drugs."

Moni clenched fingers around her phone. Shekinah!

"I spent the best part of an hour talking to both girls, and they insist they're not selling drugs to other students. For us, it's a huge relief, but they haven't been forthcoming about where they got the Molly from." He paused. "As per our protocol, the police were notified, and they're on their way. I'll advise that when you and Mr. Badmus meet the youth officer here at school, it's to discuss the next steps."

When they arrived at the school, Moni asked for a family meeting before them speaking to the officer. Mr. Scott agreed.

For the first time, Moni saw stark fear on her daughter's face. "Mom, Dad, I'm sorry," she said between sobs. "I didn't mean to."

Sam who'd been quiet since she picked him up from work, snapped. "Shekinah, saying I didn't mean to is acceptable when you run into someone in the hallway. It doesn't work when you're caught with illegal drugs." He shook his head. "I'm so disappointed in you."

Shekinah hung her head.

Moni had never heard Sam speak to their daughter in such a stern voice. "Shekinah, look up."

She did. "Tell me, where did you get the drugs?"

"Jean had said it would make me feel good." Tears rolled down her face. "I was just curious."

"Curious?" Sam's voice rose. "Who is this person?"

"Allie's older sister," Shekinah whispered.

Shekinah told them Jean, a third-year university student, came home the previous week on a holiday break. While Allie was busy getting them snacks, she and Jean started the conversation which had led to Jean giving her the drugs. She had been showing them to Allie when another student saw them.

Her heart thumped as she asked the question. "Did you take them?"

Shekinah was silent.

Sam's loud bang on the table made Moni jump. "Didn't you hear your mother?" Shekinah shook her head as she began crying.

She placed a restraining hand on Sam's arm. "You're not helping matters."

He shook off her hand. "Stop it! I'm tired of you telling me what to do say or do."

Shekinah continued to sob. Moni stared at her bent head and wondered if her child now had a drug addiction.

***

Moni fanned her legs under the Formica table as the youth officer stressed that drug possession was not a minor infraction. "Since Shekinah is a first-time offender, I'm going to recommend her case be diverted away from the juvenile justice system. It would give her a chance at avoiding a trial and getting a criminal record. However, if Shekinah does not complete the terms of the youth diversion program, we will proceed with a trial."

She glanced at Sam. He'd been staring into space since they entered the room. "Please, what are these terms?"

"Well, Shekinah will need to complete some community service hours and attend our drug education seminar. I'm also going to make a referral for some personal counseling." The officer raised an eyebrow. "I understand she's been struggling at school and home?"

Moni nodded. She hadn't said anything to Mr. Scott about behaviors at home. What had Shekinah told them?

The officer's gaze softened as it swung between her and Sam. "I have three teenagers at home. Believe me, there are days when I find policing easier than parenting. While this is not a requirement for the diversion program, I'm also going to recommend family therapy. We can discuss available services in the community. Shekinah's going to need a lot of support to stay focused while she's in the diversion program. It would be good for you all to be on the same page."

"We can access family counseling through my employee assistance program." Again, Moni glanced at Sam. Was he not going to say anything? "Do we need to get Shekinah tested for drugs?"

"I'm going to leave that decision to you. I will caution against the use of a home drug test kit. It's better to leave that to the professionals." The officer stood. "I'll have Mr. Scott bring Shekinah in. I think we should jointly present the plan to her."

***

The first thing Sam did when they got back home from the school meeting was remove Shekinah's bedroom door. He refused to listen to her pleas. "How is this going to help?"

"Moni, I can't believe you're defending her. We need to know what Shekinah is doing in her room. No child is going to be sniffing or shooting anything in my home."

She was scared, too. Still, Shekinah was not a baby. "Sam, she needs some privacy."

"I hear there's no privacy in jail. It's better Shekinah suffers some discomfort now."

"Sam, calm down. She's not a drug addict."

He turned to Shekinah who was snivelling beside her. "Your mother was right all along. I've been too soft on you. You better believe things are going to change."

Grunting, he carried the door down to the basement.

"This is not fair! I didn't even take the pills!" Shekinah ran into her room and flung herself on the bed. Her shoulders heaved as she buried her face in a pillow.

She wanted to hold Shekinah, but it wasn't the time to make her feel better. Dangerous actions always had consequences. It was better Shekinah learned the hard truth before she paid with her life.

Moni walked away.

Chapter Twenty-Six

"Did I tell you I was going to the U.S. this weekend?" Sam asked.

Moni sat next to him on the couch. Balancing the bowl of popcorn on her lap, she looked away from the television. "No, you didn't. What's going on?"

"Sorry. It must have slipped my mind. Coach Mike and I are taking the grade twelve boys to a basketball camp at Michigan State University. If things go well, we should get some scholarship offers."

"That would be nice," Moni said as her eyes flickered between him and the television. The suspect in her crime show had just found another target. Moni moved to the edge of her seat. "Girl, don't open the door!"

He had to call her name twice. "Can you please focus?"

"Oh, sorry. When do you leave?"

"Right after school on Friday. Our camp starts bright and early on Saturday. We should be back by lunch time on Sunday."

"I don't have any plans for the weekend. Shekinah and I will be home."

Sam was surprised she didn't ask him any more questions. Usually, he was subjected to a rigorous interrogation.

Moni's eyes were still glued to the screen when he left the room to call Ngozi. Odosa was away on a business trip which made it a perfect time for an overnight getaway. Ngozi's mother was visiting and able to take care of their daughter.

She picked up his call on the first ring. "Michigan, here we come."

Ngozi laughed. "I can't wait."

***

He and Ngozi had agreed to meet in the city of Guelph which was about an hour away from home. Before heading to the secluded motel he'd picked out from an Internet search, Sam stopped at an ATM and withdrew some money. There were things he needed to get from the grocery store, and it was best he didn't leave a paper trail for Moni to follow.

At the grocery store, he picked up several bags of Ngozi's favorite potato chips, a box of chocolate, a bottle of wine and a case of pop before walking toward the family planning aisle.

The pregnancy scare Ngozi had during the summer had made them cautious for a while before they went back to breaking the swinging group's cardinal rule. Debo had stressed that the paternity of the children born to members had to be unquestionable.

Sam picked up the box of condoms and headed toward the checkout counter.

His next stop was at a barbershop. He intended to arrive at the motel looking his best.

Ngozi's car was waiting outside the motel when he arrived. He parked beside her but didn't walk over to her car. To avoid being seen together, they had agreed he would go in and pay for their room while she would join him later.

The young man at the front desk looked as if he wanted to be somewhere else. His bored expression changed when Sam said he was booking a room for him and his wife.

"Spending time with the Mrs., eh?"

Sam counted out the payment. "It's our wedding anniversary."

He smirked. "Aww, a romantic weekend. You're at the right place. We get lots of honeymooners."

Sam didn't think peeling paint and a musty interior smell were attractive features. "I can see why," he said as he signed the receipt. "This place has the Taj Mahal Palace vibe."

"You wouldn't be the first person to connect those dots. That would be Mr. and Mrs. Smith, right?"

Smart-aleck. Sam gave him a tight-lipped smile. "No. It's Mr. and Mrs. Jones."

"Right, right." He lifted a key from a hook on the wall behind him. "Room 12A. You can't miss it. I'll send the one and only Mrs. Jones up when she arrives."

Mumbling some derogatory words under his breath, Sam headed toward the stairwell after he was told the elevator was temporarily out of service. He hoped the weekend would be worth all this hassle.

Minutes later, Ngozi entered the room. "That boy downstairs was rude to me." She closed the door and dropped her bags.

"Forget him. He's just having fun at our expense." He walked over and pulled her into his arms. "I've been looking forward to this all week."

The annoyed look on Ngozi's face went away. "When I arrived, and I didn't see your car, I thought maybe you had changed your mind about coming."

"Nothing was going to stop me from coming. I went to pick up some snacks for you."

"And I brought food to last us for the weekend."

Her thoughtfulness was one of the things he appreciated about her. Ngozi rubbed her hand on his scalp. "You got a new haircut."

"I knew you would notice." He couldn't remember the last time Moni noticed any haircut changes.

"So what do you want to do first?"

Ngozi looked around the room. "First, I'm going to change those sheets. I brought a set. Then, we'll eat dinner, watch a movie if they have something interesting on Pay-Per-View and we'll see what happens."

It wasn't his preferred order of things. "What happened to spontaneity?"

Ngozi batted her eyelashes. "Good things…"

He smiled. "Come to those who go out and wrestle them to the ground."

Ngozi removed her sheets from the bag and made the bed. She also served their dinner on China she had brought from home. Unlike Moni, she didn't put up a fuss when he had asked to be fed. She also dabbed his lips with a napkin. "I could get used to doing this every day."

"Knowing you, you would get bored with it sooner or later."

He shook his head. "You can never bore me."

"Stolen moments are always exciting," Ngozi said. She stood from his lap. "What kind of movie do you want to watch?"

"I was thinking we should do something else before we watch a movie."

She gave him a wide-eyed look. "What did you have in mind?"

He pulled her down on the bed and answered her with a kiss.

Chapter Twenty-Seven

Moni closed her eyes and released a long plume of air. Somehow, she'd made it to the end of the month without causing Sam grievous bodily harm. Caught up in the throes of enforcing his parental authority, he was making everyone miserable.

In addition to her bedroom door, Shekinah lost her cell phone and laptop. To protest what she had termed a great injustice, Shekinah went on a hunger strike that lasted two whole days. The more Moni begged her to eat; the harder Shekinah dug in her heels. Only when Moni had agreed to allow her to spend the weekend at her grandparents' home did Shekinah agree to eat.

She and Sam had agreed not to tell her parents about the drug possession incident. Given her mother's previous concerns, there was no way Shekinah's behavior wouldn't be seen as a result of their less than stellar parenting.

Fortunately, Mummy hadn't asked questions when she called and told her Shekinah and Sam were going through a difficult patch and they needed some time apart.

Even though she had not told Shekinah to hide the incident from her grandmother, she had a feeling Shekinah would keep the news to herself. She was smart enough to know the behavior wouldn't earn her any gold stars from her super-conservative grandparents.

As she ran the loofah sponge along the length of both arms, the plum & sakura blossom scent of the body soak filled her nose. She had been excited when Debo had sent an email to let everyone know Ngozi and Odosa were hosting the weekend's play party. Moni slid further into the bubbles. The night was going to be about her needs. She had earned it.

Wrapped in a bathrobe, Moni eyed the clothes she'd laid out. She smiled when she remembered Odosa's comment about how the color red suited her.

Moni opened her drawer to search for the red and gold silk scarf her father brought back from a mission trip to India. It was time it finally got an outing.

All dressed up, Moni smiled as she tied the scarf around her neck. The vibrant colours complimented her pale yellow blouse. She couldn't wait to see Odosa's eyes light up.

Sam's eyes ran over her when she came downstairs. "You look especially lovely tonight. I'm sure Odosa will appreciate the extra effort."

Eyebrow raised, Moni reached for her purse. Like he hadn't taken the time to shave and trim his nose hairs for his darling Ngozi.

"*Odosa?* I guess you forgot we're hanging out with the new couple?"

Sam's grin turned to a scowl. "Talk about cutting your nose to spite yourself."

Moni lifted her chin. "I have nothing to lose." But the truth was she was hoping the couple wouldn't show up. Otherwise, she would have to follow through just to prove her point to Sam.

***

Eyes averted, they both gave audible sighs of relief when they arrived and found the new couple absent. Sam marched toward Ngozi and Odosa.

In his haste, Sam barely acknowledged Debo's and Adele's greetings. She didn't make eye contact.

Moni looked across the room and watched Odosa's large eyes widen with excitement when he saw her. Heart thumping, she returned his smile. Her fingers twisted the red scarf draped around her neck.

She was ready to go upstairs when Debo ended the meet and greet segment. Under the dim lighting of the stairwell, Odosa, reached for her hand. "I wasn't sure you were going to show up tonight," he said. "I had wanted to call the house, but I couldn't take the risk that Sam would pick up the phone."

One of the group rules was no individual contact outside the play parties. But Moni didn't think breaking the rule would harm anyone. "Next time, just call my cell phone."

Odosa squeezed her hand. When they reached the stairway landing, he held a finger against his lips as they walked by the guest room. Ngozi and Sam who had gone ahead of them were inside.

She gave Odosa a puzzled look when she realized they were going to the master bedroom. Since she'd refused to go back to his daughter's room, they'd been spending their playtime on an inflatable bed in a corner of the basement. She hesitated by the door. "Are you sure?"

Odosa pulled her into the room and locked the door.

Moni's breath caught as her eyes zoomed in on the king-sized bed. She couldn't tell why the sight of crisp white sheets and sheer canopy bed drapes made her feel so unclean.

What was Odosa thinking? "But you told me Ngozi didn't want to use your bedroom for play parties."

Odosa wrapped his arms around her waist as he gently guided her toward the bed. "It's my bedroom, too."

Moni hesitated. "Are you sure?"

"This is where I want to be tonight," Odosa said as he untied her scarf. "Even though this looks beautiful on you. I've been itching to take it off since you got here."

Successful, Odosa flung the scarf on the bed. Moni squirmed as his fingers caressed her neck. "Your muscles are a little tense," he said. "If it will make you feel better, then you should know Sam has been in this room, too."

She had wondered why Odosa's face tightened whenever he glanced at Sam. Lost in Ngozi's eyes, her dear husband had not noticed the looks.

"So, is tonight all about playing tit for tat? If it is, I can head back downstairs."

"And what would you gain from doing that?" Odosa asked as he kissed her neck.

Moni struggled to stay focused. "Would you like me using you to get back at Sam?"

Odosa nibbled on her earlobe. "Moni, we can spend the evening talking about our spouses, or we can make good use of our time together. It's your choice."

She didn't say a word as Odosa unbuttoned her blouse.

It was as if being in his bed had unleashed something ferocious in Odosa. Drenched in sweat, he fell asleep while she freshened up in the master bathroom.

Gently closing the bedroom door, Moni headed downstairs to get herself a well-deserved glass of orange juice. Thankfully, the living room was still empty. She sat on the couch to enjoy her cool drink.

When she heard beeping sounds, Moni looked around for some minutes before realizing they were coming from her purse. In her haste, she had left it on the dining table. Moni walked over and pulled out her cell phone to check her messages. All three messages were from Mummy, and they were frantic.

Moni began to shake when she heard Mummy say Shekinah had overdosed on some pills and had been transported to the Trillium Health Centre.

By the third voicemail, Mummy's words were muffled by loud sobbing. She had never heard her mother sound so out of control. The situation had to be serious.

Lord, please don't let my child die. She's all I have.

Moni dumped the contents of her purse on the table in a desperate search for her bunch of keys. Where could they be? She remembered they were hanging on a hook at home. Sam drove to the play party. She ran upstairs and barged into the guest room.

Ngozi pulled the sheets to cover herself. "Moni, what do you think you're doing?"

Sam put his arm around Ngozi's shoulders. "You better have a good explanation."

"Shekinah's in the hospital," she said in a robotic voice. "I need the car keys."

Sam pushed Ngozi aside. He was almost at the door before he realized he was still naked. Moni paced as he ran back and put on his clothes. "Is she hurt? What happened?"

"Just let's go!" She spun around and headed for the car.

As they drove down the highway toward the hospital, the thought of what she'd been doing while Shekinah needed help brought a lump of half-digested shrimp to Moni's mouth. She began banging on the dashboard. "Pull over!"

Sam parked the car and held her until all she had coming up was bile. Moni wished she had the energy to tell Sam to shut up when he kept repeating sorry as she washed out her mouth and face with the bottle of water he'd found at the back of the car.

Shekinah. Her stomach twisted into several knots. For all she knew, it was already too late.

Chapter Twenty-Eight

Her mother's tear streaked face was the first thing Moni saw when she stepped into the hospital room. "Moni, where were you?"

The brokenness in Mummy's voice forced Moni to her knees. "We were at a friend's house."

"A friend's house? Moni, you knew how agitated Shekinah was when you dropped her off," she said. "Yet, you didn't answer your cell phone." Mummy pointed a trembling finger at Sam. "And yours was switched off. Shekinah kept asking for both of you."

Sam hung his head. "We're sorry, Ma."

From where she knelt, Moni's heart pounded at the sound of the IV pump and monitors hooked to Shekinah. She hadn't moved since they entered the room. But she was still alive.

Sam supported her as she stumbled to her feet. She moved closer to the bed, gripping the plastic guard rail. "Please, what happened?"

"Shekinah told me she was going downstairs to get a drink," Mummy said. "At first when I heard noises downstairs, I thought your father had returned from his outing. "Then I heard furniture being moved around. I came down and found Shekinah talking to herself as she knocked over another kitchen chair. When she saw me, she started tugging at her blouse, saying she had taken some pills and they were trying to make her heart pop out from her chest."

Tears filled Mummy's swollen eyes. "I was still trying to understand what Shekinah was saying when she began to shake. Within minutes, she was on the floor, convulsing. It was then that I called 911."

Was Shekinah trying to kill herself? Moni wondered. "What pills did she take?"

"I don't know the name. I found the yellow pills in her jeans pocket." She lowered her voice. "The paramedics and nurse said the pills were street drugs. Moni, when did my child start using drugs?"

She and Sam exchanged a look. Yellow pills. Did Shekinah keep some of the Molly? Sam moved toward the door. "I should get an update from the nurses."

Her eyes sent him a silent plea. *Don't leave me.*

Sam faced Mummy. "I'll be back soon, Ma."

Before she could open her mouth, he was gone.

"Moni, what is going on?"

She glanced at her sedated child. It was time to tell the truth. Mummy heard it and dragged herself toward a chair. "How could you children have kept such a thing from me? If I had known, I would not have left Shekinah alone."

"Mummy, it's not your fault. We didn't want you to be disappointed in us."

Turning her palms, Mummy moved them up and down like a weighing scale. "Tell me, my disappointment, your child's life, which one is more important?"

Moni couldn't meet her eyes.

"Your father is on his way. Given what you've just told me, I think it is best I wait for him downstairs. Shekinah won't be able to talk to him anyway. I'll let you and Sam decide on what to tell him. You know I will not lie for you."

"Mummy, I'm sorry."

The lines on her face had deepened from her obvious disappointment. "Moni, I have nothing more to say to you. Just take care of my child."

Before leaving, Mummy bent over Shekinah and prayed. She left without saying another word to her.

Sam brought back two cups of black coffee. "I didn't mean to stay away for so long," he said with an apologetic look. "I thought this would help."

Moni took the cup and set it down untouched.

Holding on to his cup, Sam sat beside her. "I spoke to the nurse and she told me Shekinah had overdosed on Molly. It was what caused her elevated heart rate and hallucinations."

The news didn't come as a shock. "But why was she sedated?"

"Shekinah was still agitated after they gave her some activated charcoal," Sam said. "Because she had a couple of seizures, they want to keep her for the weekend."

She had no intention of going home until the doctors could assure her Shekinah was fine. Gripping the chair's armrests, Moni stared at her sleeping daughter. She could not imagine life without her.

God, please let her live.

Finishing his coffee, Sam stood up and dumped the cup in the garbage can. Coming back to her side, Sam tried to hug her; she pushed him away. "Don't touch me."

Sam ran his hand through his hair. "What did I do? I'm just trying to comfort you."

"I can smell her all over you," she whispered.

He backed away. "I'm sorry."

She didn't want Sam around her. "Just go home."

"Go home?" Sam gave her an uncertain look. "Shekinah will want to see me when she wakes up."

"She'll most likely sleep through the night. I'll call if anything changes."

Sam walked over to the bed and stood over Shekinah for several minutes. "You'll call me when she wakes up?"

"Yes." Sam looked still undecided. "Just go."

He turned and left the room.

Moni cradled her head with both hands. She should have kept up with her searches of Shekinah's bedroom. If she had, she might have found the Molly.

Moni hurried to Shekinah's side when she heard a whimper. Shekinah settled back without opening her eyes.

She wished her mother had stayed. Shekinah needed prayers, and she didn't know where to start.

Repent ye therefore, and be converted, that your sins may be blotted out.

Crying, Moni fell to her knees. The words just began to flow. "I'm sorry, Lord. I'm so sorry. Please, spare my child's life. I promise, I will never attend those parties again. I will come back to you and trust you for my home. Please."

All night, Moni stayed on her knees, crying out for mercy.

The following morning, she and a groggy Shekinah came back from their walk to the shower room to find a woman waiting in the room.

The woman gave Moni a firm handshake. "My name is Lynda. I'm the social worker for the pediatric ward. I'm checking to see if there's anything I can do to help."

Leaving Shekinah in the care of her nurse, she reluctantly followed the worker to the little kitchenette stocked for patients and their families.

Even though her throat was closed up, Moni accepted Lynda's offer to make her a cup of tea. She needed the warmth. "When do the police come to the hospital?"

Lynda gave her a puzzled look. "Having the police come to the hospital for a drug overdose is not standard protocol. Since Shekinah isn't resisting treatment, the police don't have to be notified."

She feared that if the youth officer were told about Shekinah's overdose, the officer would change his recommendation of diversion. On the other hand, hiding the news could lead to a disastrous result. She shared her dilemma with Lynda.

"I think you should let the officer know about the overdose," Lynda said. "In these cases, transparency is the best approach. The most important thing is for your daughter to receive the help she needs."

She accepted Lynda's business card and some cafeteria vouchers for meals before Lynda walked her back to Shekinah's room. "It's usually a lonely road for parents when their children face addictions or mental health issues," Lynda said before she left. "If you need any help, please don't hesitate to give me a call."

"Thank you."

"All the best."

The following day, as she watched Shekinah nap, her mind went to the conversation with Lynda. The social worker was right about the loneliness. Mummy was the only person who had visited. When Shekinah was admitted for an appendectomy, there had been visits from the pastor and other members of their church. The women's league had also delivered warm meals to the house so Sam would not have to cook.

To be fair, they didn't know about Shekinah's condition. She didn't think it was possible to share the news of a child's drug overdose in church and expect privacy.

She was surprised when Sam visited her father and told him what had happened. Daddy called the hospital. Their conversation was brief, but from Shekinah's relieved look, Moni knew her grandfather had not come down too hard on her.

"Mom, I'm sorry," Shekinah said when she handed back her cell phone. She settled against her propped up pillows. "I know Grandpa and Grandma are going to be mad at you."

She sat at the edge of the bed. "What matters most is that you're alive for me to be mad at you."

Shekinah's look begged for understanding. "I just wanted to feel something." She tapped her chest. "In here, it felt dead."

Moni knew how it felt to be numb. She hugged her daughter. "We will get over this. Trust me."

Shekinah was discharged on the fourth day.

Sam picked them up. She sat with Shekinah in the back. Feeling the warmth of her daughter's body, Moni was thankful she wasn't the mother who had awakened the entire ward with her blood-curdling screams. One of the nurses told her a woman's son was never going home.

God had done His part and saved Shekinah's life. But despite her promise to Shekinah, she didn't know if she was strong enough to do her part. Then she remembered Mummy's words about fighting a battle that was not hers to fight.

Behold, I am the LORD, the God of all flesh: is there anything too hard for Me?

Moni tightened her grip around Shekinah and whispered the words, "Lord, I surrender. Your will, not mine."

Chapter Twenty-Nine

Sam was relieved when the motel came into view. He hadn't planned on being late for their rendezvous. It was a miracle he had not received a speeding ticket for racing down the highway so that he could get to Ngozi at their Taj Mahal motel in Guelph.

Flustered, Sam was glad the snarky guy who usually manned the front desk wasn't working. The reason for their motel stay had become the young man's standing joke. At their last visit, he had asked if they were celebrating Mother's Day.

The sweet faced woman behind the desk told him Mrs. Jones had checked into the room. He raced up the stairs.

Ngozi didn't look pleased to see him. "Thanks for keeping me waiting."

"Hello, Mrs. Jones. You look lovely as always."

"I was just about to leave," she said in a frosty tone. "Where were you?"

"I'm sorry for being late. Remember I told you Shekinah hasn't been feeling well. I had to take her to a doctor's appointment."

Ngozi moved from the doorway, and he walked in. "Still, you should have called to let me know what was going on. I also left a child at home."

Scratching an itch on his sweaty scalp, Sam wasn't sure how men who had two wives managed their schedule. Keeping things straight between Moni and Ngozi was causing him a lot of unneeded headaches.

Sam stared at the sullen woman standing akimbo in front him. "I'm sorry," he repeated. "Believe me. I got here as fast I could."

Still frowning, Ngozi plopped down on the bed. "I understand you need to take care of your child. It's just that you didn't come to the last party and you haven't been responding to my messages."

It had been hard to respond to Ngozi's numerous text messages. Each time his phone buzzed, Moni glared at him. It was as if she knew the sender.

"Ngozi, believe me. I'm not trying to ignore you." He knelt in front of her. "Listen, nothing has changed between us. It's just a matter of bad timing.

Once Shekinah is feeling better and back at school, I won't have to spend so much time at home."

She cocked her head to the side. "Are you sure?"

He nodded. "Positive."

Ngozi gave him a reluctant smile. "I guess I can stay for an hour or two."

"That's my girl," Sam said as he wrapped his arms around her. As he rested his head on her lap, he noted that she felt a little thicker around the waist. Sam kept his mouth shut. He knew pointing out a woman's weight gain wouldn't earn a man any points.

***

Ngozi propped her chin up on her hand. "Have you ever thought about leaving Moni?"

"Hmm." Feeling drowsy, Sam closed his eyes. He didn't want to talk. He wanted a nap.

She scooted closer and poked him in the ribs. "Sam, I'm talking to you."

Sam groaned Ngozi's name. Why did women always have to spoil a good thing? He opened his eyes and sat up. "And why is that such an important question?"

"I just need to know," she insisted.

That morning, Moni had told him she was no longer going to attend the swinging parties. Based on her renewed Bible reading and prayers, he had not been surprised by the decision. Grateful for Shekinah's life, he had told Moni he was fine with the decision. Ngozi and trips to Triple X were enough to keep him occupied.

Sam picked his words carefully. "Like most married people, there have been times when I have thought about it. However, things have gotten better between us."

Ngozi's hand rested on his chest. "Leaving Odosa never crossed my mind. That is, not until we started spending these special times together."

Sam went over her statement in his head. If he had heard right, she was thinking of leaving her husband for him. He had to shut those thoughts down. "If you left Odosa, it would be hard on your daughter."

"These days, I wonder if Odosa would even notice if we were to move out of the house."

Sam became alarmed. He wasn't looking to fill the position of a replacement daddy for Ifueko. He had his problems with Shekinah. He stroked her cheek. "Ngozi, I have a feeling this is getting hard for you."

She seemed to be reflecting on his words because there was a long pause before she replied, "It is."

"Perhaps it's best we end this now before someone gets hurt." Once the words were out of his mouth, he felt like a jerk. Her lashes fluttered, and her eyes began to shine with wetness.

"It's too late for that."

"Ngozi, look at me." She lowered her head instead. "I'm sorry. We both knew this was temporary. I didn't make any promises. I never told you I wanted to leave my family."

"You're right, you didn't. I just thought you felt the same way about me."

He did care about her. He just couldn't offer more. "Do you want me to leave now?"

"No. You stay. I'll go first." Ngozi rolled away from him. He was silent as she dressed and packed up her things. He stood up from the bed when she told him she had to take the sheet. She rolled it up and put it in the tote she carried and walked toward the door.

"I guess I'll see you at church?" The question felt ridiculous as soon as it left his lips.

"Not likely. Odosa has been talking about moving to a new church. I guess he was right about us needing a change." She lifted her chin. "Odosa will miss your wife. She must have been special to him. I found her scarf on our bed."

Sam frowned. Ngozi had told him their bed was off-limits. Before he could respond, Ngozi walked out of the door.

Chapter Thirty

Shekinah's progress at school and home became the silver lining in Moni's life. To her delight, Mr. Scott had intervened, and Shekinah could participate in the diversion program.

One of her responsibilities was to find where she would complete her community service hours. Determined to use the search as an opportunity to work on their communication, they talked about their options. They narrowed it down to a soup kitchen, a homeless shelter and a food bank close to home. Shekinah decided on the soup kitchen, and they were both welcomed as volunteers.

To her delight, Shekinah had adjusted well to spending Saturday mornings' washing greasy pots and peeling endless bags of potatoes even though the work ruined her pampered fingernails and she had to cut them. "They're just nails, Mom," Shekinah said with a nonchalant shrug. "They'll grow back."

Shekinah tried to escape when she wanted to kiss her on her cheek. "Mom, I'm too old for that stuff."

"No one ever gets too old for their mother's kiss," Moni said as she planted a big kiss on Shekinah's forehead.

While they worked, she and Shekinah talked about their day. Time together no longer felt like a chore. Seeing the long line of people they served and hearing their stories, the soup kitchen was the perfect venue for Moni to count her blessings.

She wasn't surprised when chatty Shekinah made friends with a young lady who attended the soup kitchen, with her grandmother.

During one of their potato peeling sessions, Shekinah asked if she and her new friend could go hang out at the mall the following weekend. Given what had happened with Allie, Moni had decided future friendships would be better scrutinized.

"You've only spoken to her a couple of times. How about you ask to see if she would be willing to volunteer here on some Saturdays? That way you guys can get to know each other better."

"Thanks, Mom. I hope she says yes. It would be nice to have someone young to talk to."

Moni placed a hand on her waist. "Are you saying I'm a dinosaur?"

Shekinah gave her an apologetic look. "Sorry, Mom. I didn't mean to be rude."

"Just teasing. To be honest, I'll be happy to have your friend join us. These aging lips would appreciate a break from talking."

Shekinah giggled.

"Now, more peeling and less talking," Moni said with a wave of her potato peeler.

"Yes, ma'am."

***

Later in the day, Moni admitted to herself when it came to her and Sam, she'd been expecting a road to Damascus experience, an instant transformation. They were finally doing the right thing.

Sam was not pleased when she told him she no longer wanted to experiment with sex toys. Apart from the flashbacks the acts brought, it became clear that what Sam wanted in bed, she was unwilling to give. He was still looking to capture the excitement of the play parties, and she needed to stop cold turkey. He had told her she was selfish.

Moni was conscious of Sam's piercing eyes as she folded their clean laundry. She didn't want, nor had the energy for an argument.

Her husband thought otherwise. "Moni, I have been very considerate. We've done everything your way. This is the one thing I have asked of you."

She began matching up his socks. "Sam, I can't. Every time we do those things, my mind takes me back to the parties, to being in Odosa's arms. It's not where I want to be."

"It's not that complicated."

"Tell me you don't think about Ngozi. About the things you did together."

Sam couldn't respond.

"I thought so."

Sam stood from the rocking chair. "I'm going for a run."

While she continued to pray and worked on finding different ways to banish the erotic images from her head, Sam worked through his mounting restlessness by joining a neighborhood running club. Regardless of the weather conditions, he was out on the streets on a daily basis. She wondered if he was punishing his body. "Be careful out there."

"I'm sure a part of you would be relieved if a hit and run accident made you a widow. You wouldn't have to deal with me."

Moni gaped at him. "Sam!"

He picked up his sunglasses from the dresser. "I'll see you later." The door slammed behind him.

Moni abandoned the clothes she had been folding and began to pray.

***

Things were in a much calmer state between her and Sam when Odosa called to ask for a meeting. The sound of his voice stripped away Moni's fragile sense of control. She said yes.

Moni decided against telling Sam. He wouldn't be able to understand her need for closure.

The following Saturday, leaving Shekinah in trusted hands at the soup kitchen, she headed for the Tim Horton's restaurant around the corner.

Moni's courage wavered when she saw Odosa's pensive face through the restaurant front window. Like her, Odosa looked like he had lost a lot of weight. Taking a deep breath, she walked through the sliding doors.

She stopped by his table. "Hello, there."

Smiling, Odosa stood. Before he could hug her, Moni stuck out her hand. He gave her hand an awkward shake. Placing her purse on the table, she sat in the chair across from his.

"Thanks for coming. It's so good to see you."

"I hope you haven't been waiting long."

"No, I've been here for only a couple of minutes." Odosa held her gaze. "You look even more beautiful than the last time I saw you. I missed you when I woke up."

Moni's breath caught. She didn't want to think about that horrific night. "How's the family?"

He ignored the question. Instead, he asked if Moni wanted anything to eat or drink.

"No, thank you."

Odosa stood. "I need a caffeine boost." He cast an apologetic grin. "Let me get a double-double. I'll be right back."

He took a sip of his coffee and Moni felt convicted when she thought she saw hope in his eyes. She should have declined the invitation. "Odosa—"

He interrupted her. "Please, hear me out. I need to know if there's any hope for us."

"Sam and I are trying hard to make our marriage work."

He peered at her face. "Moni, you don't look happy to me. Something tells me things have not been successful."

"As I said, we're still working on it." She held his gaze. "Odosa, I'm not prepared to leave my husband for you."

"I see." Sighing, he ran a hand across his face. "Yesterday, Ngozi told me she'd had an abortion last month."

She was at a loss for words. "Oh."

"Because of the complications Ngozi experienced with Ifueko's pregnancy, we had decided not to have any more children," Odosa said in a monotone voice. "To prevent any accidents, I got a vasectomy."

As Odosa's words sank in, Moni gripped the edge of the table. *Sam.*

Silent, they stared at each other for a couple of minutes. Breaking eye contact, Moni shook her head. "I need to go."

"Moni, those evenings we spent together were some of the best times of my life."

"Odosa, no." Moni pushed back her chair.

"Wait, I have something for you." Odosa reached into his coat pocket, pulled out her red and gold scarf and handed it over.

She placed the scarf on the table. "You shouldn't have bothered. I forgot all about it."

They both knew she wasn't just referring to the scarf.

"I didn't." Odosa's voice was solemn, and his eyes were sad.

Squirming in her seat, she found herself touching the scarf. Odosa leaned over and placed his hand on top of hers. A warm sensation shot up Moni's arm from the familiar feel of his touch. She jerked her hand away.

Beloved, flee from every appearance of evil.

Moni picked up her purse, then reached for the scarf. "It's best I leave now."

Odosa gave her a resigned look. "I understand. Take good care of yourself."

Moni swallowed the lump in her throat. "You, too."

At the door of the coffee shop, Moni took a deep breath. Her fingers clenched around the scarf for some minutes before she flung it inside an open garbage can. Some mementoes were too dangerous to keep.

Chapter Thirty-One

Debo looked up when Adele walked into their bedroom.

"We need to talk." Adele's accent always thickened when she was nervous.

He gave her his full attention. "I'm listening."

"I can't do this dancing back and forth anymore," she said with a shake of her head. "I want a divorce."

Because he had rehearsed various versions of the unfolding scene in his head, he could ask his question calmly. "Why?"

"I don't love you anymore."

"That's not an acceptable response," he said. "Do you have anything else?"

Adele muttered some French words under her breath before throwing up her hands. "What difference would giving you another reason make?"

They both knew who she was leaving him for. But he wanted, needed, to hear her say the name. Perhaps then, his brain could process what his heart found hard to accept. "Adele, we have four children, have been in each other lives for over twenty years, so I think I deserve more than the standard 'love don't live here anymore' break-up line."

Adele took a deep breath. "Edet values me."

The words were like picks dug deep into his skin. "He values you?"

"How could you have suggested we start swinging?" she asked. "Was I not enough for you?"

"Those are two separate things."

"They are not," Adele insisted. "Listen to this. The man, Debo, didn't think Adele was good enough not to be shared. The man, Edet, thinks Adele is good enough to keep to himself. Guess who Adele wants to be with?"

Debo remembered Moni's statement about him being the serpent that had wandered in her garden. In his foolishness, he had handed his wife a poisoned apple and destroyed his home. "You've made up your mind?"

Adele nodded. "Yes."

For several minutes, he thought about his options. "I will sign the divorce papers after you fulfill three conditions."

Adele's face perked up. "I'm listening."

"One, we'll both visit Pastor Iginla to let him know we're moving to Moose Jaw."

She frowned. "But, I'm not—"

He held up a finger. "I'm not done. Two, to keep up the charade, you'll go with me to Moose Jaw for two weeks. Your mom can watch the kids. Three, you will not have that man around my children until the divorce is final or I will fight you with everything I have. Together, we'll break the news to them."

"But, what's the point of my going with you to Moose Jaw?"

"Hmm. How do I put this? Well, I don't think the church would welcome an assistant pastor who is in the middle of divorcing a wife who is bent on committing adultery with another church member's husband."

Adele's face turned beet red. "I get the point."

Even though his heart was breaking inside, he gave her a big smile. "So, what do you say?"

"You have yourself a deal. I have one condition of my own," Adele added. "It's either you move to the guest room or camp out on an air bed on our bedroom floor."

"I'm staying in our room," he said. If he got his way, the boys would never get to know dad and mom had ever considered divorce.

***

Dressed in matching navy blue tops, he and Adele sat in Pastor Iginla's office to tell him the good news.

"I'm sorry it took me this long to give you a response," Debo said. "I, we, are happy to say that we'll be going to serve in Moose Jaw."

A broad smile transformed Pastor Iginla's face. "Glory to God! Deacon Debo, when I was praying this morning, the Holy Spirit told me it is where you needed to be. This is great news."

He turned to Adele. "Sister, my wife said you had called her."

"Yes, sir. She gave me some valuable advice."

"Good. Are you all going to move next month?"

"No, sir," Debo said. "With the children in the middle of their school year, we thought it was best for them to stay here until the summer months."

Pastor Iginla nodded. "The children's well-being is important. I'm sure the church would make the necessary accommodations for you." He stood and walked around his office desk to give them both a hug.

"We will miss you dearly. Deacon Debo, please rest assured that we'll take care of Sister Adele and the children in your absence. With your permission, I will make the announcement this Sunday so we can begin preparation for an appropriate send-forth service."

Guilt rose inside him. He would have preferred to leave Ontario without any fanfare. "I'm fine with the announcement, sir. But I don't want to inconvenience anyone."

Pastor Iginla patted him on the shoulder. "Your humility is commendable. But, you are part of our family. We must make you miss us enough to come back."

"Thank you, sir."

Before you leave, we should pray," Pastor Iginla said. "This is not a commitment to be taken lightly." He reached for their hands and closed his eyes.

As the warmth from the Pastor's hand seeped into his, Debo kept waiting for the moment where the pastor would sense the filth in his soul and pull away.

Pastor Iginla's booming voice filled the room. "Our dear Heavenly Father, before whom all hearts are open and no secrets, hidden. I bring before You this evening, Your children, Debo and Adele. Today, they have committed to serve You and Your people.

"I know and prophesy in part. Therefore, I hand Debo and Adele over to You as they start this new journey. Please, go ahead of them, go with them to make their paths smooth. And may Your peace which passes all human understanding guard their hearts as You work out Your purpose in their lives. Amen."

Fear stricken, Debo was unable to say amen.

Chapter Thirty-Two

Moni's heart skipped when she saw Sam's car idling in the parking lot of the soup kitchen.

Since there was no way she could walk by without being seen, she opened the car door and slid into the passenger seat. "Hey, you. What are you doing here?"

His eyes were cold. "I came to surprise my two hardworking ladies by bringing them lunch," he said. "Where were you?"

"Uh…" *Moni, no more lies.* "I went to see Odosa."

Sam's eyes narrowed. "Did you sleep with him?"

She shook her head. "No."

"So, how long have you guys been meeting behind my back?"

"It's not like that," she said. "This is the first time."

Sam snickered. "I'm expected to believe that?"

"It's the truth," she said. "Odosa called and asked for a meeting. I decided to see him because I wanted to get some closure."

"If it was all innocent, then why didn't you tell me?"

"Would you have let me go?" she asked.

"What kind of question is that? Would *you* have let me go to see Ngozi if she had called?"

Ngozi. "Did you know she was pregnant?"

Sam's fingers tapped a nervous beat on the steering wheel. "Last summer, Ngozi thought she was pregnant."

"*Last summer?*" Something clicked inside Moni's head. "Was that why she was crying at the church picnic?"

"Yes. She told me Odosa wasn't too happy about having another baby. Later, she said it was a pregnancy scare."

"Well, Odosa said she had an abortion last month. The baby wasn't his."

Sam looked at her as if she had suddenly sprouted horns. "What?"

"Any guesses as to the paternity?"

Sam avoided her eyes as he shrugged. "Ngozi is a married woman."

"Well, Odosa got a vasectomy years ago."

"Then, whose child was it?"

"Since you were her regular swing partner, your guess is as good as mine."

Guilt flashed across Sam's face as he sank into his seat. "Oh, my God."

"You didn't use protection."

"It was only a couple of times."

"You do know it only takes one time to catch an STD or to get someone pregnant? Sam, a baby's life was taken."

Sam's face hardened. "Before you go all sanctimonious on me, remember, your hands aren't squeaky clean either. You gave Odosa your cell phone number. I saw his text messages."

Moni looked away. Sam was right about her unclean hands. It was the reason why she still had a hard time believing God would forgive her when she couldn't forgive herself.

"Sam, trying to suppress what happened is not working for me," she said. "If you'd be honest with yourself, you'd admit it's not working for you either. We need help."

"Help from where?"

"The church," she said. "I'm sure Pastor Iginla will be able to help as we figure this out."

Sam gave her an incredulous look. "You want us to tell Pastor Iginla that we're part of the swinging group they're trying to hunt down? How do you think Debo and the others would handle that news? You're so caught in forging your new beginning you're willing to sacrifice everyone."

"That's not true. We don't have to say anything about them," she said. "This is about us getting right with God."

"You do realize once we tell him, we can't take the words back?"

A sense of shame settled over her. "I know," she said. "But our life now is based on a series of lies."

"Telling the pastor would be like shooting ourselves in the foot."

"But, we have to do something."

He started the car. "I have to go. Shekinah is waiting for you."

Moni opened the door and stepped out. "I'm sorry for messing up your plans. Another time?"

He looked surprised by her words. "That's okay," he said in a gruff voice. "See you at home."

"See you at home."

***

Sam went down to the basement, locked himself inside their home office and wept. Spent, he sprawled out on the carpeted floor.

Since leaving the soup kitchen parking lot, all he had thought about was how the baby could have been the son he'd always wanted. He felt betrayed. Regardless of the challenges involved, Ngozi should have told him about the pregnancy. The decision about what to do was rightly his and hers. It was not hers and Odosa's.

A mocking voice echoed in his head. *Sam, stop kidding yourself. Do you think another man's wife would carry your baby only to hand him over to you?*

His mind went back to their last meeting. Ngozi had probably terminated the pregnancy because he had told her he wasn't ready to leave Moni. Sam dug his face into the carpet. It was all over.

Sam was still down in the basement when the doorbell rang. He ran upstairs to see who was at the door. It was Debo. "Hey Bro, what are you doing here at this hour?"

"I know it's late. But, I needed to see you."

"Come in." He closed the door. "What's going on?"

"I'm moving to Moose Jaw, Saskatchewan," Debo said. Sam heard the weariness in his friend's voice.

He did a double take. "Are you kidding me?"

"Not a joke. I'm moving."

Sam placed a hand on Debo's shoulder. "Let's go talk downstairs. I don't want to wake Shekinah and Moni."

Debo shook his head. "How about we go outside? I could use the fresh air."

"Fine. We'll take a walk down the street."

He joined Debo outside, and they fell into step beside each other. "What happened?"

"Adele has found true love with Mr. Bassey."

He couldn't believe his ears. "Adele picked him over you? Is she on some street drugs?"

"I don't think so. We've been going back and forth on this issue for the past two months. I didn't want to burden you."

Sam stopped on the sidewalk. He had sensed something was bothering Debo. But he had been having too much fun to care. He scratched his head. "I'm sorry."

Debo looked as if he was on the verge of tears. "Adele wants a divorce. Sam, I don't want our marriage to end. I love her."

"Then, why are you moving to Moose Jaw? It will be hard to win her back from there."

"I know. But, I need to get away from here. I don't trust myself not to harm Mr. Bassey if I were to run into him. I wouldn't do too well in prison." He chuckled, but it held no joy.

"Moose Jaw is too far away." Sam was thinking of himself. Debo had always been around him. The thought of him living across the country was hard for him to wrap his mind around.

"When I'm all settled, you have to visit," Debo said.

"Of course. I'm sure Moose Jaw would have fun spots for us to explore."

"That's the last thing on my mind," Debo said swiftly, and Sam knew then his friend was truly hurting over the situation with Adele.

Debo took a deep breath. "I should let you get back home. Just in case Moni wakes up and finds you gone."

He decided to give Debo a heads up about Moni's intentions. "There's something you should know. Moni wants to tell Pastor about the swinging."

Sam had never seen his friend look so scared. "She wants to share details about the whole group?" Debo asked.

"She said she doesn't plan to." He looked away. "I don't want to go. But almost losing Shekinah scared me. And some days it feels as if Moni's shielding her from me. God knows what she's told her. I feel I need to go so I can get Moni off my back and perhaps gain a chance at winning Shekinah back. What do you think?"

Debo blinked behind his glasses. "It's your call. You can tell from my mess, I'm no marriage expert. I do need this assistant pastor job while I figure things out. Promise you won't say anything about me to Pastor."

"I won't." He extended his arms for a hug. "I'm going to miss you, Bro. As soon as you give the go ahead, I'm buying a plane ticket to Moose Jaw."

Debo stepped into his embrace, and they gave each other a tight hug. He would miss his friend.

Chapter Thirty-Three

Moni was drenched in sweat as she stuttered over her lengthy confession to Pastor Iginla. Sam watched Moni squirm under Pastor Iginla's gaze. He wished he hadn't caved in and allowed her to do this. His only relief was that she didn't say that it was he who had introduced them to swinging.

Pastor Iginla turned to him. His nostrils flared with every disgusting word he said. "Brother Sam, you're the head of your household. Why did you decide to do this evil thing?"

He had found the whole experience quite enjoyable. Since he didn't want to talk about the affair or his feelings about being overlooked, his response was flippant. "It was the devil. Things had just spiralled out of control."

The pastor shook his head. "Brother, the Bible says, there is a way that seemeth right unto a man, but the end thereof are the ways of death." Standing, he walked over and got his Bible.

"It's always best to check the lies thrown by the devil with God's word."

Sam fidgeted through what he considered a rather long-winded sermon about how there shouldn't be a hint of sexual immorality amongst God's people and how it brought dishonor to God's name.

While the Pastor's words had bored him, it had reduced Moni to tears. He didn't feel sorry for her. She had insisted on airing their dirty laundry in public. If he were to conduct a church-wide poll, he was sure everyone had issues they kept private.

"Since you are part of our family, the church will pay for Christian counseling should you decide to attend," the pastor said. "We have a list of counselors. However, until the counseling is completed, I think it's best you both stop serving at the church."

Moni's crying grew louder. Irritated, Sam kept his eyes fixed on a spot above the pastor's head. He shouldn't have let Moni weaken his resolve not to come.

The pastor handed Moni a box of tissues. "Please believe me. My intention is not punishment. My hope is to see you restored to full fellowship in love and dignity."

Moni shook her head. "Pastor, this is hard."

"Sister, by coming and making this confession, you've already taken the hardest step," Pastor Iginla said in a gentle voice. "The time away from your ministries here will help you focus as you work on your relationship with your husband and God. Our minds and bodies need discipline. When they are out of control, we wander down questionable paths."

For a brief moment, Pastor's eyes settled on his fists. Feeling uncomfortable, Sam flexed his fingers.

"If we want to enjoy the fullness promised to us, it can't be about chasing the euphoria of serving Jesus. We have to pick up our crosses on a daily basis and walk the path of righteousness. Even on the days, we don't feel like doing it."

Pastor Iginla moved to the edge of his seat. "Before you leave, there's something I need to know. Are there other members of Faith Assembly involved in this practice?"

They were both quiet.

Moni nodded her head.

"Sister, what are their names?"

He gave Moni a pointed look. She had promised not to divulge any names. If she opened her mouth, he would make her pay.

Moni looked down. "Pastor, I'm sorry," she whispered. "I cannot say."

"Brother Sam?"

"It is not my place to talk about people's problems."

"Let me be clear that this is a serious issue. It is a sin that is threatening to destroy the fabric of our church family."

Pastor Iginla stretched out his hands. "Please, let's say a prayer of agreement before you leave. I'll continue to lift you up in prayer. This is not going to be an easy battle."

***

Sam slammed the car door shut and faced Moni. "Are you happy now? I said you were going to regret coming here for help."

"I wasn't expecting Pastor to throw us a pity party. Sam, this is serious business."

"I'm sure you weren't expecting him to say you couldn't lead worship or do all the other stuff you love. Oh, poor you. What are you going to do?"

"Why are you so spiteful?"

Sam cut his eyes at her. It was always her way. Always and he was sick of it. "Last Sunday, I'm sure you saw Mr. Bassey standing by the church entrance in his head usher jacket," he said. "And Adele is still in the choir. Even Debo is getting what he wants. He's quietly going about his business before he leaves for Saskatchewan. You know why no one has suspended them? It's because they've kept their mouths shut."

"I don't care what anyone else is doing," Moni said. "We're not going to sprint into heaven as a group. I'm just focusing on my soul."

Sam slapped his thigh. "Finally you make sense! Since this is all about individual journeys, Moni, please stop dragging me along on yours. I'm more than your husband or Shekinah's father. I have a mind, too. Let me decide what is best for me as a person."

Moni threw up her hands. "Fine. I give up. Do it your way."

"Thank you. I intend to."

During the drive home, Sam could barely contain his excitement as he thought about his next move. Who would have thought that a visit to Pastor Iginla would set him free?

He shouldn't have to sit in a church pew while his heart was somewhere else. No need to restrain himself because of other people's expectations. At long last, he was going to experience abundant living.

Chapter Thirty-Four

He rubbed his fingers across the door name-plate as he mumbled the name and title under his breath. *Debo Ajala, Assistant Pastor.* The white plastic made the nameplate look a little cheap, but it would do until he could arrange for something appropriate.

Shoulders squared, he turned the doorknob and stepped into the office. The room size pleasantly surprised him.

A warm shade of green, the room was large enough to accommodate an oak executive desk and a couple of leather upholstered armchairs. He pictured himself seated in them as he ministered to church members.

Debo placed his briefcase down before walking toward the large window. He pulled back the long drapes to reveal an unobstructed view of Moose Jaw River. There were several people out skating on its frozen waters. Debo inhaled as he traced a circle in the frosted window.

Even though he had been told Moose Jaw's weather made Brampton feel like Florida, he hadn't expected to feel so cold.

He opened his briefcase and brought out a large framed family picture, and the family Bible passed on by his father before he left for Nigeria. He placed the picture frame at the right angle for visitors and placed the Bible to the right of his chair.

For a fleeting moment, his smile slipped when his eyes settled on the faces of his four boys. Even though he had seen them that morning, he missed them. It would be a temporary separation, he promised himself.

To shake off the heavy feeling, he sat in the chair and swirled himself around several times. He had been given a second chance, and he wasn't going to blow it.

A loud knock on the door made him bring the chair to a stop. Schooling his expression into the somber look befitting a pastor, Debo cleared his throat. "Please, come in."

The door creaked open, and Deacon Gabriel walked in. Debo had forgotten that the man was waiting for him in the main sanctuary. "Do you need anything?" Deacon Gabriel asked.

Debo stood. "No." He gave the older man an apologetic look. "Sorry for taking so long. I could not help saying a prayer."

"I just wanted to make sure you were fine," Deacon Gabriel said. "If you're not done, I can wait downstairs."

"There's no need to. I finished just before you knocked on the door." Debo reached for his briefcase. "I appreciate you bringing me here." He had wanted to see his new office on day one.

"I'm always happy to serve where needed," Deacon Gabriel said. "I must say we were surprised when Pastor Ezekiel announced your impending arrival. A group of us started the fellowship that evolved into this church. We were hoping that leadership would choose someone local. Someone who understood our vision. Nevertheless, we're happy that you're here."

Debo had the sense that the local person Deacon Gabriel had in mind was himself or one of his cronies. "As you know, we have all been given different gifts," he said. "Sometimes, so-called outsiders are more equipped for the job."

"You're right. But there's also a difference between anointed and wrongly appointed," Deacon Gabriel said before heading towards the door.

Okay. Feeling uneasy, Debo gave the retreating back a thoughtful look. He couldn't help wondering if Deacon Gabriel knew something about him.

***

Throughout their three-and-a-half-hour flight from Toronto to Regina, Adele spoke to him twice. During the hour drive from Regina to Moose Jaw, he had been able to draw her into a stilted conversation, but he knew she had tried because of Deacon Gabriel's presence.

He walked into the hotel suite bathroom. "I'm back."

Adele was drying her hair. She glared at him. "I guess you forgot how to knock."

"An unlocked door is an invitation," Debo said as he stared at her. He still remembered what it felt like running his fingers through her hair, drawing in the faint smell of vanilla from her shower gel.

"It's only an invitation for someone who doesn't understand the concept of boundaries," she said. "Please, stop staring. You're making me uncomfortable."

He grinned when Adele turned away her face as he unzipped his trouser. "This isn't the first time we've both used the bathroom."

Adele switched off the dryer and left, slamming the bathroom door behind her.

He couldn't understand how she could have gone from loving him to hating him. There had to be something left, something he could hang his hopes on. Blinking back frustrated tears, Debo zipped up and washed his hands. Adele was in front of the television when he came out. "Since there's no air mattress here, I guess we're sharing the bed."

"I thought you would be sleeping on the couch."

"No. You're free to join me on the bed," he said as he sprawled out. "Perhaps one last snuggle for old times' sake?"

"Very funny. I didn't come here for that. My presence is in exchange for an uncontested divorce. Don't make all this harder than it has to be."

He had only been trying to lighten the mood. Not that he would have forced her to do anything against her will. "Adele, don't be silly. I'm not going to jump on you."

"I'm fine over here," Adele said as she curled on the couch.

"Suit yourself. Are you ready to Skype with the children?"

She gave him a guilty look. "I spoke to them while you were at the church. They should be in bed by now."

He had been looking forward to the call. "You are already trying to keep my children away from me."

"Debo, no. Maman was exhausted. She needed to rest."

He gave her a disbelieving look. Since Adele was no longer on his team, he no longer trusted her.

"Fine, you can call her."

He wasn't going to disturb a seventy-year-old woman's sleep. "You can sleep on the bed. I'm going to walk the hallway."

He would need a special kind of grace to survive the next two weeks without losing his mind.

Chapter Thirty-Five

Sam soon began to get bored with attending Triple X. If he was going to please himself, he was going to do things right. A chat with one of the bartenders proved invaluable as she turned out to be a walking encyclopedia on online sex chat rooms.

Sam found himself spending hours just browsing through the message boards. There were hundreds of them, and he felt like a child set loose in a candy store.

Moni had kept her word about letting him be, and he planned weekends around his activities.

In a matter of days, he was spending time with people he'd met online. It was easier than he had thought. First encounters were held at coffee shops far from home, while motels and homes were used as party venues.

Despite the variety, the parties were not enough to fill a yawning hole inside him. It became all about finding the next thrill. Given the variety of sexual acts the people he had met wanted or were offering, he knew it was out there. And time was on his side.

Back from an extended overnight date with a couple of women he'd met on one of his websites, Sam dragged himself past Shekinah's bedroom. She was sprawled out on her bed. The door had been replaced with the condition that it be kept open at all times.

Shekinah looked up from her book and gave him a tentative smile. "Hi, Dad."

"Hello, Princess." Moni had been successful in turning Shekinah against him. Clutching their matching Bibles, they stepped aside whenever they ran into him in the hallway. Most times, Moni's eyes were flashing the Morse code for the words "big sinner". His jaw clenched. Like she had the right to judge him.

"Dad."

He turned and saw Shekinah standing by her doorway. "Dad, are you coming with us tonight?"

"Going with you where?"

"Church. I told you I was getting baptized and you had said you would attend."

"Don't think so, Princess." Unable to face Pastor Iginla, he had not been back at church since the day they met with him. There was also no point in going to church to sing, "I surrender all," when he wanted to hold on to a fair number of things. When Shekinah had asked him, he didn't have the heart to tell her he couldn't go. It had been easier to lie.

"I need to catch up on my sleep," he explained. "And with the way I feel, it's unlikely I would make it out of bed before tomorrow afternoon. Make sure your mom takes plenty of pictures for me."

Her obvious disappointment had pulled down Shekinah's lips. "I'll tell her," she said. She disappeared into her room.

Sam found himself grappling with guilt. He could tell that Shekinah had wanted him at her baptism. But attending the event meant facing his in-laws. He would prefer not to speak to them until he knew the direction he was going to take.

Despite what Moni must have told them, they'd been kind enough to stay in their home, while he had stayed in his.

Sam continued on his way. He would get Shekinah a nice gift to make up for his non-attendance. There would be other events.

***

The sound of his Akon's "Mama Africa" ringtone made him pick up his cell phone from the coffee table. Seeing Debo's number flash across the screen, he took the call. "Hey, Bro."

"Hey," Debo said in a tired voice. "Thought I should let you know we got here safe and sound."

"Great. What's the place like?"

"I haven't seen much of the town, but the church looks good. We're having dinner with the senior pastor later tonight."

"How's Adele? Any progress?"

"No. I'm not giving up yet, though."

Debo could be delusional at times. From what he'd heard through others at the group, Adele had moved on. "That's the spirit," he said. "Keep at it."

"Thanks, Bro. How are your ladies?"

"As far I know, Shekinah has been keeping out of trouble. Moni's somewhere in the house."

"That's good. I was wondering if you could check on the boys for me," Debo said. "From what Adele said tonight, I don't think Maman is coping well."

"Of course." He loved the attention the boys gave him. "Consider it done. If Maman is open to an outing, is it okay for me to take them out? I know they love that video game arcade not far from your house."

"I'm sure she'll be fine. Thanks, man. I owe you."

"No, you don't. Just paying up some old debts so we'll be square."

Sam heard Debo sigh. "This all feels like a bad dream. I want my old life back."

Sam felt bad for his friend, but he couldn't say the same about his own life. His new life was great. In the past week, he had been thinking of moving out of the house. The accusing looks on the faces around him were beginning to wear on him. "Give yourself some time," he said. "Things will get better."

"I just remembered something. The deacon who picked me up from the airport was acting strange. I haven't been able to shake the feeling that the man knows something about our group."

"I hope you're wrong. What's his name?"

"Gabriel Nkop."

The name was unfamiliar to him. "Never heard of him," Sam said. "Well, find out what you can about him and watch your back."

"Will do. Got to go now," Debo said. "We'll catch up later."

"Stay out of trouble."

He heard a bit of the old Debo when he chuckled. "I wish. Trouble keeps finding me."

Chapter Thirty-Six

"I'm ready when you are," Adele said.

Debo looked up from punching the address into the GPS and whistled. She had picked one of his favorite dresses for their dinner with the Ezekiel's.

The blue silk material flowed over her voluptuous body in the right sort of way, not tight but clingy enough to showcase a small waist that would make one doubt that she had given birth to four children.

He stood from the desk chair. "You look good."

Adele looked uncertain. "It's not too much?"

Debo picked up his leather jacket. "On you, even a dress made of jute would be too much."

"Monsieur Sweet Nothings." The tone of the words was not complimentary.

"Adele, a simple thank you would have worked."

"Just so know, I'm going to leave the talking to you." Adele grabbed her coat. "You're the one who needs to make a good impression."

There were many uncomplimentary things he could say to her, but he didn't want them to arrive at the Ezekiel's with Adele in a bad mood. "They're expecting us at six, so it's best we leave now."

"Fine with me." Adele picked up her purse, and they headed out.

They arrived at the Ezekiel's doorstep with five minutes to spare. Adele held the potted plant she brought back from her shopping trip as he pressed the doorbell.

From pictures on the church website, Debo recognized the pastor as he opened the door and held it wide. When he came to the door, he said, "Welcome."

Standing behind him, Sister Unoma, his wife, looked delighted to see them. "We hope you didn't have any trouble finding your way?" she asked.

"It was very straightforward," he said. "It's a pleasure to meet you, sir."

Pastor Ezekiel offered his hand. "The pleasure is all ours."

Even though Debo was over a head taller, there was something about the pastor that made his presence filled the room.

Pastor Ezekiel led the way to a formal dining room. "I didn't invite the rest of the pastoral staff. We thought you are not ready to meet a crowd."

Debo nodded. "It had been a long day. Leaving the kids was difficult."

"I understand you have four children," Sister Unoma said.

Adele promptly brought out pictures of boys from her purse. "We took these last Christmas."

"Aww, they are precious." Sister Unoma passed the pictures to her husband. "Very fun ages, too. I can't wait to meet them."

Debo had been told they had fraternal twins who were in college. "Your children must be at school?"

Pastor Ezekiel nodded. "Yes, they are both at McGill." He gave his wife a teasing smile. "These days, their mother lives for the summer months."

Sister Unoma raised an eyebrow. "Says the man who does a countdown to their arrival by crossing off the days on his calendar."

They all laughed.

"McGill is a wonderful university. Adele and I met there."

"I didn't know that," Pastor Ezekiel said. "Montreal is such a beautiful city."

"It is. I'm biased since it's my home city," Adele added.

"Do you still have family there?" Sister Unoma asked.

"I'm an only child, so it's just my mother and some extended family members. My father passed away a couple of years ago."

"Sorry to hear that," Sister Unoma said.

"Thank you."

"How did you meet each other?"

He reached for Adele's hand knowing she would not be able to ignore him. "Adele got my attention by tripping and dumping a cup of scalding coffee in my lap."

Adele pulled her hand away under the pretext of reaching for the platter of roasted vegetables even though she hated eggplant. The brief contact made him long for more.

"I made up for it by accepting your dinner date offer," she said as she heaped her plate.

"And here you are today," Sister Unoma said with a happy sigh. "Parents of four beautiful boys."

Unless a miracle happened, their love story was over. "Yes, here we are." He watched as Adele stuffed her mouth with eggplant. What had happened to his Adele?

"Our story is a little different," Pastor Ezekiel said in a smug tone. "I snatched Unoma out of a convent."

Sister Unoma chuckled. "Here we go again. He didn't snatch me. I left."

Pastor Ezekiel faced him. "Back in those days, I used to do a lot of street evangelism. She had heard my voice through the megaphone and had looked out of her window to see the gentleman whose baritone voice was charming the crowd. I think it was love at second glance."

"I saw him that day," Sister Unoma said as she gave her husband an indulgent look. "We couldn't understand why he had decided to do his evangelism in front of our premises."

"It was the perfect spot," Pastor Ezekiel said.

"Of course it was. I didn't see him again until after I had left the novitiate."

Debo was speechless.

"You were going to be a nun?" Adele asked.

"Yes. Leaving the convent wasn't an easy decision. My desire to serve Jesus hadn't changed. What changed was the way I wanted to serve him."

They all heard the loud beeping sound of an oven timer. Sister Unoma pushed back her chair. "The shrimp balls are ready."

"So what do you think of our little city?" Pastor Ezekiel asked as his wife hurried to the kitchen. "Do you see yourself staying here?"

"I must admit the weather would take some getting used to. I was surprised when Pastor Iginla told me there was a parish of Faith Assembly up here. Most Nigerians stay in the Greater Toronto Area."

Sister Unoma came back to the table with a plate of brownies. "Our work brought us here," she said as she set it down.

"Unoma and I work in a potash mine about fifty kilometers north of

Moose Jaw. I'm a mining engineer. She works in the human resources department. I'm sure you're aware that at this time, the church is not able to support a full-time pastor. We're very grateful that the school would continue to pay you while you serve here."

"As the church grows, I'm sure things will change," Debo said.

"The local church is important but we have the heart for missions, and we've been praying for growth in this area," Pastor Ezekiel said.

During their university days, they'd spent hours on benches as they talked about changing the world for Jesus. "There was a time when Adele and I had thought about being missionaries."

"Perhaps God sent you here to prepare you," Pastor Ezekiel said. "God works out His purpose in our lives through the things that happen to us. We sent our first missionary team to Zambia this past year. There is a huge community of Chinese workers there who have been able to hear the word of God for the first time because they are in Africa."

Debo glanced at Adele. "Adele has never been to Africa."

"Really?" Sister Unoma said. "Brother, why haven't you taken her?"

"We keep postponing our trip to go see the grandparents," Debo said. "It's a long trip for little ones."

Sister Unoma nodded. "Relocating across the country when you have little ones can't be easy either. We'll be happy to help you look for a suitable daycare, a family doctor or employment. Sister Adele, I know you are a teacher, but we often don't think about the transferable skills that we can bring from one job to another job. If you have a resume available, I can start looking out for opportunities."

"I'll need time to work on one," Adele said. "I've been at my current job for six years."

"No pressure," Sister Unoma said. "We just want to make you so comfortable you won't want to leave us."

"I don't know if you'll be able to keep us here. The church in Brampton wants us back," Debo said.

"I love a good challenge," Sister Unoma said.

Pastor Ezekiel shook his head. "You've been warned."

"Don't scare them off." Sister Unoma turned to him. "Tea or coffee to go with your brownies?

"Tea will be fine."

It was almost eleven p.m. by the time they left to head back to their hotel. Ten minutes into the drive, Adele had nodded off. She drifted to the side until her head rested on his shoulder. The familiarity made his heart ache.

For the first time in a long while, Debo found himself praying in earnest for Adele and their marriage, but a mocking voice in his head told him too little, too late.

Chapter Thirty-Seven

He watched as Adele brought out her toiletries bag from the bathroom. She placed it in her suitcase. "This wasn't our deal. We had agreed you would stay for two weeks."

"Debo, I need to go home," Adele said in a firm tone. "I'm done. This constant badgering is more than I can handle. I've played my part here."

He had not expected Adele would call the airline and change her flight home. The proximity had him on edge as Adele frustrated his attempts to repair their relationship.

Even though he would miss her, a part of him was relieved by her decision to leave earlier than planned. "So, this is it? See you whenever?"

"I wouldn't do that to the boys," she said. "They need you in their lives. We'll just have to figure out a schedule for visits and calls. I don't imagine your responsibilities here would give you a lot of free time."

He stopped to gape at her. She was putting him on a timetable? "How generous of you," he sneered. "I don't want to interrupt your precious adult time."

Adele straightened her African wax print skirt and blouse. The *dashiki* and *sokoto* outfit he wore was made from the same material. His parents gifted the material. They had no idea about the current situation. Debo sighed. He'd made such a mess of things. His mother loved Adele.

"Does your mother know about your plans?"

"I'm a big girl," Adele said. "I don't need her permission or her approval."

"She would be so proud to know that her married daughter is dating."

Adele's eyes flashed a challenge. "Are you sure you want me at the church service?"

"We had a deal."

"Our deal didn't include my being subjected to insults."

"Why are you so angry? I only said the truth."

"I'm sure your parents would be proud to know their golden boy was in charge of the swinging group."

"Adele—"

"Now that we've established that we're huge disappointment to our parents, I would like to leave for church."

Since he didn't have an appropriate response, Debo followed her out of the room. He had a church to win over.

***

Debo's heart thumped as he prepared himself for the podium. A part of him almost expected the building roof to roll back as a booming voice announced that he was a fraud.

He and Adele stood when Pastor Ezekiel and the choir led the church in a welcome song. Debo couldn't help feeling excited. Things had not worked out the way he'd planned them, but he was still moving forward.

"Family, as I invite Pastor Debo and Sister Adele up here, please, let us give them a warm Faith Assembly welcome."

For a moment as he stood under the spotlight, an intense feeling of fear gripped him. He didn't belong on the stage.

He took the microphone from Pastor Ezekiel and faced the congregation. *One, two, three, action.* "Good morning, Faith Assembly. We bring greetings from everyone at our home church in Brampton."

Debo laughed when someone in the pews said Moose Jaw was now his home. "Yes, this is our new home. We look forward to getting to know you all."

He handed the microphone to Adele who mumbled a few words and handed the microphone back to Pastor Ezekiel. "You can tell who the talker in the family is," Pastor Ezekiel teased as they went back to their seats.

At the end of the service, he and Adele stood in the lobby to greet the people in the receiving line. Deacon Gabriel and his wife were the last people in the line. "Nice seeing you again," Debo said as Deacon Gabriel introduced his wife, Sister Prudence. She gave his hand a vigorous shake before hugging Adele. "I understand you and the children will not be joining us for a while."

"We didn't want to disrupt their school year." Adele's smile was strained, and for the second time that day, Debo was relieved she was leaving. He wasn't sure she could handle much more of the pretense.

Debo could feel Deacon Gabriel's eyes on him. He was used to being liked and didn't know how to handle the man's covert animosity. Perhaps if he went to him for advice about church matters, he would feel appreciated. He wasn't going to worry about it. There was time for him to figure things out.

"We'll take good care of him for you," Sister Prudence said to Adele.

"He's quite used to other people taking good care of him." Adele cut her eyes to him and then returned them to Sister Prudence.

"Are there any particular meals your husband likes?" Sister Prudence asked as if he wasn't standing there. Debo shifted from one foot to the other. The last thing he needed was different women dropping off food for him and staying behind to chat.

"Anything you make would be fine," Adele said.

"I do know my way around the kitchen," Debo said. "I don't want to be a bother."

"It's the least we can do," Sister Prudence insisted. "Perhaps you can join us for dinner before you leave for Ontario?" she said to Adele.

"My plans changed, and I'm leaving this evening."

"That's too bad. It's been a while since we visited Ontario. My cousin attends your church."

"Who is that?" he asked.

"You must know them," Sister Prudence said. "The Bassey's. Sister Ekaete and I are first cousins."

We know them all right, Debo thought as he glanced at Adele.

Adele had gone pale. "We are...friends. I'll be sure to pass on your greetings to them."

Deacon Gabriel who had wandered away came back for his wife. "The children are hungry." This time when his disapproving eyes swept over Debo, he knew why. At least his instincts had been dead on.

"Pastor Debo, see you at Wednesday Bible study," Sister Prudence said before they walked away.

"I thought my heart was going to pop out of my chest," Adele whispered to him. "Mrs. Bassey wouldn't say anything to her cousin, would she?"

He mulled over the question. He didn't think so since she also had something to lose. "How's she handling her upcoming divorce?"

Adele looked away. "She doesn't know Edet is leaving her."

From what he knew of her, Mrs. Bassey had a fiery temperament. "Well, in that case, your guess is as good as mine."

***

Adele had asked to be dropped off at the Air Canada terminal. He parked curbside. "So what's the next step?"

"I'll send you the divorce papers when they're drawn up," she said. "At some point, we will have to talk about our joint assets and how to go about dividing them."

He didn't want to think about getting a lawyer or attending court proceedings. "Are you staying in Brampton?"

"We haven't decided yet."

They used to be the 'we' in Adele's sentences, Debo thought. "Well, I hope you find whatever it is that you're looking for." He parked the vehicle.

He was surprised to see tears in Adele's eyes. "I know you think I hate you," she said. "I don't. I can't. You'll always be the father of my children. And I'll love you for that. I hope you find whatever it is you're looking for in this place."

Her words just made him feel worse. It sounded like a "let's throw Debo a bone" speech. There was nothing for him in Moose Jaw. He just needed somewhere to hide while he figured out his messy life.

"I'll call when I get home," she said as she brushed her fingers against his cheek.

His skin tingled from her touch. "Adele, please—"

Not waiting for his words, she turned away, and a big part of his life ended as the door closed with a gentle thud behind her.

Chapter Thirty-Eight

It wasn't how she had planned to break this news to her mother, Moni thought as she leaned against the kitchen table. Mummy's request to meet with the both of them had left her with no choice. "Sam couldn't come because he moved out of the house two weeks ago," she said.

Mummy gave her an alarmed look. "Moved to where? Why?"

Sam had told her since he still intended to file for divorce, it was best they start their one year separation period. She couldn't meet Mummy's eyes. "He's staying in an apartment somewhere in Toronto. He has, em, asked me for a divorce. He already brought the papers home."

Mummy didn't look shocked. "Sam's absence from church and family events clued me in that something was seriously wrong." Her mother paused for a long moment and then asked, "Moni, are you finally ready to tell me the truth?"

Moni watched her mother age before her eyes as she told her about Sam's affair, her behavior towards him, the swinging, the divorce request, everything.

"Please don't tell Daddy," she begged. "He would probably ask me never to come back to this house."

"Your father strives to live like Jesus. And Jesus does not reject sinners. I will let you decide whether to tell him," Mummy said as she rested against the kitchen table and took a deep breath. "Child, the Bible says, except the Lord build the house, they labor in vain that build it. Committing adultery was no way to save your marriage. It dishonors God, and you're supposed to honor Him first, more than anything else."

"Mummy, it felt as if I had no other choice."

"It was a lie from the enemy, right from the pit of hell," she said. "His plan is always to keep believers down until they are destroyed. Moni, humility is the secret to redemption. For things to change, you must take yourself out of the equation and give it all to God."

Her gaze flickered up to Mummy's face and back to her hands. "But Sam wants out of our marriage," she said. "I can't make him stay."

"Do you want a divorce?"

It was a question she'd asked herself daily.

Sam's choice to see other women had set her free. He had hurt her again, and the anger which overwhelmed her pain left no room for other emotions. Placing all the blame at Sam's feet would be easy. But she had chosen to swing with him.

The irony was his departure had brought both relief and a desire for reconciliation. Moni wanted to see if they could salvage their marriage just because she still loved him.

Moni shook her head. "No. But what else can I do?"

Mummy gave her a pointed look. "Have you been consistently praying for Sam and your marriage?"

The prayers she said were mostly about Shekinah and her struggles. She hung her head.

"Moni, I'm not going to tell you to sign or not sign the divorce papers. As a Christian, you cannot make it through this trouble-ridden life by piggybacking on someone else's convictions. You have to know the Lord's will for your life. And you can only do that by asking Him. Child, He's always near. Let's pray."

She held on to Mummy's hands.

"Father God, I have come before Your throne of mercy to ask You to help my Moni become the person You meant for her to be. I also ask that You bring about a transformation in her husband. And in Your perfect timing, may these two completely turn back to You and each other. Amen."

***

Moni sat in the car outside her parents' home for a couple of minutes. She rested her head against the steering wheel before reaching over to turn on the radio.

Since deciding to take control of her mind, it was left permanently on their local Christian station. She was determined to saturate her mind with the Word anyway, anytime she could. The afternoon show hosts were discussing Psalm 91.

Moni listened as they discussed how the secret place was more than the intimacy and familiarity of the presence of God. The pastor said the secret place could also be a physical place, a prayer closet where one could be alone with pressing thoughts and with God.

At home, she heard Shekinah moving around in her room. She walked by. All she could think of was that she needed to be in a secret place.

Moni locked the door behind her and looked around the room. Before their lives were turned upside down, the bedroom had been her place of refuge.

She bit her lip when the sight of the king-sized bed brought back memories of her last time in Odosa's arms. On the heels of the memories, came phantom scents from the body oils and fragrant candles they had used during the play parties.

Moni choked back tears. She had to find another room. Turning on her heel, she unlocked the door and ran down the stairs. She wandered through the living room and kitchen and ended up in the basement. Claustrophobic, the tight crawl space under the stairs would have been her last choice. She opened the door and huddled inside. Feeling as if air was being drawn from her lungs, Moni wrapped her arms around herself.

"Lord, I confess my sin of sexual immorality and pride. I pray for Your mercy and forgiveness."

Between her gasps, she recited Psalm 51. "Be merciful to me, O God, because of Your constant love. Because of Your great mercy wipe away my sins!"

By the end of the psalm, she was drenched in sweat. It felt as if she'd been running up and down a hill.

Beloved, your shame is removed.

"Mom, where are you?"

She lifted her head at the sound of Shekinah's voice.

"I'm in the crawl space."

Moni was surprised when Shekinah asked to join her. She didn't like tight spaces either. Shekinah wedged herself in. Moni pulled the light cord and saw her eyes drowning inside pools of sadness.

"Honey, what's wrong?"

Shekinah searched her face. "Are you and Dad getting a divorce?"

The fear in Shekinah's voice made Moni draw her daughter close. Inside the lanky teenager was a child who didn't want her world to change.

Lord, what do I say to her?

The truth.

The truth was it took two people to work at a marriage. And based on their conversations, Sam had checked himself out.

Moni continued to hold her close and kissed the top of her head. "I don't know, honey. What I do know is prayer helps when things get hard. Will you pray for Dad and us?"

"I'm not sure what to say."

"Just tell God what's on your heart."

Shekinah nodded. They held each other's hands and bowed their heads.

Chapter Thirty-Nine

Grocery bags in hand, Debo kicked the door shut and headed towards the kitchen. He had moved into the three-bedroom apartment at the end of the previous month. A one-bedroom would have been suitable for him but trapped in his lie, he'd been forced to rent a bigger, more expensive place since the church thought his family was joining him.

His groceries put away, he drank a glass of cold orange juice before plopping down on the sofa one of the church members had gifted him.

On most days, between running the church benevolence program and carrying out all the tasks assigned to his portfolio, Debo was thankfully too busy to think about his messy life. When alone, he couldn't escape the thoughts.

Restless, he picked up his Bible from the side table. He had barely opened it since his arrival in Moose Jaw. He knew he had to do better. He was the Assistant Pastor for crying out loud. Clenching his jaw, he flipped through the pages. Nothing caught his attention. He decided to choose where to read by closing his eyes and allowing his Bible to fall open at a page.

When he opened his eyes, he was in the book of Revelation. His eyes were drawn to Revelation 3:16. *"So then because thou art lukewarm, and neither cold nor hot, I will spew thee out of my mouth."*

He frowned. Revelations was not one of his favorite books in the Bible. Debo closed his eyes again. When he opened them, he was still in the New Testament, in the book of Hebrews. He read the Scripture closest to his fingers. It was Hebrews 4:13. *"Neither is there any creature that is not manifest in his sight: but all things are naked and opened unto the eyes of him with whom we have to do."*

Where were all the Scriptures about God's unfailing love and promises? Debo dropped the Bible on the sofa. He would have to get himself a proper devotional guide.

He heard the notification sound on his cell phone and reached into his pocket. The text message was from Adele. She was letting him know they were available for a Skype call. He logged into Skype through his phone and Adele's face filled his screen. "Where are my boys?"

"Hello to you, too," she said. "They're here. Hold on."

He exhaled when Number One's face came on. He looked so much like his mother.

Debo cleared the lump in his throat. "Hey, big boy."

"Hi, Dad."

He stopped himself from rubbing his fingers on the screen. "I miss you."

"I miss you, too. Uncle Sam came and took us out."

Debo smiled. Sam was a true friend. "I know. Did you guys have fun at the arcade?"

"I did. Bolu was crying 'cause he lost," he said.

"That's none of your business," he heard Bolu say in the background.

Their second son was a fierce competitor and a sore loser. "I'll talk to him. Take care of yourself and your brothers, okay?"

"I will, Dad."

Bolu was pouting when he sat in front of the computer. "I cried because that one was laughing at me," he said.

He settled the quarrel between the big boys, spoke to the younger ones and promised to send them pictures of their new bedrooms. When they told him they wanted to visit, he said it was up to their mom.

The boys left the room at their mother's request. "Thanks for throwing me under the bus."

"We both know you're in charge. When are you bringing them?"

"Bye," Adele said as she signed out.

Debo paced the room for a few minutes. Avoiding his dark thoughts, he dialed Sam's number. Sam picked up the call on the third ring. From the background noise, it sounded like he was at a party. "Hello."

From the slurred voice, Debo could tell Sam had been drinking. "Where are you?"

"Triple X. We're having mad fun here."

On a weekday? "I bet," he said in a wry tone. "I just wanted to thank you for taking the boys out."

"Anytime."

He heard a woman's voice. "Sam, are you coming upstairs?"

"Debo, please hold on."

He wanted to talk about Adele, but he had the sense Sam was too busy to care. "How are Moni and Shekinah?" he asked when Sam came back.

"I'm sure they are doing fine," he said. "I moved out of the house last week."

He sank back into the sofa. "Sam."

"I know what I'm doing."

"It doesn't sound like it."

Sam's mocking laugh made him flinch. "You're not in the position to give any advice."

"Message heard loud and clear," Debo said. "I'll talk to you later."

The line went dead.

Debo couldn't believe Sam had left his family when all he wanted in the world was to have his back.

Frustrated by Adele and now Sam, Debo decided to burn off some energy by running up and down the apartment building stairs. He kept at it until he was drenched and the muscles in his thighs cried for mercy. He took a shower, changed into his pajamas and sat in front of the computer.

He was giving his first sermon the following Sunday, and he had no idea what he was going to say. He had once heard there were websites where pastors could purchase ready-made sermons and video illustrations. A Google search brought up a lot of links. The good ones also offered accompanying praise and worship music. Blown away by the choices, Debo rubbed his forehead. Thanks to Papa Badmus, he was a competent piano player so he could weave some piano playing into his sermon.

The problem became settling on a particular sermon. Debo thought back to the sermons he had heard as a young man. Moni's father was a fiery preacher and many Sundays, he had left the church with fear and trembling branded into him.

He was more of the "catch them by sharing honey rather than vinegar" kind of guy. Debo frowned as he browsed through several websites. It would be bad if he ended up buying a sermon someone at church had seen online.

His eyes flickered to his Bible. He picked it up. The third attempt at finding a Scripture to read brought him to Matthew 14. He remembered the first time he heard the story of Peter walking across the water. He had wondered if one day, he could do it.

His Internet search listed several sermons. All he had to do was merge several of the sermons into his unique version, and he would be fine. There was no point punishing himself when inspiration wasn't coming.

Two hours later, he had a reasonable sermon. He did a quick spell check, composed an email to Pastor Ezekiel, attached the sermon document and clicked the send button.

He decided the job well done had earned himself a plate from the tray of spicy Jollof rice Sister Prudence made for him. He pushed back his chair and headed towards the kitchen.

Chapter Forty

Sam could only describe his current situation as living in a double state of blessing.

He'd been browsing the papers when he came across a job ad for a cushy city job. They were looking for a manager to work in community relations. The compensation caught his attention. A six-figure salary would go a long way. The only snag was that apart from working at fast food restaurants as a student, all he had was teaching work experience.

He had told himself he had nothing to lose as he applied for the job. To his utter amazement, he was called for the first set of interviews. He had scaled that, made it to the second round and ended up as the lucky candidate.

On his first pay day, he visited a nearby Ford dealership and picked out a new gold Mustang convertible. It had felt like a dream until he woke up the next day and still saw the car parked outside.

Three months into his new job, he moved out from the basement room he had been renting at Brampton into a spacious two-bedroom apartment in downtown Toronto. From his living room bay window, he had a stunning view of Lake Ontario. His long-term dream of buying a house in Debo's old neighborhood no longer seemed unattainable.

To Moni's credit, she hadn't kept Shekinah away from him. He was free to pick Shekinah up from the house, and he could also call her whenever he wanted. Since he had no intention of being a deadbeat Dad, he sent Moni generous monthly checks. Even though she was yet to cash the checks, he had done his duty.

Sam smirked when he remembered the stunned look on Moni's face when he had shown up at the house in his new car. She and probably the other folks from church were likely expecting him to fall flat on his face just because he had decided to follow his path. If he had known things were going to turn around for him completely, he would have moved out months earlier. It almost felt as if Moni's presence had blocked his blessings.

Sam stretched out his long legs on the leather ottoman. He picked up the remote control and turned on the surround sound system. He found jazz music calming.

He logged into five chat sites to see if he had new messages from the women he had been talking to online. His eyes widened when he read one of the messages. The things people said they were willing to do and did continued to blow his mind.

The sound of his ringtone made Sam pick up his cell phone from the coffee table. Debo's number flashed across the screen. He debated with himself for a couple of minutes before placing the cell phone down. It rang several times and then it stopped.

Sam squashed his guilt. He didn't know how to handle the new Debo who called mainly to complain.

There were instances when he had wanted to tell Debo to shut up, man up, and handle his problems. He had done that for years without going around acting as if the sky was falling.

The day he had bought the car, he had not been able to tell Debo about it because he didn't want to make him feel bad. A part of him resented being placed in that position. He shouldn't have to minimize his joy because things were not going well for Debo.

As far as he was concerned, Debo was responsible for his current situation. There was no point in him being a martyr by allowing Adele to run him out of town. If she wanted her lover, then she should have packed her bags and left. He liked Adele, but a part of him had always felt Debo should have married someone in their league. Adele came from money and had the sense of entitlement that came with it.

He decided to drop off some presents for Debo's boys. While he was in the neighborhood, it wouldn't hurt to drive around to see if there were any for sale signs. He wasn't there yet, but it was only a matter of time.

Chapter Forty-One

The caffeine buzz from downing three cups of black coffee was taking over. Hands on his head, Debo spun around in his chair.

The church secretary knocked and waited for his response before poking her head into his office. "You have someone waiting on you."

Debo glanced at the wall clock. "That would be the last person for today." Benevolence ministry time ended half an hour before church began.

"Yes, Pastor."

Minutes later, the door creaked open. From the air around her, Debo could picture the steep walls erected around the gaunt woman who took tentative steps into the room.

Uninterested in her story, he pointed to the chair and opened the metal box in front of him. "Good morning. So how much do you want?"

She cocked her head to the side. "How much do I want?"

Debo forced a smile. She must be a newcomer. "Yes. We usually give out $25 gift cards, but there have been instances where we've given an extra $10 card depending on the expressed need."

She gave him a puzzled look. "You're not going to ask me why I need the money or ask if I was ready to say the sinner's prayer?"

He had been wrong about her. Debo smirked. "I get the sense that you're not new at this."

"Not new at what?"

"I'm sure you go around to various churches for these cards, and you've been asked to give your life to God more times than you can remember."

She lifted her chin. "And what's that got to do with anything?"

Debo reclined back in his seat. "Well, unless you're here to tell me that things have changed and you are now willing to give your life to the Lord Jesus Christ, why should I bother to ask those questions?"

Blood drained from her face. "What?"

"Like I said before, how much do you want?" When she didn't respond, he reached into the metal box for a $50 card and held it out. "Here you go. Since you're my last visitor, you get one of the big ones."

To his surprise, instead of thanking him, she burst into tears.

As her sobs grew louder, Debo debated on whether or not to page the secretary. As he reached for the phone, just as abrupt as they started, her tears stopped.

The woman knocked over the chair as she backed away from his desk. "It wasn't just about the cards you know. I always came here because it's the only place where I was told God would never give up on me. I figured if God was as big as He was and cared about me, maybe things would turn out all right."

She looked at him through narrowed eyes. "What are you doing in that chair? You don't belong there."

Debo gritted his teeth. Only the enemy could have sent the woman to destabilize him on such an important morning. "God bless you, sister."

"Save your blessing!" She hurried out, leaving the door open.

Minutes later, the senior pastor walked into the office. "I just ran into Ethel at the door. She was on the verge of tears. What happened?"

"*Ethel?*" Was she supposed to be someone special?

"I was told she just came in to see you."

Debo shrugged. "I'm not sure. She refused the gift card I offered her."

"That's strange. She's been coming here since we opened."

"Perhaps she was unhappy to see a new face."

"Hmm." Pastor Ezekiel shrugged. "Oh, well, I'll let you get ready for service."

***

Debo swayed as the choir led them in worship. All around him, eyes were closed, hands lifted up.

When it was time for him to preach, he moistened his mouth by taking a sip from the glass of water placed on the pulpit. "Good morning, Faith Assembly."

He smiled when some church members returned his greeting. "It is with a deep sense of gratitude to God that I stand before you," he said. "Before we move into our study of the Word, let us pray."

Debo bowed his head as he tried to organize his thoughts. He calmed himself with a mental image of running water.

"Today's sermon begins a three-part series titled, Faith Boosters. I'll be talking about three different groups of people; the boat people, the market people, and the city people. Please open your Bibles and let's read Matthew 14:22-36."

After he read the Scripture, Debo scanned the room. They all looked attentive. Good.

"The first time I read this Bible passage, I was a little boy amazed by the apostle Peter, a man who had walked on water. As I prepared for this series, I thought about that event on the Sea of Galilee, particularly, about those who had stayed behind in the boat. I call them The Boat People. Amongst this group of people, we have four sub-groups."

"The first group believed that due to their past actions, they deserved to be trapped in a boat going nowhere. Nothing anyone said had convinced them otherwise. They rejected mercy and were bent on sinking under the huge waves in atonement of their sins.

"The second group were the planners, the ones who found it hard to give up control. They made contingency plans, waited for the right weather conditions, tracked whale migration to avoid a Jonah story repeat because faith in an unseen, untouchable God simply defied their logic."

Debo brought out his new handkerchief and dabbed his forehead. He wasn't sure why he suddenly felt hot. He drank some water to moisten his mouth.

"The third group was excited about leaving the boat until they saw Peter begin to sink. If Peter, a bold man of faith could sink, they thought, what hope was there for them? Like Peter, who began to sink because he took his eyes off Jesus, their eyes were not on the savior."

"The fourth group stayed because they were comfortable in the boat." He shook his head. "You see, they had lived there for years. It was the place they knew. The place where people knew them."

He gave a mirthless laugh. "Then, the devil showed up, and their boat was repossessed. In a twinkle of an eye, they ended up in the water, helpless in the absence of the life jacket of faith. Remember what Job said? The thing I feared most has come upon me."

"Brethren, what mental boat has the enemy trapped you in? Where is that place or situation you need to leave? The devil will use everything he can to keep you trapped in a boat going nowhere."

He paused to take another sip of water. "Church, listen up. Sometimes, the enemy uses well-meaning friends who drag you out of the water and bring you back in the boat just when you're about to let go of your fear and let God. Does someone here know what I'm talking about?"

He smiled as a loud hallelujah came from a pew in the back. "We have to be discerning when it comes to choosing our friends and living our lives according to their lives."

"Only one thing is going to move you out of the boat and keep you walking on water. It is your faith in Jesus Christ. Jesus is a lifesaver; He is the saver of your soul. Jesus is a lifeguard. He will guard your life. You just have to step out and believe."

Debo moved away from the pulpit, sat at the piano and began playing the chorus to the hymn *Turn Your Eyes upon Jesus*.

Turn your eyes upon Jesus,

Look full in His wonderful face,

And the things of earth will grow strangely dim,

In the light of His glory and grace.

To close out the service, Debo did an altar call for those who wanted to rededicate their lives. The numbers surprised him. He thought about Ethel and her words that intended to curse him. *What did that delusional woman know?* Debo thought as he counted bowed heads. He was where he belonged.

Chapter Forty-Two

Sam clenched his teeth as he emptied his bladder. The pain from the burning sensation matched the soreness in his throat. The flu-like symptoms he'd begun to experience made him call his family doctor's office for an appointment since the over-the-counter medication he bought had not helped. The earliest he could see the doctor was in two weeks.

He turned on the faucet and spent some minutes washing his hands. A colleague of his had just returned from the part of British Columbia where there had been an outbreak of avian flu. He knew it would be foolish not to get himself checked out.

Back on the couch, Sam signed into one of his online sites and cancelled his weekend dates. He didn't have the energy to entertain.

Sam was contemplating a nap when his cell phone rang. The call was from his daughter.

"Hello, Dad."

Sam smiled at the sound of Shekinah's voice. "Hello, Princess. Is everything okay?"

"Yes. I just wanted to talk to you," Shekinah said.

"I'm glad you called." The previous day, he had cancelled their bowling outing because he didn't want to pass on any of his germs. "Did you do something fun yesterday?"

"I didn't go out. But Mom and I made a new Nigerian dish. I saved some for you."

His Shekinah was all grown up, he thought with pride. "What was it?"

"The YouTube lady had called it *moin moin* with seven lives. I was like really?" He could picture Shekinah rolling her eyes. "Apparently some versions of the dish have fewer lives."

Despite being in pain, Sam laughed. His mother used to make the steamed Nigerian bean cake when he lived at home. Mama Badmus' *moin moin* often had four protein types or lives: hard-boiled eggs, chopped liver, dried fish and corned beef.

"Hmm, that must be very tasty."

"It is. I can't wait for you to try it. Are you feeling better now?" Shekinah asked.

"I'm staying home tomorrow."

"Do you want me to come over?" Shekinah sounded worried.

After the previous weekend's party, his apartment needed to be tidied, and he didn't have the energy to do the work. "Not now. I'm not good company."

"I just want to see you."

"I'll talk to your mom about you coming for an overnight visit when I'm feeling better."

He knew Moni would probably say no since she didn't want Shekinah exposed to his "unsavory" activities.

"I'll be praying for you."

"Don't worry about me," he said. "You take care of yourself."

"I will."

"How's your mother?"

"She's in the bedroom. Do you want to talk to her?"

"Just tell her I said hello." He told himself it would nice to surprise Moni by sending some flowers to her office. Despite everything, she was doing a good job with their daughter. He furrowed his brow. He couldn't remember if Moni liked roses or carnations. He would just send both.

"Dad."

"Yes."

Shekinah sounded hesitant. "There's something I wanted to ask you."

"What is it?"

"I'm getting an award at school, and I was wondering if you would come."

He had thought it was something serious. He remembered the expression on Shekinah's face when he had told her he couldn't attend her baptism. It was time he faced his soon-to-be ex-in-laws. "Of course I'll come," he said.

"Will you remind me?"

"I will. Thanks, Dad. Love you."

"Love you, too."

Chapter Forty-Three

Within the week, Sam's condition worsened. He had been able to keep his fever under control with painkillers, but a pus-like discharge forced him to buy some disposable underwear.

While waiting for the doctor, Sam rubbed away the tension forming in the back of his neck. He just wanted to get the antibiotic prescription and leave.

Things were not that straightforward. The doctor said he seemed to have a virulent form of flu, but he also needed to get tested for sexually transmitted diseases. "How long do I have to wait for the results?"

"The results will be back by the end of the week," the doctor said. "For your privacy, you'll need to come back here for your test results. I'll need a swab of the discharge."

Embarrassed, Sam couldn't look the doctor in the face as he swung his feet off the exam table.

The doctor handed him a specimen container. "I'll also need a urine sample."

"Can't you prescribe an antibiotic while I wait for the results?" He was missing out on a lot of fun.

The doctor shook his head. "It's best to wait. I'm sure you'll want me to prescribe the appropriate medication." He sat at his desk and reached for his prescription pad. "I can prescribe something for the flu. It may help." The doctor tore off the script and handed it to him. "I'm also prescribing some rest."

He was ready to try anything. "Thank you."

***

Four days later, Sam was back at the doctor's office for his test results. From the moment the doctor walked into the room, Sam tried to read his expression. The deadpan expression gave nothing away. "Hello, Mr. Badmus."

Sam acknowledged the greeting with a mumble.

"I'm sorry to tell you that you've contracted gonorrhea and a nasty strain of it," the doctor said.

He mouthed the word. "Gonorrhea?"

The doctor nodded. "The good news is, nothing else was found. I must let you know HIV and syphilis testing has been known to come back with false negatives. I would recommend a re-test in three months."

Hearing the words HIV, Sam felt as if something had settled on his chest. He couldn't catch his breath. The room began to spin. As he held onto the arms of his chair, he heard the doctor calling his name. "Mr. Badmus, can you hear me?"

"I may have HIV?"

"I don't think you need to worry about that at this point. Let's focus on the gonorrhea."

Despite his lifestyle, contracting a STD was the last thing on his mind. "Is it curable?"

"Oh, yes. Hopefully, all you need is a single-dose of an injectable antibiotic."

Sam felt the pressure on his chest ease. "That's it?"

"Yes. You should tell your wife to get tested, too," the doctor insisted. "She may need treatment."

"I think Moni will be fine." He cleared his throat. "We've not been intimate in months."

"Symptoms of gonorrhea often show up early in men, so this is most likely a recent infection. I would advise you to let your sexual partner know of your condition. If your partner is not tested and treated, you may become infected again."

Sam licked his dry lips. He didn't even know the names of some of the people he'd been with. How was he going to ask strangers to present clean STD results? "Can I get the medication today?"

"Yes. I will advise abstinence for at least a week. If your symptoms return following treatment, please let us know. It may be a treatment failure, and we'll need to try another antibiotic." The doctor stood. "I'll have to administer the shot in the buttocks."

His face pressed into the exam table, Sam flinched at the prick of the injection. Life was unfair.

Chapter Forty-Four

"Mom?"

Moni looked up from her book and gave Shekinah her full attention.

"I'm anxious about Dad. I haven't heard from him all week."

When Shekinah began moping around the house, Moni knew it was because her father had not come to see her in a while. Since he moved out, to his credit, Sam had tried to see Shekinah on a regular basis. Knowing how addictive his pastime was, she had assumed he had gotten too busy. It was the reason she had not tried to contact him herself.

Moni closed her book. "I'm sure your father's doing fine," she said. "Did you call his cell phone?"

"I did. But Dad did not answer. It keeps going to his voicemail. I left several messages, too."

Shekinah said as she flopped beside her on the couch. "Is it okay if I go over to his place to check on him? Please."

Since her father left, Shekinah had been begging for an overnight visit. She didn't want Shekinah exposed to any filth.

Moni shook her head. "He'll call you."

"Mom, he wasn't feeling fine the last time we spoke," Shekinah said. Her eyes widened. "Maybe he's been admitted to the hospital."

"If he's at the hospital, I'm sure someone would have called to let us know. I'm still his next of kin."

"But what if he's unconscious in his apartment and he can't call for help?" Shekinah was begging her for something. Moni knew she had to relent.

"Oh, Shekinah. Your imagination is something else."

"It happens. Can we just check on him? *Please.*"

"How about I go and check on him for you?" she offered. "That way if there's anything wrong, I can get him appropriate help."

Shekinah's face lit up. "Thanks, Mom. Can I come along?"

"I plan on stopping there on my way to work tomorrow. You have to go to school."

"Promise you'll send me a text to let me know he's doing okay," Shekinah said.

The child was persistent. Moni smiled at her. "Deal."

***

The next morning, Moni called the office to say she'd be late before making the short drive to Toronto. Thankfully, unlike many downtown complexes, Sam's apartment building had ample visitor parking. She took the elevator up.

Heart pounding, Moni stood in front of Sam's apartment door. Since he moved out of the house, they were yet to be alone.

She sent up a quick prayer for help on what to say or do before knocking on the door. There was no response. Moni thought of giving up. But Shekinah would worry if she didn't know her father was in good health. Unsure of what to do, she stood in the hallway.

She was about to leave when the brushed nickel handle turned, and the door opened.

Sam's bloodshot eyes peered at her. Moni pursed her lips. She had probably woken him up from a drunken stupor.

"What are you doing here?" His voice was hoarse. He must have been wearing his clothes for days, Moni thought. He looked worse than he sounded.

"Your daughter asked me to come and check on you. She's been leaving messages on your cell phone."

"Oh." He scratched his head. "My cell phone is dead. I've not been feeling well." He held the door wide open. "Come in."

Moni hesitated, before stepping in. Taking a closer look at Sam's sweaty face, he did look feverish. A foul smell in the room made her wrinkle her nose. "What is that smell?"

Sam looked embarrassed. "It's probably the half-eaten box of pizza on the kitchen counter. I haven't been able to take out the trash in a week."

She continued to look around. The apartment didn't look like what she had imagined in her head. She had thought Sam would decorate the space with pornographic images.

"Before you start giving a lecture about the mess, remember I didn't ask you to come," Sam said in a weary voice. Taking shallow breaths, he leaned against the wall.

Moni stared at him. Lord, what do I do now?

Take him home.

Sam wasn't a child she could march to her car.

Take him home.

"I didn't come here to fight. I know I can be militant, but I won't kick a man while he's down." She moved closer. "Why don't you spend the weekend at home? You know Shekinah would love the opportunity to play nurse."

"You want me to come with you?"

She nodded. "I can't leave you in this state."

He gave her a wary look. "Moni, a lot has happened between us. Why do you still care?"

"You are Shekinah's father. And what would Jesus do?"

Sam twisted his lips. "I don't think Jesus would do anything for me. We gave up on each other a long time ago."

Something turned inside her at the sight of the bleak look on Sam's face. "Please," she begged. "I can't leave you like this."

"Don't you have to go to work?"

"Work can wait. I'll call and let them know I have a family emergency."

He still looked uncertain, but she sensed he wanted to come. "Are you sure?"

She wasn't. But she had heard His clear directive and she was going to obey it. "Yes."

"I'll come on one condition."

"What is it?"

"I don't want to be subjected to any preaching while I'm at the house. Deal?"

The battle for Sam's soul was not hers to win. She would love him and pray. "Deal."

"Okay, I'll come." Sam watched as she packed his overnight bag. "You don't have to do this."

"I know I don't," she said. "But I've learned that when He says something to listen. It's the best way to live."

"Didn't I say no preaching?"

"I thought it was okay since we're still at your house."

Sam gave her a half-smile. "I should have known you'd find a loophole."

When she was done, he held on to her arm as they walked over to the car.

Moni's heart thumped as she drove home. *Thank You, Lord Jesus.*

Chapter Forty-Five

Sam felt like a stranger when he stepped into the house he had lived in for over ten years. It was his first time back since he packed his bags. The house looked the same, yet so much had changed.

He declined Moni's offer to take his overnight bag and took slow steps up the stairs. He opened the door to the spare bedroom, set the bag down and laid on the freshly made bed. His eyelids began to flutter, and he soon fell into a deep sleep. He woke up mid-day to find a covered lunch tray in the room.

The meal was a bowl of goat meat pepper soup. His favorite dish. A gentle knock on the door made him replace the lid. "Who is it?" he asked.

He heard Shekinah's voice. "Dad, I'm home."

"Come in."

The door opened, and Shekinah bounced into the room. "I told Mom something was wrong," she said. "I'm so glad she brought you home."

"Don't come too close, Princess," he warned. "I don't want to give you any bugs."

Shekinah sat at the other end of the bed and pointed to the food tray. "Do you need me to take that downstairs? Is there anything else you want?"

His heart expanded. Just watching Shekinah fuss over him was enough medicine for him. "I've not eaten yet."

She gave him a stern look. "Dad, you're not going to get better if you don't eat."

Sam smiled. "Is this Nurse Shekinah talking?" When she was a little girl, Shekinah spent hours sticking Band-Aids on her stuffed animals. She also gave them shots with a toy syringe.

"That's right. And I'm a senior nurse now. Got promoted. Mom said she had made you some pepper soup. I'm sure it's cold by now." She stood and walked over to the bedside table. "Should I warm it up and bring it back?"

"Sure. You're the medical professional."

The soup was piping hot when she brought it back. She sat until he drank the last drop.

"Lunch checked off," she said. "What do you want for dinner?"

He didn't want to think about more food. "How about we decide on dinner later? I need to take a shower first." He was covered in sweat from eating the spicy soup.

"Okay, Dad." Getting up, Shekinah took the tray downstairs.

He took a cool shower and changed into his pajamas since he had no intention of going downstairs. Lying down, he drifted off again.

The digital clock on the dresser said it was 8:00 a.m. when he opened his eyes. Sam got out of bed to use the bathroom. He wasn't sure if he had been dreaming, but he had a faint recollection of Moni coming into the room during the night and touching his forehead.

A short while later, Moni brought him a breakfast tray. "Good morning. I'm the one on duty since your nurse is still asleep. I hope you had a good night."

"Good morning. Yes, I did."

Moni set the tray down on the bedside table. "Since I wasn't sure what you'd be able to eat, I made oatmeal and eggs. "Shekinah and I are going to the soup kitchen, and we won't be back until later so your lunch, spaghetti and meatballs are inside the blue food warmer on the kitchen counter."

"Thank you." Moni's pampering was unsettling him. He had not done anything to deserve it. Guilt over what he was yet to tell her struck hard.

When Shekinah came to say goodbye, she brought him a wrapped gift. "I thought you might have missed this."

He tore away the gift wrap to see his old Bible. The pages had been straightened out, and it also had a new cover. The beautiful green leather had 2 Timothy 3:16 inscribed on it.

Sam knew the words by heart. *All Scripture is given by inspiration of God, and is profitable for doctrine, for reproof, for correction, for instruction in righteousness.*

He couldn't tell Shekinah he no longer read the Bible. "Thanks, Princess. That was thoughtful of you."

The big smile on Shekinah's face told him he had said the right thing.

Minutes later, Sam decided to go downstairs to watch television. At the last minute, something compelled him to bring along his Bible.

He walked downstairs and sat on his favorite recliner in front of the television. The Saturday morning sports talk show was on, but he kept flipping through the Bible, skimming through the Scripture passages he had highlighted in two colors. Yellow for Scriptures that encouraged him during the times he had felt down and green for teaching Scriptures.

Before he knew it, he spent the entire time Moni and Shekinah were away reading through and trying to remember what had been going on in his life when the Scriptures were highlighted.

The following morning, he didn't see Moni before she and Shekinah left for church. When Shekinah brought him a breakfast tray, he had wanted to ask how her mother was doing but changed his mind. Shekinah might see the concern as a desire for reconciliation. Given the news he was yet to tell Moni, it would be unfair of him to give Shekinah any false hope.

Upon their return, Shekinah came to the room and invited him down for lunch. "We eat together now."

Sam came back to the room to rest. His eyes were drawn to the Bible as he kicked off his house slippers. Picking up the book, he slid under the bed covers.

By the time he had gone through half of the highlighted Scriptures, Sam was convicted. He could not go back to his apartment without telling Moni about his gonorrhea diagnosis. Even thought it had nothing to do with her, it may convince her to get an STD screen. The thought of telling her made him break out into a sweat.

The opportunity for a conversation came when Shekinah went to bed. "There's something important I need to tell you."

Looking alarmed, Moni tightened the sash of her house robe and followed him.

Telling Moni about his condition was one of the hardest things Sam ever had to do. His marriage intervention continued to cast a shadow over their lives.

Face blank, she just stared at him with vacant eyes. She was clearly in a state of shock. "Moni, please, say something."

She took a deep breath. "Is it something Shekinah could have been exposed to?"

Worried about her exposure he had done his research. "No," he said. "She's fine."

"The doctor thinks I may have this…infection?"

He was too scared to mention HIV. "A clean test will put your mind at ease."

Moni sighed. "Is that why you're sick?"

His symptoms came back. The doctor said the strain of gonorrhea he had was most likely resistant to the antibiotic he'd received. Sam had been prescribed a different drug. A sense of shame made him reluctant to tell her. "Yes. I think my body is also worn out from doing too much."

They both knew what he had been doing.

He would have felt better if she had yelled or cried. Her stillness made him wonder what she was going to do next. "I'm sorry."

Moni looked away. "I need to be alone now," she said, dragging herself from the porch swing as if her body weight had doubled since she sat. "Goodnight."

Chapter Forty-Six

His troubles started when the check engine light came on. Within minutes, the car began to sputter and it stalled by the side of the road. Debo banged on the steering wheel. Why couldn't he catch a break?

Unsure of what to do, he opened the car hood to take a look. Nothing looked out of place. He slammed the hood shut. With the exorbitant cost of shipping his Mercedes to Saskatchewan, he had bought the used car with the hope that it would last him the year.

Debo pulled out his CAA card. The car dealer had offered him a one-year membership at the automobile club as a sales incentive. He kicked the front car tire. The man must have known he was selling him a lemon.

An hour later, his car was towed to the nearest auto repair center. The news he received only made his frustration rise. "I can't afford a new transmission."

The mechanic shrugged. "I may be able to get a used one from a salvage or junk yard. No guarantees on the performance."

"I'll take the chance."

He was in the middle of filling out paperwork when his cell phone rang. It was Pastor Ezekiel. "I need to see you at the church this afternoon for an emergency meeting."

Debo was pensive. What emergency could there be? "Sir, is there a problem?"

"It's best we talk when you get here," Pastor Ezekiel said.

He couldn't think of any assigned task he had left undone. "What time do you want me there, sir?"

"As soon as possible," Pastor Ezekiel said, and this time Debo recognized that the man's tone was terse.

Debo interpreted the response to mean now. Squashed behind the wheel of the loaner vehicle offered by the auto center, Debo pushed the speed limit. He couldn't shake off an ominous feeling. The egg sandwich he had forced himself to eat before he had left home sat like lead at the bottom of his stomach.

The secretary told him Pastor was waiting for him in one of the board rooms. The five men seated had varied expressions. Deacon Gabriel's expression held a hint of a smile... he was gloating on the inside, while Elder Supo's pained expression would have been more appropriate at a funeral.

No one had to tell him it wasn't going to be business as usual.

Pastor Ezekiel pointed to the sole empty seat. He spoke as soon as Debo sat. "We just received some alarming news from Brampton."

His heart skipped. "Is my family okay?"

"As far as we know, they're fine. The disturbing news is about your leadership position at a swinging group." Pastor Ezekiel searched his face. "Is this true?"

Technically, he no longer belonged to the swinging group. "Actually," he began. "I—"

Deacon Gabriel cut him off. "There is no actually in this matter. Pastor, please ask him to tell us the real reason behind his family's absence."

Deacon Michael who had been quiet since the meeting began looked him straight in the eye. "Pastor Debo, what is the situation with your wife and children?"

Looking at the faces before him, he decided he had nothing to lose by throwing himself at their mercy. "Adele and I are getting a divorce."

"A divorce?" Pastor Ezekiel asked. "Why?"

"Adele is in love with a married member of our church." Debo realized the magnitude of what he had said. The words cut like a sharp blade against his ear drums clear down to his heart.

Elder Supo's eyes bulged. "The devil is a liar!"

Pastor Ezekiel straightened up in his chair. "We have no choice but to ask you to step down from your pastoral position immediately. I was asked to let you know the school will pay your salary for two months as part of a severance package. They feel it would be unfair to make your children starve while you find other employment."

Where was he supposed to go? "I made a mistake. A terrible mistake for which I am ashamed and sorry. My coming to Moose Jaw was a re-dedication of myself. And since my arrival, I have done everything right in a bid to move beyond what happened in Brampton."

The men's faces remained as frozen and placid as the Moose Jaw River, but Debo continued his plea.

"We go around town telling folks about our marvelous God who offers second chances. Don't I deserve a second chance, too?"

"Brother, your job is being terminated because you covered your sin and violated the trust we had in you," Elder Patrick said in a firm tone. "We're not asking you to leave the church. You just can't stay in a pastoral position."

How could they think he would step down as pastor and continue to attend the church? He might as well attach a big dart board to his shirt and wait for all the insults that would be thrown his way.

Because he did not doubt that Deacon Gabriel had contributed to his downfall, he wasn't going to let him off. "Since it's the day for uncovering secrets, I must let you know Deacon Gabriel knew about this from the first day we arrived in Moose Jaw. Adele's lover is related to his wife."

Pastor Ezekiel's brow furrowed. "Deacon Gabriel, is this true?"

Deacon Gabriel shifted in his seat. "Yes, Prudence is related to Mrs. Bassey, but I didn't know for sure what was going on until Mrs. Bassey confessed to their pastor."

"You had some suspicions," Pastor Ezekiel said. "How could you have kept such a thing to yourself?"

With all eyes focused on Deacon Gabriel, Debo walked away from the table. As he closed the door behind him, he could still hear the raised voices.

He flung his things into the cardboard box waiting for him at his desk.

Debo's mind went back to his first night in Moose Jaw. He remembered standing in front of the door and rubbing his fingers across the plastic name plate. The more befitting name plate he ordered had arrived the week before. He had been waiting for the opportunity to broach the matter with Pastor Ezekiel before having it installed. Debo opened his desk drawer and brought out the golden name plate. The sight brought a deep pain. He flung it into the trash can.

Unable to see through his tears, Debo tossed the framed family picture on his desk into the box. The glass pane shattered into pieces. Broken, just like his life. Just like his family. He picked up the box and walked out of the office.

***

Back at his apartment, Debo dumped the box on the ground, pulled out his telephone and dialed Sam's number. The call went straight to Sam's voicemail and he was unable to leave a message. He sent Adele a terse text message: "Skype now."

Adele's eyes were swollen when she signed into Skype. Her distress didn't make him feel better; it only infuriated him. His life was over because of her choice. "I just lost my job," he said to her. "What happened?"

"It was Mrs. Bassey," she said in a low voice. "Three days ago, Edet had asked her for a divorce. When he refused to change his mind, she went to Pastor Iginla and gave him a list of names. She outed herself as the mystery letter writer."

"Where is she now?"

"On her way to Nigeria."

"She causes all this ruckus and then escapes the fallout? That's just fantastic. She and her wife stealing husband should be glad I'm nowhere near them."

"Debo—"

"Don't Debo me!" He took several calming breaths. "I want to speak to my boys."

"I sent them on a walk so I could talk to you."

"You sent them out on a walk? Adele, are you losing your mind?"

She looked away from the screen. "They are not by themselves. Edet is out there."

He hadn't thought it was possible to go from near calmness to rage in one second. "I thought we had agreed you would keep that wife thief away from my children until the divorce is final?"

"Listen, we're both adults so there's no need for any name calling," she said. "Edet has been very kind to your sons."

"Well if loverman Edet thinks he can just waltz in and take my place—"

Adele interrupted him. "Do you still want to talk to your children?"

Her prissy tone irked him. "What's the point?" he said. "You already gave them a new daddy, or should I say, grandpa, since you're not that much older than his children."

"Debo—"

Snarling, he yanked the computer plug from the wall.

Chapter Forty-Seven

Moni was unable to sleep. The results of her STD tests were due the next day. Her agony and unrest were evident in the tangled sheets around her. She remembered conversations with Shekinah about actions and consequences. With the dire consequences of her actions staring her in her face, she could only beg for God's mercy.

Dragging herself down to the side of the bed, Moni closed her eyes and began to pray. "Lord Jesus, please, let this cup pass over me…"

My grace is sufficient for you.

Moni repeated the Scripture to herself until she drifted away into untroubled sleep.

The following day, Moni walked out of the doctor's office in a daze. Her STD screen came back clean.

The peace in Moni's heart told her the screen would be fine. Later that day, she was laughing and crying in her bedroom when she called Sam to tell him the news. The anguish on his face as he told her about his diagnosis had stayed with her. Perhaps the news would help.

He must have felt her excitement through the telephone. "To the glory of God, the results came back clean!"

She heard his huge sigh of relief. "Moni, that's great news. I can't tell you how happy I am."

"Me, too," she said.

As Sam fell quiet, she wanted to ask if he was alone. Instead, she asked him how he was doing.

"I'm fine. Taking things easy."

Easy could mean many things Moni thought. "I have to go. Take care."

"You, too."

Moni placed the telephone back on the charger before picking up her Bible. She needed the Word to hold her up. She would not let the thoughts of what could have been or what could still be, rob her of the day's peace.

***

The following morning, Moni woke up to a quiet house. Sitting in the rocking chair bought when Shekinah was a baby, she faced the large bay window in her bedroom.

Bright, warm rays streamed into the room. Head tilted back, Moni closed her eyes as the warmth wrapped her face. She felt at peace. His peace that passes all human understanding. There was no other explanation for her state of mind.

Moni's eyes flew open at the sound of the bedroom door opening.

Rubbing her eyes, Shekinah walked in. "Good morning, Mom."

"Good morning, young lady."

Dropping to the ground, Shekinah sat cross-legged in front of her chair. Her hair pulled into a tight bun, Shekinah looked like a feminine version of her father. "You're up early."

Most Saturdays, she had to drag Shekinah out of bed. "Why are you up so early?"

"I couldn't sleep." Shekinah looked around. "Some days, I forget dad no longer lives here."

There were days she expected Sam to walk through the front door or moments when she wondered what Sam would want for dinner as she drove home from work. "It takes some getting used to."

"Is there a chance you and Dad will get back together?"

Seeing the longing on her daughter's face, Moni took her time to answer the question.

"I don't know," she said. "Remember, it has to be a mutual decision."

"Do you still love him?"

It was hard to explain to a teenager who had yet to explore love herself how her emotional pendulum swung between love and indifference. "I'll always love him for being your father."

"Parents always say that. Dad still loves *you*. I could tell from the way he was talking about you yesterday."

Moni sat up. What had Sam been saying about her? "Did he ask you to say something to me?"

"No. He wouldn't do that, but I want him back home." Shekinah sighed. "When I told Grandma, she said we are to call those things that do not exist as though they are. Isn't it setting yourself up for disappointment?"

"It's called exercising your faith."

"But what if it doesn't happen?"

"Then you have to accept that God has another plan for you."

"The faith business isn't easy," Shekinah said.

"Your right, it isn't. But it's harder to figure out life without God." Inside, Moni chuckled at herself. She was one to speak.

Shekinah gave her a thoughtful look. "That's what Grandma said."

"Grandma is a wise woman."

Shekinah played with the strings of her pajama pants. "Grandma said we get impatient because we can't see the big picture as God does."

"We sure do." Moni reached over and stroked Shekinah's cheek. "I don't know what's going to happen, but I know God is in control. We're going to be fine."

"I hope so." Yawning, Shekinah stumbled to her feet. "I'm hungry."

Moni stood also. "Next time, please bring a cup of coffee. Making me answer all these hard questions on no caffeine isn't fair."

Shekinah raised her hand over her eyebrows to salute her. "Yes, ma'am."

Moni grabbed her around her shoulders and hugged her tight. "I love you."

"I love you, too," Shekinah replied.

Moni released her and raised a hand to stroke her daughter's beautiful cheek. "We're going to be fine," she repeated. They made their way down to the kitchen.

Chapter Forty-Eight

Hungry, Sam opened the refrigerator. He had been stunned when Moni sent him back with a care package. "Just something to tide you over until you're able to cook," she'd said.

The warmth of the gesture nearly broke him down. He'd been so busy picking and looking for what was wrong with his wife, he had not focused on what was right.

He brought out a bowl of Jollof rice and baked chicken wings and warmed himself a plate. It had been hard watching Moni and Shekinah drive away. The visit had been nice.

Sam sat at the kitchen table with his plate of food and a glass of water. Since his return home, he had gone from reading the rest of the highlighted Scriptures to picking a topic from the list at the back of his Bible and reading the comprehensive list of verses addressing it.

Reading the Scriptures about sexual immorality, he confirmed that Debo was right about the absence of Scripture on the topic of swinging. But he also found plenty of references on adultery and holy living.

Scriptures about prosperity had reminded him that material prosperity wasn't always a sign of God's favor. And God's blessing didn't only manifest in material wealth. He thought about how he had felt when he bought his Mustang. Owning the car of his dreams had made him happy when he first acquired it. Months later, it had become just another possession.

One thing he had envied Debo and Moni for was how sure they had been about their salvation. For him, as the initial euphoria of giving his life to Jesus faded, it became a constant struggle to sustain his joy. He had thought doing as many good works as possible would help him regain that joy. The Scriptures he read on the topic of grace showed him his priorities had been misplaced. He couldn't earn God's grace.

Sam placed his plate inside the sink. Back at his favorite spot on the couch, he turned on his computer to Marvin Sapp's *Never Would've Made It*.

One of the advantages of living alone was no one could complain as he sang along to the song at the top of his croaky voice. In the past week, the song had become his anthem.

The song lyrics sank into his spirit and his thoughts went back to Moni. She had been on his mind all day. He had woken up that morning with a reminder of the night he had prayed to God to send him a wife. He and Moni began courting in a matter of weeks.

He also remembered the story of the prodigal son. Like the prodigal, he had also been living a dirt-filled life. He had abandoned his Moni and Shekinah. He wondered if there was still a chance for him as a prodigal husband and father. He had no idea, but he needed to find out.

***

Sam stood outside the door of his house and attempted to slow down his breathing. He was nervous. He wasn't sure what to expect. Moni's voice was void of emotion when she'd agreed to meet with him. He rang the doorbell.

He heard Moni's raised voice speak, "Come in." Sam waited a couple of minutes before realizing she wasn't making her way to the door. Come in, meant come in. This was his house. He had keys. He removed them from his pocket, turned the lock and stepped in.

He found a somber looking Moni in the living room. From her seat opposite the living room's bay window, she would have seen him walking up the driveway. He sat on the chair next to her. "Thanks for agreeing to meet with me. I appreciate it."

Moni had her hands clasped in her lap. Her calm countenance unnerved him. "You said you had something important to say?"

He wasn't sure he could bear the pain for one more day. "I came to ask for your forgiveness."

"And I thought you were coming to persuade me to sign the divorce papers." She sighed, and if he had to identify why, he'd say it sounded like relief.

Sam shook his head as he moved to the edge of his seat. "Moni, I no longer want to get a divorce."

He strained to hear Moni's words. "You no longer want a divorce?"

He shook his head. "I know I've hurt you and Shekinah. My selfishness ruined our lives. The excitement wasn't worth the cost." Sam paused, measuring each word he spoke, knowing they mattered more than anything he'd said in a long time. "If you will have me, I want to come back home. I'm ready to work on our marriage, to be the husband and father God intended me to be."

Moni continued to stare at him. Sam found himself talking faster. "I don't want to pressure you. I'm willing to wait on your decision."

When she didn't say anything, he stood. "I'll leave now."

Moni held out a hand. "Please, stay."

He sat.

"First, I need to ask for your forgiveness, too," she said. "Remember my first visit to the Bassey's?"

"The night you ran out?"

"Yes. Debo said some things to me that I hated hearing, but I knew his words were true."

Sam frowned, but let her continue without questioning her.

"He told me long before any serpent wandered into our perfect little garden, we had let the weeds grow untamed. I hated him for the statement, but he was right. My pride and unforgiveness led me down the wrong path." She looked him in the eye. "And I did develop strong feelings for Odosa. If Shekinah had not taken the Molly, I don't know where we'd be."

Sam realized their story could have been so much worse if not for God's grace. "You have my forgiveness. Do I have yours?"

"This pastor's daughter found her missing forgiveness a long time ago," she said. "When are you coming home?"

It was his turn to gape at her. "You want me back?"

Moni nodded. "Yes."

"The doctor wants me to do a repeat STD screen in two months." He willed his eyes to stay on her face. "I've done things I'm too ashamed to talk about."

"I'd be lying if I say I'm not scared about what the future could hold. But, I've also learned faith and fear cannot exist in the same space."

Even though it was what he had prayed to hear, Sam fought his doubts.

"My dear husband, intimacy in a marriage is much more than sex," Moni said. "These past months have taught me that."

Kneeling before Moni's chair, he placed his head on her lap and began to weep. Wrapping her arms around him, Moni wept along. A Scripture he'd read earlier settled in his soul: *Mourning may tarry a night, but joy comes in the morning.*

Sam was ready for divine joy.

Chapter Forty-Nine

Debo stayed in bed for three days straight. On the fourth day, he forced himself out of bed to take a hard look at his situation. He sat down and crunched the numbers. No matter how he manipulated them, he couldn't make the figures look good.

Even with the severance package he had received from the school, he needed to find a job. He was stuck in a rental lease he couldn't afford to break.

The sound of his cell phone ringing made him look up from the calculations. He frowned when he saw Sam's number. All of a sudden, Sam was calling him every day. He didn't want to hear about how Sam was enjoying his life. He'd pass on that. He ignored the call and instead gave his attention to an advertisement for a cashier/stocker at one of the nearby grocery stores. The biggest attraction was the proximity to his apartment. His car was still at the auto repair shop and from the quotes he had been given, it would be cheaper for him to sell it for scrap and take public transportation.

The minimum wage pay offered by the grocery store was not appealing, but it would help until he could find something better paying. The minimum wage pay offered by the grocery store was not appealing, but it would help until he could find something better paying. He applied to the online job bank.

The next day, he was thrilled to get a call for an interview. Clutching a little plastic binder with his resume to his chest, Debo sat outside the manager's office. Five other middle-aged men sat beside him. Giving each other silent nods, they didn't make prolonged eye contact.

The Nigerian saying, no paddy for jungle, came to Debo's mind. With one advertised position, it was war. No point getting friendly with the enemy.

They all straightened up when the manager's office door opened.

His bleached blonde hair slicked back with gel, the young man wrinkled his nose as he peered at the paper in his hand. "Mr. Ha-jar-la?"

Debo had become accustomed to the different pronunciations of his name. "Excuse me," he said. "Please, do you mean Ajala?"

"I didn't mean to butcher your name," he said. "It's a…different one. Come on in. I'm Jason."

During the interview, Jason's face gave nothing away. Debo couldn't tell if he was doing well.

At one point, Jason leaned forward. "Can I call you Dee?" he asked. Without waiting for a response, he went on. "D, I'll be honest with you, we're looking for a younger dude. A stocker would need to move heavy skids around. Lots of them. We don't want someone popping out their back on the floor. Too messy for us."

He would have welcomed the opportunity to flex his muscles. None of the men seated outside looked as fit as he did. "I'm in excellent physical shape."

Jason didn't look impressed. "We might as well get to the last question. So tell me, what are the important things you should remember when putting out new stock on the shelves?"

His head began to ache. "Em…em…It's important to arrange them neatly and check for damaged merchandise?"

Jason tapped a pen on the table. "Anything else?"

"I should make sure glass items are not broken?"

"True. The more important task is for you to remove expired items. You would then move the older stock to the front and arrange products with the labels facing the aisle."

He had a feeling things were not looking good for him. Debo licked his lips. "Jason, I'll be straight with you. I need this job."

"This isn't a charity organization."

"I know. You need a hardworking man. Someone who would give you value for your money. I am that man."

Jason nodded. "I like your confidence." He stood and held out his hand. "Welcome to the Northern Food Market family."

Smiling, Debo stood and shook the offered hand.

***

He spent a couple of weeks stocking shelves before being moved to a full-time cashier position. Some progress was better than none, he'd thought when Jason handed him the job change letter. And the new position had the advantage of not breaking his back, literally.

Debo finished a customer's order, handed over the receipt and bid her a good day. The next person in line moved up, and he began ringing her items without looking at her face.

"Don't I know you from somewhere?" the customer asked.

His heart sank when he recognized the face. It was Ethel. The woman who had rejected the benevolence ministry grocery cards. Of all the people he could have run into from Faith Assembly, it had to be her.

Debo gave her a blank look but replied politely. "You must have me mixed up with someone else."

Her snicker made it clear she knew she was not mistaken. "Is that so? I could have sworn you were the assistant pastor at Faith Assembly."

Debo watched as the next person in line moved closer. Nothing like juicy gossip on a slow Thursday morning. He lowered his voice. "As I said, you must be mistaken."

"I guess they figured you out," Ethel said, handing over her grocery gift card. "Too bad for you. I'll keep you in my prayers."

Bile filled his mouth, but he still managed to say a cheerful, "have a good day" when he was done with her order.

The rest of his shift passed in a blur as he kept playing over the encounter in his head. The mocking look in Ethel's eyes had stripped away the shreds of dignity he had wrapped around himself. Now that she knew where he worked, he wouldn't be surprised if she came to the store to taunt him.

During his walk home, he came across a cook wanted advertisement posted on a store front. The job was at one of the many casinos in Moose Jaw. From what he had been told by the street evangelism team at Faith Assembly, gambling and prostitution had thrived in Moose Jaw for years. He wrote down their website address. There was no way he could function as a cook, but he thought they might have other positions.

He browsed the job listings on the employment page of the casino's website. He was right about them having other positions. They needed someone to work in the security department. He didn't have the required job experience, but as Sister Unoma had pointed out to Adele, he did have transferable skills. He was also persuasive once he got an opportunity to sell himself.

The next day, he showed up at the casino door with an edited resume. He didn't think that leaving assistant pastor as his last full-time employment position would give him the street credit he would need for the job, so he omitted that information.

The gentleman at the door gave him a welcoming smile that lost some wattage when he told him he was there to drop off a resume. The big smiles must be reserved for customers. "Do I drop this with you or is there someone else I can see?"

"I'll get you someone from HR."

He was ushered in and served a warm drink. To his surprise, he was given an interview on the spot and told he could begin the following week. Debo could barely contain his happiness. Not only was the pay competitive, but it came with a benefits package.

Feeling on top of the world, he headed to the grocery store and gave his notice. Unless they visited the casino, he would no longer have to worry about seeing Ethel or any church members. He chuckled at the thought. That would make for an exciting reunion.

Chapter Fifty

"What are you people doing?"

They sprang apart at the sound of Shekinah's voice. His arm had been around Moni's shoulder.

"We are a married couple."

Shekinah dropped her backpack and ran towards them. "You guys are getting back together," she exclaimed.

Sam stood and hugged their daughter. "Yes, Princess. We are."

With tears running down her face, Shekinah ran around the room. "He did it, mom. He did it!"

Moni still remembered their early morning conversation. "Yes, He did it."

Shekinah stopped in her tracks. "Oh, my God. I have to tell Grandma."

Moni laughed. Shekinah knew her grandmother well. "We are all going over to see your grandparents. Do you want to change first?"

Shekinah grabbed her arm. "No, let's go now!"

They arrived at Moni's parents' house. Shekinah sprang from the car and raced ahead of them to the door. "I can't wait to see Grandma's face."

Mummy's mouth flew open when she opened the door and saw them. "Sam, is that you?"

Prostrating before Mummy, he greeted her. "*Ekaasan*, Ma."

"Get up, get up," she said. Her gaze swung between the both of them. "Tell me you're back at home?"

Sam kept his gaze low. "I'm moving back soon," he said. "Ma. I'm so sorry for my behavior."

Waving her hand up in the air, Mummy beamed. "Glory to God! *Oluwa modupe* o!"

Mummy's loud voice brought her father to the living room. Moni knelt to greet him. "*Ekaasan*, sir."

Daddy motioned for her to get up. He turned to Sam who hung his head. "I'm so sorry, sir."

"Son, we're glad to have you back," Daddy said to Sam as he patted his back. "Glory to God! We have been waiting for this day." He turned to his wife. "Mummy, this calls for a special celebration."

"Yes, oh," Mummy said as she held on to her gown and danced around the room. "The Lord has answered my prayers. I will sing praises to Him."

They all burst into laughter when Shekinah held the bottom of her tee shirt and danced behind her grandmother.

Moni knew her mother would ask for a private meeting before they left, so when her mother summoned her to her bedroom, she followed and took a seat next to her on her parents' bed.

"Is there a reason why Sam is not home yet?"

The reality was that the relationship would never go back to the way it was before Sam's affair. There were lingering doubts to deal with, ghosts of the strangers they'd allowed into their beds to chase out.

Amongst other things, they needed marriage counseling. She had accepted that there was hard work ahead as they built back trust between them with the goal of having a stronger marriage.

Moni picked her words. "Mummy, we're trying not to rush through this. We have to get to know each other each again. Also, Sam has to give two months' notice at his apartment."

"So, you're not afraid Sam would change his mind about coming back home?"

There were times when she had wondered if Sam would have come back if he hadn't been shocked to his senses by the STD diagnosis. But there was no point dwelling on the past. "Mummy, God brought him home. It wasn't my doing. He will keep Sam as we walk through this period."

Mummy nodded. "Will Sam be coming back to Faith Assembly?"

They were yet to talk about church attendance. "I don't know. I hope so. I do know he has re-dedicated his life and knows he should be part of a local church."

"I will continue to pray for you both," Mummy said before wrapping an arm around her shoulder and pulling her close for an embrace.

***

It had not been hard to convince Sam to spend the evening with them.

They had to persuade Shekinah to go upstairs when she began nodding off.

"Okay, Princess," her father said. "I'll call you tomorrow."

Shekinah looked puzzled. "You're not staying here?"

"Not tonight," Sam said.

To Moni's relief, Shekinah didn't argue with her dad. Shekinah hugged them. "I'll check on you before I go."

She nodded. "Goodnight, Dad."

Moni and Sam exited the house and took a seat on the porch swing. Moni spoke first. "So, that wasn't so bad, was it?"

"No, it wasn't." Sam shook his head. "Can I ask what you and Mummy talked about?"

"She wanted to know why you weren't moving home now and whether you were coming back to Faith Assembly."

Sam hesitated for a long moment before replying, "I'm ready to do whatever you want."

"No, Sam," Moni said with a shake of her head. "This is no longer going to be The Moni Badmus Show."

A small smile tugged at one side of his mouth. "You mean that?"

"Yes. You're not going to hide behind your old 'you made us do this' statements."

Sam grinned. "So, this is about you?"

"Of course it is," she replied with a teasing grin.

Sam took her hand and linked their fingers before placing them in his lap. "I was thinking that we should get a new place," he said. "I... I mean we can afford the dream home we've always wanted in Debo and Adele's old neighborhood."

She knew how much Sam wanted to live in that neighborhood. It would be a perfect backdrop for the gold Mustang winking at her from the driveway.

"There's nothing wrong with wanting a house in Gordon Woods," she said. "But in less than three years, Shekinah will be leaving for the university. What are we going to do with all the space?"

Sam sighed. "I guess you're right."

"I'm not saying we have to stay here," she said. The idea of their moving did bode well for a fresh start. "I'm just saying let's stop and think about this.

There are other nice neighborhoods in the city. I'm ready to go house hunting if that's—"

Sam interrupted her. "Can I kiss you?" he asked. "Please."

Moni's pulse quickened at the request. Sam had seemed reluctant to initiate anything apart from brief hugs and hand holding.

Sam cracked his knuckles as the silence between them lengthened. "Forget that I asked," he said with a hollow laugh. "It's understandable that you're afraid to catch something."

A sentence from a book she had read on re-building a marriage after adultery popped up in her head. Building trust required vulnerability. Moni leaned forward and planted her lips on his.

For a moment, Sam froze before he gave her a long, soft kiss. He left that night, but it wasn't long before he came home for good.

They had a special celebration the day Sam moved back home. Her parents had insisted on holding a belated twenty-first wedding anniversary dinner for them.

Pastor Iginla and his wife were the only guests invited. She and Sam had gone back to see him, and he had welcomed them with open arms.

Daddy presented them with a packet. "Your mother and I think you will both greatly benefit from attending this program," he said. "All expenses have been paid. You just need to pack your bags and go."

Opening the envelope, Moni found out her parents' gift was a weekend away at a marriage retreat in Vancouver. She had never been out west. "Thank you so much."

"The greatest way you can both thank us," Mummy said, "Is for you to go, learn and come back rejuvenated."

Sam and Moni agreed they could both do that.

Chapter Fifty-One

Debo yawned, removed his glasses, and rubbed his eyes. Staring at security cameras for hours on end was wearing on him. Thankfully, it had been a quiet night, their guests were behaving, and there had been nothing suspicious to report to the security personnel on the casino floors. He had worked three, consecutive night shifts. Although he appreciated the overtime that afforded him the ability to replace his car, he looked forward to a day off.

Debo began rubbing his palms together. No matter how hard he tried, he couldn't keep his hands warm. He turned at the sound of the door opening.

"Hey, Watcher." Elyse, one of the casino nurses, walked in with a plate of muffins and a cup of coffee.

He had been surprised when he found out the casino had full-time nurses on staff to help the guests, particularly those in the senior population. Some of their diabetic guests had a habit of sitting for hours at their slot machines because they didn't want to get up and have someone else claim their jackpot. Some even wore adult diapers to avoid using the restroom.

"Top of the morning to you, Needles," he said. Blessed with a petite figure, a pretty, heart-shaped face and a smile which showcased her one dimple, Elyse was always a welcome visitor.

"I thought you might want a healthy breakfast," Elyse said as she placed the plate on his desk.

"Thank you. I needed a warm drink."

"Are you feeling cold?" Without waiting for a response, she reached for his hands. "Let me warm for those up for you."

As she rubbed her hands over his, Debo told himself not to get excited. Elyse was just her usual, helpful self.

"Ever heard of the saying, 'cold hands, warm heart'?" Elyse asked.

"No." Debo withdrew his hands. "Is that your way of telling me you think I'm kind?"

Elyse grinned but didn't reply. She had a way of being friendly that he wasn't sure how to take.

He raised the cup and took a sip. "Thanks for the food and the hand rub."

"Anytime." She leaned against his desk. "Any plans for your day off?"

"There are no exciting things to do in this town."

Elyse shrugged. "It depends on what you're looking for."

Debo rubbed his head. "Right now, I just want to take a shower and go to bed."

"One of these days, we should do something fun."

Now it was his time to shrug. "I have been thinking of going on a whale watching excursion."

"That would be nice. You just let me know when you're ready."

"Sounds like a plan."

He ate his meal, completed his paperwork and went home.

Debo had just crawled into his bed when his phone rang. It was Sam. His friend has left many messages that Debo had deleted without even listening to. He realized he couldn't put him off forever and he didn't want to, so this time he decided to answer the call.

"Bro, long time no speak," Sam said. "I left you several messages."

"I've been busy." Debo sprawled out on his bed. "How are things in Ontario?"

"Good." Sam hesitated. "But are you angry with me?"

He was, but he denied it. "No. I understand personal fun can get in the way of friendship."

"Buddy, I'm—"

He interrupted. "Let's just drop it."

Sam sighed. "Well, I thought I should let you know Moni and I are back together."

"Great news. So you've moved home?"

"Yes, I have," Sam said. "We're actually in the process of buying a new place."

"Wow. I'm happy for you guys." He meant it. "Please keep me updated, so I know where to look for you when I'm in Brampton."

"Are you moving back?" Sam sounded excited.

"I don't have definite plans yet."

"That reminds me. I stopped by your place twice in the past week. No one came to the door. Did they travel somewhere?"

Debo frowned. Adele had not informed him of a trip. "Was it during the day?"

"No. To make sure they were home, I went at dinner time."

"Thanks for the heads up. I'll get in touch with Adele."

"Sounds look a good plan," Sam said. "We'll talk later."

"Thanks, Bro. Say hello to Moni."

"I will."

He sent Adele a text message. She had better not have eloped with his children in tow. His text received an immediate response. Adele agreed to a Skype chat.

He didn't bother with a greeting. "What's going on? Where are you?"

He could tell there was something wrong from the way Adele had her arms wrapped around herself. "We're in Montreal."

"Montreal? You pulled the kids out of school so you could introduce your lover to Maman?"

"No. Edet and I are done." She lowered her eyes and then raised them again. "He couldn't take on the responsibility of caring for the boys." Her laughter held a bitter edge. "He's been there, done that."

The news was music to Debo's ears. "Oh. That must have been unexpected."

"He didn't bother to tell me until he had bought his ticket to Nigeria," Adele complained as if he cared. "I came to Montreal. I needed a change of scenery."

"When are you going back home?"

Adele shook her head. "We're not going back to Brampton."

His jaw dropped. "You moved my children to another province, and you didn't think it was important to tell me?"

"I'm sorry. I wasn't thinking straight."

"You haven't been thinking straight since that man got in your head."

"I don't have to listen to this."

This wasn't the way to get her back, he thought. "I can't pretend I'm not devastated things didn't work out between us. You know I haven't stopped loving you. If you're sure you want to leave Ontario, fine. We'll sell everything, I'll join you in Montreal and we'll start over."

"It's not that straightforward."

"It's not as complicated as you make it sound," he said. "All you have to say is, Debo, come to Montreal and I'll wrap up my life here."

"I filed the divorce papers yesterday. Once you've been served the divorce papers, you'll have thirty days to respond. You promised me an uncontested divorce, so please, Debo, stay in Moose Jaw."

Chapter Fifty-Two

Debo came to work with a fireball churning inside his chest. He had started the day by opening his door to a process server. Even though he knew that the divorce papers were coming, receiving them had still been a shock.

"What's wrong with you?" Elyse asked when he stopped by the nurse's station during his break. "You look tense."

"I was served with divorce papers this morning."

Elyse gave him a sympathetic look. "That sucks. I haven't gone through one but I've been told by friends that it feels like a death of something. You'll need some time to grieve."

"Right now, I'm just angry."

"It's okay for you to be angry," she said. "That's part of the process."

Debo didn't want to spend any more time grieving over someone who obviously hadn't cared for him. "I'm not the grieving kind of guy. I think it's the perfect time to go out and celebrate a new beginning."

Elyse raised an eyebrow. "Oh, yeah? Maybe we can go whale watching this weekend?"

He had something else in mind. "How about I come over to your place tonight? It seems like a perfect time to take you up on the offer of a proper Saskatchewan meal."

Debo could tell from the expression on Elyse's face that she was conflicted. "Are you sure you're ready to try my cooking?"

He didn't know what he was ready for. He just didn't want to go back to his empty apartment. "Is the offer still on the table?"

Elyse's hand went to her hair. She began wrapping the long strands around her finger. "I think a relaxed evening will be good for you. So, yes."

"Is there anything you need me to bring?"

"Nothing I can think of. Just bring yourself."

Feeling better, Debo went back to his office. It would be good to spend the evening laughing enjoying the company of someone who wanted to be with him.

Hours later, Debo was driving out of the parking garage when he heard a woman's screams. Debo turned the corner and brought his vehicle to a stop when his car headlights settled on Elyse and two men. She was trying to fight them off. He remembered that the camera in that part of the parking lot was not working so there was no way the guy who'd just started his shift could send them some help. Key left in the ignition, he jumped out of the car and ran towards them. "Let her go!"

When they realized he was alone, one of the men started laughing, "And if we don't, what are you gonna do about it?"

He pointed to the camera. "Look, I don't want any trouble. The police are on their way, so just take whatever and get out of here."

"You can take my purse," Elyse offered. "I have some cash in there."

Debo moved closer. "No one has to get hurt."

"Who told you that's all we want?" the man holding Elyse said as he ripped her blouse.

Propelled forward by Elyse's terrified scream, Debo slammed his body into the other guy. They both crashed onto the cement floor.

Debo scrambled to his feet. Just before he could grab on to the other guy, he felt something crash into the back of his head. The pain buckled his knees. As he tried to get up, another hit on the side of his head sent him back to the ground.

He heard Elyse's terrified screams. But there was nothing he could do. His eyes began fluttering. Just before he slipped off into darkness, he heard a harsh whisper, "Next time, mind your own business."

***

Somewhere in the distance, he could hear a woman's voice. "Sir, can you hear me?"

Even though the voice was unfamiliar, the soothing tone made him turn his head in its direction. His eyes however refused to open and her voice drifted away.

A little whimper escaped from Debo's mouth as he tried to let her know he could hear her. He felt a soft hand on his bare arm. "Just relax," she said in a soft voice which washed over him and stilled his body. "You'll feel better by the morning."

When she took away her hand, he wanted to call her back. He couldn't understand why his head throbbed the way it did.

Debo squinted as a memory came to him. He heard the boys laughing as his oldest son threw a soccer ball in his direction. It knocked into the side of his head.

A familiar smell wafted up to his nostrils. It was the rose scent of Adele's perfume. He rolled to the side, thinking that she was lying next to him.

He couldn't understand why she had to wear perfume after taking her nightly bath. Adele told him it made her feel beautiful. She didn't need anything to make her more beautiful in his eyes.

Bumping into a cold metal bar, Debo grimaced. Where did the bar come from? And where was Adele?

Exhausted by the thoughts running through his mind, Debo let himself drift away into a restless sleep filled with dreams of strangers chasing him.

The following day, when he opened his eyes, the first thing Debo saw was a blur of unrecognizable shapes. He reached out to pick up his glasses but both the glasses and his night stand were missing. What was going on?

He blinked, and the blur turned into a stark white wall. He had a feeling he wasn't in his bedroom. He lifted up his hand to rub his eyes and realized he had an IV line sticking out from it. Why was he in a hospital?

He was wondering what to do when a worried looking woman walked in. "Oh, thank God, you're awake," she said. The woman's soft voice brought an image of a cinnamon bun on a plate. "I've been so worried."

Somehow, the woman thought he knew her. "I'm sorry but I don't know who you are."

Her mouth opened as she stared at him. "You don't remember me?"

When he tried to sit up, he felt the room move. He settled his body back against the bed. "I don't."

Bursting into tears, she hurried out of the room.

Where in the world was Adele, he wondered. Why had they not called her about him?

He was relieved when a nurse walked into the room. "I heard you're awake. How are you feeling?"

"I need to call my wife."

The nurse reached for the phone and gave it to him. "Do you remember her number?"

He gave her an odd look. "Why wouldn't I remember my wife's number?"

Lips pursed, she handed him the phone. "You'll need to dial one before the number," she said on her way out.

It shouldn't be a long-distance call, but he added the extra digit as he dialed Adele's cell-phone number. She picked up on the third ring. "Hello?"

"Thank God! I was wondering where you were!" he exclaimed.

"You know where I am." Her voice sounded off. "What do you want? I have things I need to do."

"Are you coming here soon? I don't know what's going on with the staff."

"Coming where?

Why would she even ask the question? "To the hospital of course."

"Look, Debo, I don't have time to play your games this morning. I have a job interview to get to. Flying to Moose Jaw wasn't on my to-do list for today."

He didn't think it was possible for the pain in his head to get worse. "Moose Jaw? Nothing made sense. "Please, can I talk to the boys?"

There was something wrong with all the females he had spoken to since he'd woken up. The boys would let him know what was going on.

"There's no need to get them all worked up with your talk about being in a hospital when you know they're still adjusting to everything," Adele said. "We have our scheduled Skype chat for tomorrow. You can talk to them then."

The next thing he heard was a click. Debo stared at the receiver in disbelief. Adele had never hung up the phone on him before. What were the kids still adjusting to?

Chapter Fifty-Three

Moni left home expectant. The marriage retreat was a Friday evening to Sunday morning event. To get some rest before the first session, they caught an early flight from Toronto's Pearson International airport. It helped that the event location was in their hotel conference room.

Refreshed from lunch and a nap, they signed in at the registration desk and picked up their name badges and handbooks before heading to the conference room. Finding two empty chairs at the back, they sat.

Moni looked around. There had to be at least fifty couples present. "There're so many people here," she whispered to Sam.

"Guess lots of people are struggling, too," he whispered back as he reached for her hand and squeezed it.

A short while later, a middle-aged couple stood on the front stage. The woman picked up the microphone. "Welcome to New Beginnings Marriage Retreat," she said. "My name is Abby. And this is my husband, Dave. We'll be facilitating this evening's session."

"For first-time attendees, please know the goal of the retreat is to help build healthy, God-centered marriages. Whether you've come for a tune-up or are hanging by a thread, our prayer is that God will bless everyone here."

She handed the microphone over to Dave. "Over the next couple of days, we're going to have serious conversations about why marriages fail, the importance of communication, the role of sex in marriage and how to fight fair."

"What my wife and I have come to realize is that any weakness in our spiritual or physical relationship can and will be exploited by the enemy of our souls."

During the break period, she and Sam went over Abby and Dave's teaching. "I was a bit skeptical about coming," Sam admitted with an apologetic grin. "I thought we were going to be doing all kinds of group activities. I'm glad we came."

Moni smiled. Sam normally would have hated to talk about his feelings in front of strangers. After the break, Abby started on the topic of why marriages fail. She glanced at her husband. Sam was focused on the speaker.

"Fifteen years ago, we came to our first New Beginnings Marriage Retreat in a state of distress," Abby said. "Barely two years into our marriage, I cheated on my husband. And we were in the process of getting a divorce when a friend invited us to the retreat. It changed our lives."

"Most people don't start a marriage with the plan to cheat on their spouse or to divorce. I didn't. Neither did Dave. But at a certain point in our marriage as in most failing marriages, things began to change. The reasons why they do are as long as my arm. I'm sure if I polled the room, I'd get answers ranging from unfaithfulness, selfishness, lack of communication, addictions, cultural differences, and the list goes on and on."

"The reality is any weakness in our spiritual or physical relationships can and will be exploited by the enemy. And as a couple, you're either working hard towards oneness or drifting towards separation."

Sam gave her hand a gentle squeeze. Moni squeezed back. Abby was spot on.

Time flew by and during the Saturday morning session, as part of renewing the "wow" in their marriages, the men were given the task of organizing a romantic evening. And they were each asked to write something to share with their spouses that evening. During the afternoon, she and Sam spent time apart to work on their project.

Moni knew why Sam had insisted on a stroll when she came back to a candlelit dinner set out on the balcony of their hotel room. Sam admitted to arranging the evening with the concierge's help.

When it was time to share their write-ups, she asked him to go first.

Sam dug out a piece of paper from his trouser pocket. "I'll admit I didn't write these lines. But they perfectly capture how I feel about you."

He cleared his throat. "How fair is thy love, my sister, my spouse. How much better is thy love than wine."

Moni giggled as she read from her sheet of paper. It was funny they had both picked verses from the book, Song of Solomon.

"His mouth is most sweet: yea, he is altogether lovely. This is my beloved, and this is my friend, yea, he is altogether lovely. This is my beloved, and this is my friend, O daughters of Jerusalem."

Sam reached for her hand. "Thou art all fair, my love; there is no spot in thee."

Moni's heart fluttered. How come she never knew Sam had such a romantic side to him? "Let him kiss me with the kisses of his mouth: for thy love is better than wine."

"Until the day break, and the shadows flee away," Sam said. "I will get me to the mountain of myrrh, and to the hill of frankincense."

She smiled at him over the flickering tea lights. "I am my beloved's, and my beloved is mine."

When they were done, Sam reached for her other hand. "Are you ready for our marriage renewal in the morning?"

Moni had been delighted when Abby said couples could renew their vows at the retreat. She stood, walked around the table and sat in Sam's lap. "I can't wait."

Moni sighed as Sam's lips found hers.

The next morning, the emotional marriage renewal ceremony was witnessed by Abby and one of the retreat volunteers. She and Sam stood before them as Israel Houghton's "Moving Forward" played in the background.

Sam couldn't stop smiling when Abby handed them a covenant certificate.

When it was time to leave for the airport, she didn't want to go. It was so easy to feel optimistic in such an environment. "I know we've been doing well, but look at all the people who came for the retreat."

Sam smiled at her. "The statistics don't have to apply to us. Remember, greater is He that is in us, than He that is in the world. We have to keep trusting Him."

She took a deep breath. Yes, she would trust Him. Holding hands, they walked out of the building.

Chapter Fifty-Four

His memory came back in the middle of eating lukewarm green beans and mashed potatoes. Debo dropped his fork, pushed away the hospital bedside table and forced the half-eaten mass in his mouth down. Adele's reaction to his telephone call now made sense. How could he have forgotten that?

The strong wave of grief overtook him. Debo sobbed into his pillow until he fell into an exhausted sleep. An hour later, pain from his taped ribs woke him up.

Nauseous, he pressed his bedside nurse's call button. As he waited, his stomach heaved. There was no way he could get to his puke basin without assistance. To his embarrassment, the nurse walked in as he vomited all over himself.

He was given a stern warning against leaving his bed since he had developed vertigo from the head injury. Even though he resented her irreverent tone, he knew hitting his head again wasn't ideal. He wanted to go home, and Debo doubted they would let him leave while he was unable to walk on his own.

He opened his eyes at the sound of a soft knock on the door. "Come in."

Elyse walked into the room holding a huge floral arrangement.

"Hey, Needles."

"Hey you," Elyse said as she placed the vase on his bedside table. "Compliments of the casino."

"Wow. That must have cost the company something."

Elyse rolled her eyes. "Chicken change. I'll bet they're buttering you up, so you don't sue them."

It was the last thing on his mind. "I'm sorry about your last visit. I can only imagine how you felt."

'Don't worry about it. I had always thought I had an unforgettable face. I guess I was kidding myself."

He patted a spot beside the bed. "How are you doing?"

"Some days are better than others," Elyse said as she sat. "That night, I was so scared when you wouldn't respond to your name."

"Did they hurt you?"

"No. A group of guests came out of the elevator and scared them off."

He reached for her hand. "I'm glad."

"Me, too." Elyse handed him an envelope from her purse. "A little thank you from me."

Debo smiled when he saw the greeting card Elyse must have had custom made. The cover had his image in a superhero costume.

His mind went to Sam. "An old friend has always accused me of trying to save everyone."

Elyse winked. "You can save me anytime."

"As long as we can think of other less painful superhero rescues damsel in distress scenarios, I'm game."

Elyse stood. "On my way in, I was told by the nurses not to tire you out."

He didn't want her to go. "Are you going to come back?"

"How about we plan a lunch date when you're out of the hospital?" Elyse asked.

"That sounds even better," he said.

He watched Elyse mouth her phone numbers as she punched the digits into his cell phone. "You call me when you're ready."

"I'm ready now. Our date will be a world spinning experience."

Elyse moved close to give him a gentle kiss on the forehead. "Be well, my friend."

He was somewhat sad to see her leave. "Thank you."

Shortly after she left, there was a knock on the door. A man entered the room.

"Hello, my name is Akiak Brown. I'm one of the hospital chaplains. May I come in?"

Debo had opened his mouth to say no, thank you, but he found himself raising a hand to usher him in. "Sure. I could use some good company."

"I know a joke or two." Akiak pulled a chair closer to the bed and sat.

"I must let you know I'm not interested in hearing about God right now."

"That's okay. I'm here to listen and lend support in whatever way you need it."

He hadn't expected the response. Debo felt the need to explain himself. "I'm not an atheist. I'm just a Christian on a hiatus."

"Can I ask why you're on a hiatus?"

For a moment, Debo studied the chaplain's face. Akiak had high cheek bones, long dark hair swept into a ponytail and a mesmerizing glow in his eyes. The glow both intrigued and intimidated him. He found himself saying things he had not planned to say.

"Well, there's a whole lot going on in my life right now. I'm far away from everyone, and I'm not sure what to do."

"May I ask where you family is?"

"In Québec."

"It must be lonely without them," Akiak said in a low voice.

The loneliness caused him physical pain. "We're in the middle of a divorce."

"That's a tough situation," Akiak offered. "And now you're lying here in a hospital bed."

"Yes." He did have a right to be mad at God. "Prior to landing here, I had also been kicked out of my pastoral position," Debo added. "And with the way things are looking, it may be months before I can go back to the new job I found."

Akiak looked thoughtful. "I guess that's why you're on a hiatus from God?"

"Wouldn't you run far away from a God who only deals you pain?"

"Since you don't want to talk about God, is it okay if I don't respond to that question?" Akiak asked.

"I guess." He did want to have the conversation. "Perhaps we can talk at another time?"

Akiak nodded. "I would love to. I'm off for the next couple of weeks." He handed over his business card. "I doubt you'll still be here by then."

Debo looked at the card. Akiak was a coordinator at the Friendship Centre on Main Street. "What's a Friendship Centre?" he asked.

"We serve the needs of urban Aboriginal people by providing culturally appropriate services in urban communities," Akiak explained.

"Something like a home away from home?"

"Yes. Our children need to know their heritage."

"Interesting," Debo said as he placed the card on his side table. "Thanks for stopping by."

"Before I leave, can I say a quick word of prayer?" Akiak asked. "I'll pray under my breath so you don't have to hear it."

"I do know when He hears your petition about me, He won't listen."

"The One whom you don't want to talk about is always listening when we call upon Him." Akiak bowed his head.

Watching Akiak's mouth move, Debo wished he could hear what the chaplain was saying. Just in case he was praying for his demise. One never knew.

When Akiak was done, Debo didn't join in the audible amen. Just in case he had been right.

Chapter Fifty-Five

Alone in his basement office, Sam sat with his head bowed and prayed for his friend. Debo had sounded disoriented on the telephone, and he was worried about him. Prayers were the most important thing he could offer, but he also knew the presence of a friend in the time of trouble was invaluable. Sam knew Moni might have reservations about his decision to visit Moose Jaw, but he had to do what was right. She still struggled to accept that Debo was not the enemy. The enemy would use anyone open to him.

Minutes later, Moni came down to the basement to look for him. "What are you doing?"

"I just needed some time alone."

Her brow furrowed. "Are you okay?"

"Yes." Sam sat back in his chair to admire her. It was funny how he couldn't stop staring at her these days.

Moni cocked her head to the side. "So, how is your friend doing?"

Thank You, Lord. It was the opening he had prayed for. "Better than last week," he said. "He has been discharged, but he won't be able to work until the vertigo improves."

"That must be tough. Who's taking care of him?"

"He has some nurses coming into his apartment to check up on him." Sam hesitated before adding, "I'm going to see him. I need to check on him."

Moni nodded. "I knew you would."

No quarrel. He was relieved. Sam stood and pulled her into his embrace. "Have I told you I love you today?"

"At least five times."

"Well, here's number six. I love you. You are truly God's gift to me, and I pray He grants us many more years together."

Moni burrowed her face into his sweat shirt. "I love you, too," she whispered.

***

Standing in the arrivals lounge at the airport in Regina, Sam slung the strap of his carry-on luggage on his shoulder. Since Debo was still not permitted to drive, he had insisted on arranging his transportation to Moose Jaw from the airport.

The rental car he had booked was waiting, and during the drive to Moose Jaw, Sam prayed that he would be able to minister to his friend in a meaningful way during his three-day visit.

Although he called Debo to let him know he was on his way, he had not expected him to find him waiting in the apartment building lobby when he walked in. Sitting down, Debo looked lost in thought and didn't notice him until he snuck up on him. "Hey, Bro!"

Debo staggered to his feet. "You made it."

Sam took a deep breath as they shared a hug.

When Debo stepped away, he punched him on the arm. "You've lost weight."

"While I was at the hospital, I worked on my six-pack. You, on the other hand, have not been skipping too many meals since I last saw you."

"Since Shekinah became an Internet chef, I've become her mandated food tester. I still struggle with saying no to that child."

"Since this is for Miss Glory, taste on. I'll have to chase you down the stairs while you're here."

"That's exactly what you need right now."

Debo blinked several times. "It's so good to see you man."

He swallowed the lump in his throat. "Same here. We better go upstairs before we start bawling."

To Sam's surprise, Debo had made him some Beef Bourguignon.

"That was tasty," he said serving himself a second plate.

Debo smirked. "I'm not just a pretty face."

Their stomachs full, they sprawled on the couch. Sam gave a contented sigh. "This feels like our university days."

Debo nodded. "I miss that period of our lives. I appreciate you coming to see me."

"I should have been here earlier." He knew he owed Debo an apology for his behavior. "I know I'm no longer worthy to be called your friend or your brother; you can just call me that dude from Brampton."

Debo had a straight face. "Nah, I don't want to give Brampton a bad name."

"Ouch. I guess I deserved that."

"No, you don't," Debo said as he threw a pillow at him.

Sam knew he couldn't go back to Ontario without baring his heart. "Yes, I do. I used to be so jealous of you and Adele. About the fancy cars, the new home and all the other stuff you guys did. No matter how much I tried, we just managed to keep our heads above water."

"Bro, there was nothing to be jealous of. The house was a gift, and we borrowed against it to finance all the stuff you saw. It was all a show."

He couldn't believe his ears. "Really?"

Debo nodded. "And at the end of the day, it all doesn't matter. They're just temporary, perishable things. I would give it all away to have Adele back."

"Are you still swinging?"

"No. I gave all that up when I moved here. What I want to know is how you worked things out with Moni. Even though we have a divorce petition pending, I'm hoping I can win Adele back."

"It wasn't anything I did," he said. "God did it."

Debo looked crushed. "Then, there's no hope for me."

"There's always hope. In every situation we go through, we have to know that God is working everything out according to His purpose for us."

"You look at peace."

He didn't want Debo to think he had it all together and there was no hard work involved. "Some days are better than others." He told Debo about the marriage retreat. "It's not about how many times we fall; it's all about getting back up again."

Debo gave him a sad smile. "My legs are wobbly. I often fall on my face."

"Then lean on Him."

"Easier said than done." Picking up the remote, Debo switched on the television. "So, what would you like to watch?"

Sam decided to drop the subject. He had planted the seed. The Lord would make it grow.

Chapter Fifty-Six

"I know you don't want to talk about this, but we need to settle our affairs in Brampton. We can't just abandon everything and move on. There are owed property taxes, insurance, and many other loose ends to tie up."

Her gentle tone told a story. Adele was trying to appeal to his reasonable side. He didn't want to listen to what she had to say. He wanted his family back, so tying up loose ends wasn't high on his list of things that would help his cause. "This isn't my fault. You're the one who left Ontario without making adequate plans."

"I know I messed up," Adele said in a weary voice. "But, we can't keep throwing away money when I need to find our place. Maman isn't complaining, but I'm sure she must want her peace back. You know how loud your boys get."

He wanted the best for his sons. "You can talk to a realtor about selling the house."

Adele sounded hopeful. "You mean that?"

He remembered Adele's excitement when the house was being built. The many hours they had spent pouring over the building plans, friendly debates over furnishing choices. Everything had to be perfect for their dream home.

"Yes. You're right. It is time for us to move on."

"I'm going to Brampton next week. No point in wasting more time," Adele said. "Can you meet me there?"

Adele didn't know about the extent of his injuries. His pride wouldn't let him tell her. She may think she needed to travel down to see him. He wanted her love, not her pity.

"You can put my things in storage for now," he said. "I'll get to them later."

"And your car?"

Debo winced. It some unexplainable way, the Mercedes had become an extension of himself. "You can talk to the folks at the dealership about selling it. I don't need it here." He also couldn't afford to maintain a luxury car while pinching pennies.

"Are you sure you don't want to park it at Sam's house for now?"

He didn't want to inconvenience anyone. "There'll be other cars," he added in consolation to himself. "Just sell it."

Ending the call, aching, Debo went to his bed and wrapped the duvet around his head. Divorce was painful. Plain and simple.

***

The doubts he had battled before making the call went away when Akiak sounded happy to hear from him.

"Debo! I was hoping you would call. How are you doing?"

"Much better. Hoping to get the all clear when I see the doctor next week."

"Great news. Were you thinking of coming to visit us at the Centre?"

He had realized that the peace reflected on Sam's face had mirrored the look on Akiak's face. He couldn't stop thinking about it.

"Are you available for a visit?" he asked.

"Can you come tomorrow? I'll be at the Centre all day."

He had plenty of time on his hands. "Tomorrow sounds fine."

"Good. See you then."

***

The cab he took dropped Debo by the front door of the Friendship Centre. The receptionist paged Akiak.

"*Tunngasugit,*" Akiak said greeting him in his native tongue. "You're in time for lunch." Akiak led them down an empty hallway. He opened a side door, and they walked into a large hall. It held several round tables covered with red checkered table cloths. The room buzzed with a quiet energy as those present carried on conversations and ate their meals.

Akiak pulled a chair for him at one of the empty tables. "Let me get you a plate of *Muktuk*. It's a traditional Inuit meal. What would you like to drink?"

Debo knew how much Akiak treasured his Inuit heritage. He wasn't hungry, but he also didn't want to hurt his friend's feelings. "Sure. Any pop will be fine."

"I'll be right back."

He took a cautious look at the breaded pieces when Akiak came back. "What is it?"

"The strips are made from the skin and blubber of the Bowhead Whale."

Debo dipped the *Muktuk* strip into the soy sauce served with it. He took his time chewing. "Not bad."

Akiak smiled. "It is an acquired taste."

"I'll have to make you a Nigerian dish when you visit me," he said. "Hope you like spicy food?"

"I'll drink some milk to cool my tongue if I need to."

They left the hall and went to Akiak's office. The first thing Debo's eyes were drawn to a plaque on the wall.

Debo mouthed the words. *It is in the midst of anguish and terror that we realize who God is and the marvel of what He can do - Oswald Chambers.*

He looked away from the picture and found Akiak staring at him. "I have found that to be true in my life."

Debo took his seat. "I was hoping we could finish the conversation we started at the hospital."

"We'll do that when I come over for dinner," Akiak said. "So what are your plans?"

Debo knew he didn't want to go back to the casino. Elyse was there. He didn't want to hurt her. "I need a new job."

"Well, if you're interested, I have a job proposition for you," Akiak said. "We need someone to join our client resource staff."

"What do they do?"

"They make sure everyone is having a nice time while they're at the Friendship Centre by answering questions, making appropriate referrals and helping run the wellness groups and social programs we offer."

It sounded like something he could do. "Can I think about it?"

"Sure. Give me a call to let me know."

"Thanks for the offer."

"We'd love to have you join us," Akiak stood. "I do have to run now. There are some things I need to attend to."

On their way out of the office, he turned to Akiak. "I've been wondering about something. At the hospital, when you prayed for me, what did you say?"

Akiak's eyes twinkled. "I just kept saying, reel him in Lord. And here you are."

Chapter Fifty-Seven

At his check-up appointment, the doctor gave him the all-clear which meant he could go back to work. He was still in the medical building when he called Akiak to express his interest in the job. The interview went well, and he was offered the job on a probationary basis. He accepted and started the next day.

Debo listened as Akiak introduced him to a group of fifth-grade students who were visiting the Friendship Centre for a cultural experience field trip.

"When we sit in a circle, we are all equals," he explained. "This way, we can easily share our wisdom." Akiak grinned. "One of the best things about being in a circle is that you can't get cornered."

The kids laughed.

There was so much he had learned about Aboriginal peoples since he began working at the centre and there was still a lot more to learn.

During break time, he and Akiak spent some time re-arranging the room before heading to the kitchen to grab a mid-day snack.

"I should let you know I'm traveling home next month," Akiak said at the end as he sliced them some apples. "I'm taking some supplies to my people."

He had heard Akiak talk about Resolute Bay, but he didn't know where it was. "Is it close by?"

Akiak shook his head. "It's in High Arctic, the second northernmost community in Canada."

A shiver went through him. "It must be freezing there."

"We're used to it. Right now, we have twenty-four hours of sunlight a day, so it helps. That's why Resolute Bay is called the land of the midnight sun."

He couldn't picture it. "That would be a sight to behold."

"If you can afford the air ticket, I'd appreciate the company."

Debo considered the offer. It would be an unforgettable experience. "How much is an air ticket?"

Akiak grimaced. "A return ticket is about eight thousand dollars."

"What? That's ridiculous. Traveling within a country shouldn't cost that much."

"That is why many of us can't afford to go home. I try to go as much as I can. My only sister, Saila, still lives there."

"I wish I had the money."

"If you stay here, there will be other visits," Akiak said.

"I'd love to go on this one."

"There's nothing impossible for God to do. Ask Him. If He wants you to go, He'll make it happen."

Debo stared at his friend's face. Akiak's simple faith was still hard for him to grasp. He was amazed by the way Akiak involved God in every decision he made.

Break time conversations had led to what he tagged tentative conversations with God. He knew God could see him figuring things out. But as his father had once told him, God still loved it when his children took the time to talk to Him. Just like he did when Debo called Nigeria to say hello or I miss you to his earthly father, Mr. Ajala.

Despite their new relationship, he was reluctant to ask God ask for a favor about something that wasn't such a priority. He didn't think he had earned the right to when he'd been doing things his way. Reaping what one sowed made logical sense.

"Debo, I am convinced that God brought you here for a purpose," Akiak said as he pushed back his chair. "His will be done."

***

He'd been ecstatic when Adele called him to let him know his car was purchased by the dealership. All the bells and whistles he had insisted on made the car an easy sell. He paid cash, and they returned nearly as much as he'd given them. The sale meant he had the money to pay for his ticket.

Halfway through their nineteen-hour journey, he'd begun to wonder if he'd made a big mistake. The money would have paid his rent for months.

As the small propeller plane taking them to Resolute Bay ran into some turbulence, Debo felt his stomach heave. He was able to fight the feeling for most of the trip, but then he lost it and managed to get his brown paper bag in front of his mouth just in time. Debo went to the cramped bathroom and washed out his mouth.

They landed at Resolute Bay airport. Debo staggered down the aircraft's metal steps to join Akiak on the tarmac. They had been traveling for almost two days, and he was ready to plant his feet on solid ground.

Akiak gave him a sympathetic look. "Welcome to Qausuittuq. That was rough, eh?" He patted him on the back. "A bit of fresh air, you'll soon feel better."

He did begin to feel better as the crisp Arctic air fanned his face. Even though there were hotels and lodges, Akiak had told him his sister Saila would not forgive him if they didn't stay at her place.

"She likes to pamper me. It's a match made in heaven as I like to be pampered."

Debo saw the strong family resemblance when Saila opened the door to her house.

"Akiak!" She gave her brother a big hug.

Akiak introduced him. "This is my big sis, Saila. As the first born, she has more mileage on her than the rest of us."

"Don't you forget that while you're here, big city boy," Saila said with a hand planted on her hip.

"*Ainngai*," Debo greeted as he inclined his head. He had worked hard on learning how to say hello in Inuktitut.

His friend looked pleased. "I see someone is trying to impress big sis."

"He was successful," Saila said as she held her arms wide open. "*Tunngahugit.*"

Akiak insisted that Saila put up her feet while he and Debo cleaned the kitchen. They could hear Saila snoring on the couch. "When we're apart, I miss her so much," Akiak said as he covered her with a quilt.

Since their arrival, there had been a different air around Akiak. He held himself a little less rigid, had a bounce to his steps. "You're different here."

"It's the home factor," Akiak said. "I belong here."

To whom did he belong? Looking away, Debo began drying the dishes as Akiak washed.

"What is more important than anything is belonging to God," Akiak stressed as if he could read his mind.

Debo glanced at Akiak. He was staring into the sink full of soapy water. After a moment Akiak spoke, "I have done a lot of things I'm not proud of.

Things which brought me shame. A wise woman, my late grandmother, would say to me, 'Child, those who mock you are not your creator.' My encounter with the Lord set me free."

Debo reflected on those words. He had always thought that the worse that could happen to him was being the fixed object of another person's scorn. Everything he had strived for was to avoid being mocked. "I just want my life back." He thought about it again. "No, not the way it was. I want Adele and the children."

"Seek Him first," Akiak said.

The directive sounded too simple which meant there was more margin for disappointment. "What if I do and they don't come back?"

"His will be done on earth, as it is in heaven, not ours."

Feeling frustrated, he threw the tea towel on the counter. "Then, what's the point of it all?"

"Does the clay dare ask the potter why it was made into one type of pot and not another? I have found peace in the acceptance that we were created for His pleasure."

Pensive, Debo spent the rest of the evening dwelling on the words. After he had been escorted to the guest room, he stood by the window and stared at a sun which had refused to set. Even though he tried, Debo was unable to banish thoughts about the God who had also created the sun and placed it in the sky.

Chapter Fifty-Eight

It was almost noon when Debo opened his eyes. He had slept for ten hours. He hurried out of bed, mortified at what his hosts must think of him.

Taking slow steps, he wandered in the direction of voices coming from the kitchen. Akiak and his sister were talking at the table.

"Sleeping Beauty is up," Akiak teased when he saw him.

Hands behind his back, he faced Saila. "Good afternoon. I'm sorry for staying in bed this late."

Saila gave a dismissive wave. "You must have been exhausted from your long journey." She gave her brother a feigned annoyed look. "This one should have stayed in bed, too. The way he has been questioning me about my health, you would think he works for Statistics Canada."

Akiak laughed. "Says the person who knocked on my door to find out if I needed anything."

Lifting her chin, Saila faced him as she pushed back her chair. "Food or shower? And what can I make you?"

"I'd like to shower first," Debo said. He could smell himself. "Anything you make is fine."

"To face our weather, you'll need something hearty in your belly," Saila told him as she walked over to her fridge. "I made beef stew yesterday. I also have some homemade buns."

Debo nodded. "That would be more than welcome. Thank you."

"Big Sis just told me there's a paraskiing event taking place this afternoon," Akiak told him. "I think it would be a good way for you to see Resolute. First, I do have a meeting at the church. You're welcome to tag along."

"What's paraskiing?" He had only heard of parasailing.

Akiak turned to him. "Basically, to paraski, you put on a parachute harness, strap on skis or use a snowboard to glide. It's fun." Akiak puffed out his chest. "I used to be a paraski champion and—"

Saila interjected. "He won once."

Akiak made eyes at his sister. "I was close the second time."

Saila laughed. "So were twenty other competitors."

"Since everyone can now call themselves a hero, I can call myself a champion," Akiak said.

"A dressed-up lie is still a lie," Salia said in a firm tone.

Debo showered and ate and then dressed quickly as to not make Akiak late for his meeting. He wore his thermal underwear, thermal socks, three layers of clothing, a fleece mask and fleece lined boots before leaving the house.

From a distance, he could see the billowing parachutes. The outdoor competition had scores of people huddled together at the edge of a frozen field.

He was enthralled by a spectacle of colored parachutes set against the white snow and light blue skies.

As they watched the teams, he turned to Akiak. "This looks like a very popular sport here."

"It is. Competitors travel down from other communities," Akiak said. "Our elders work hard to make sure the young ones have positive outlets.

Like anywhere, you must give teenagers something productive to do, or they'll get into trouble. When I was a young punk, I used to go around making trouble. Before I got home, my grandmother would have been told the whole story. Since we didn't have the cover of darkness, there was no sneaking anywhere."

Akiak took him to the cooperative store for a warm drink. When he was done, Debo walked around to see if there were souvenirs he could get for the boys. Debo found some t-shirts with the slogan: 'Resolute Bay isn't the end of the world, but you can see it from here.' He picked one up. "Is that true?"

"We are the landing ground for North Pole expeditions," Akiak said. "Interested in taking another trip?"

Debo shook his head. "No, thanks. There's a reason my ancestors settled in Africa. I may be Canadian born, but cold weather seeps right into my bones."

Their next stop was at the church. Resolute Bay Anglican Church was a small building with a green and brown roof. A plain white cross topped the steeple.

While Akiak met the Reverend and some other men, Debo was told he could walk around the building. There wasn't much to see, but he was drawn to the music playing behind closed doors.

Stepping into the room, he saw a group of teens gathered at the other end. From the musical instruments, it looked like he had walked in on the church young band practice.

As they started on a new song, he took a seat at the back. It wasn't his first time hearing Chris Tomlin's *Jesus Loves Me*. But it was the first time the song lyrics came alive as they made their way through his ears to his heart.

He sang along as he rocked in his seat.

As he rocked on the spot, images of earthen water pitchers filled his head. He heard the rush of water, felt a warm sensation go through his body as if some things were being taken out. A pouring out, then a pouring in. A pouring out, then a pouring in.

Debo fell to his knees.

Less of me, Lord. More of You.

As the words sunk into his spirt, he began to laugh. From a distance, he heard a question. "Sir, are you okay?"

Unable to speak, he nodded.

Less of me, Lord. More of You.

Debo continued to laugh.

He heard Akiak's voice, felt a hand on his shoulder. "Debo, are you alright?"

Less of me, Lord. More of You.

Debo opened his eyes. He had needed to come to the end of the world to find peace. "Yes, I am."

Chapter Fifty-Nine

Debo sprawled on his bed and stared at the old popcorn ceiling. The joy he'd felt while at Resolute Bay seemed to have left him. The silence in his empty apartment had forced him to count his losses.

Hungry for the sound of another human being, he reached for the laptop on his night stand and found a Christian playlist on YouTube. He settled against his pillows as the voices filled the room.

The words 'not by sight' came to his mind. Debo thought about how he had spent his adult life chasing glittery, tangible objects, things he could see. The past year had proved they were not able to give him honor.

He glanced at the laptop when Santus Real's "Lead Me" began playing. The song lyrics struck a chord inside Debo as he imagined Adele singing to the words to him. When the song ended, he re-played the song. Debo realized that he couldn't lead his family or anyone without being led by God.

During the drive back to Moose Jaw, Akiak told him before honor comes humility. Debo knew he no longer wanted to be the emotional Christian whose faith ebbed and flowed with the frequency of his fickle emotions. He was ready to humble himself for a life of obedience.

***

Debo turned at the sound of his name. He would have recognized the voice in his sleep. "Needles!" He hurried towards her, stopping about a foot away when he remembered it would be inappropriate to give her a body crushing hug.

Elyse whispered to the woman whose wheelchair she stood behind before stepping forward with an outstretched hand and grin. "Hello, Watcher."

He shook it with both hands. "It's so good to see you."

She stuck both hands in her scrub pant pockets. "Likewise."

"What are you doing here?"

"I came to see one of my friends," Elyse said. "I also volunteer at The Alzheimer Society. Funny running into you here."

He grinned. "This is where I work."

"We heard you'd resigned. And since you didn't call…" Elyse's voice trailed off.

He should have called her. "I'd like to make it up to you. How about I take you out for lunch?"

She seemed embarrassed that he offered. "Don't worry about it."

"No. We'll do it tomorrow. You pick the time and the place."

"There's a delicatessen not too far from here," Elyse said. He recognized the name. "Perhaps we can meet at noon?"

"Done."

Elyse glanced at the woman waiting on her. "I've got to go."

"See you tomorrow."

***

"Who's that lovely looking lady you were talking to?" Akiak asked as they tidied up at the end of the day.

Debo smiled. "I thought you were busy."

"I still have working eyes. Was she someone special?"

Debo thought about the question. "Kind of. We were going to her apartment the night I was beaten."

"I see." Akiak's expression became thoughtful. "Are you seeing her again?"

"We're going for lunch tomorrow."

Akiak patted him on the arm. "I'll be praying."

There was a time when the church-speak would have made him upset. Why was it necessary to pray about everything?

During one of their conversations, Akiak had pointed out the Bible said to pray without ceasing, which meant nothing was too inconsequential to pray about. The Scripture wasn't new to him. He had just thought it was kind of silly to bother God with the small things.

"Thank you." He would need God's wisdom.

***

Elyse finished the quiche she'd ordered and settled back into her chair before saying what Debo sensed had been on her mind the entire time. "I can't help thinking how things would have been different between us if you had made it to my apartment that night."

Looking into Elyse's eyes, Debo was reminded how lonely he was. It would be so easy to care deeply about Elyse. But he knew he would only end up hurting her. And he was done hurting people. His heart was with Adele.

When he had thought about that night at the casino, it was as if while God's eyes were roaming the earth, He had seen that Debo needed to be saved from himself. "It was for the best."

"Perhaps," Elyse said as she searched his face. "You look like you're at peace."

"I am."

"I'm glad you found what you were looking for."

Something told him he might never see her again. "His name is Jesus."

Elyse gave a nervous laugh. "All that organized religion stuff is not my thing."

"I know." He wanted to tell Elyse he would be praying for her. Instead, he held out his hand. "Can I pray before you leave?"

He had never seen the angry look on her face before. "I don't have a problem with prayers, meditations, and chants. It's the only one true God thing I find to be discriminatory."

Debo reminded himself that he had been saved by grace and called to love. A mind steeped in the world's ideologies was no match for a changed heart. "We'll agree to disagree."

Elyse's fingers curled around his. "Deal."

Debo bowed his head and said five words under his breath. "Lord, please, reel her in."

Chapter Sixty

Debo was sweating when he stepped out of the Pierre Elliott Trudeau International Airport. He took off his jacket. He should have checked the weather forecast for Montreal before leaving Moose Jaw. They were worlds apart in terms of the weather.

The taxi he hailed took him straight to his mother-in-law's home in Old Montreal. To avoid an uncomfortable situation, he had called his mother-in-law to let her know he was coming to see Adele. In her blunt way, Maman had told him it was about time he showed up.

Maman gave him a warm hug and a kiss on both cheeks. "Son, it is good to see you."

Debo cleared the lump in his throat. He had thought Maman would have taken her daughter's side. "Same here. You look great."

"Your children are keeping me young." Her smile was tired. "The big boys are at school, and the baby just went down for a nap."

He followed her into the kitchen. "Do you want something to drink, eat?"

Thoughts about his conversation with Adele had unsettled his stomach. He said, "I'm fine."

"Your wife will be home soon. She's only working part-time at her new job."

He didn't know Adele had found a job. "If you don't mind, I'll sit outside to wait for her."

"I cannot express how happy I am that you came," Maman said as she walked him to the door. "Sometimes, at night, I hear your wife crying. I think she misses you."

He was sure Adele's tears were for Mr. Bassey. "I've missed her, too. I just hope she'll listen to my pleas."

Maman patted him on the arm. "Speak from your heart."

Debo nodded. He intended to give it his best shot.

From his position on the porch, he was able to watch Adele walk down the side of the cobblestone road without being seen. She had wrinkles in her brow that weren't there before. He stood. "Hello."

At the sound of his voice, Adele went pale. She looked around as if searching for an escape route. "How did you get here?"

He tried to lighten the moment. "I came by plane."

Adele gave him the exasperated look he'd never thought he would miss. "This isn't the time to be silly, Debo."

She was right. "I'm sorry."

Walking past him, Adele went into the house. He followed her.

Adele spoke to her mother in rapid French as her flint colored irises flickered back at him.

"Adele, stop being stubborn," Maman snapped. "It's time you tell me what's going on between you two. This is more than I needed a break from Brampton because Debo and I fought."

"Well," Adele said as she wrung her hands. "The truth is we're divorced."

He heard Maman's sharp intake of breath. "Oh *Mon Dieu!* Adele."

Adele stepped forward. "Maman—"

Pale, Maman shook her head. "No. Don't come closer."

Adele stopped. "I know I should have told you. I'm sorry."

"Maman, please don't be angry," Debo interjected.

Eyes narrowed, she wagged a finger at him. "You are not innocent. Both of you, out."

"Maman, please—" Adele protested.

"Out I say. And don't come back until you've figured out how to talk to each other. My grandchildren deserve parents who put them first."

They grabbed their coats and left the house.

Adele scowled at him. "Thanks a lot. If you had told me you were coming, I would have had time to break the news gently."

The previous week, he had received their divorce order in the mail. It was what made him buy the ticket to Montreal. It had not felt real. "How was I to know you hadn't told her?"

Adele gave him a pointed look. "Have you told your parents?"

"Not yet."

"Exactly."

"My situation is different. I don't live with my parents, and I don't talk to them every day," Debo said. "Anyway, if I had told you I was coming, you would have said I don't want to see you."

She shrugged. "So, what now?"

"You heard Maman. We have to talk."

"Fine. Let's go to the park."

The well-used park was one of the reasons why the boys had loved to spend summers at their grandmother's home. The fall foliage of blazing oranges, reds, and yellows was a beautiful sight.

They found an empty stone bench under one of the trees and sat. "That's an interesting pin," Adele said to him.

Debo looked down. He had not realized his fingers were playing with the brooch. It was Akiak's gift. The lapel pin brooch shaped like an iron anvil was to remind him that iron sharpens iron.

"My boss and friend, Akiak, gave it to me. I can't wait for you to meet him."

"Is he coming to Montreal?" she asked with feigned innocence.

"Adele, the battle is over. You won. I just want to spend some time my boys. Is that too much to ask for?"

He was surprised when Adele's eyes filled tears. "What exactly did I win? You think this was easy for me?"

"I'm sure it's not," he conceded. "But have you thought about how hard it must be for our children? I've been involved in their care since the day they were born."

"This was never about your abilities as a father."

Debo heard what she had left unsaid. "I couldn't have been that bad as a husband."

She shrugged. "It no longer matters. We're divorced."

"Divorced couples remarry." One of the books he had found on the topic had advocated that couples spend at least one year in courting before remarrying. "I know I can't hurry things. I don't want to. We could walk through this at the pace you're comfortable with."

"I'm sure they're eligible women in Moose Jaw. Perhaps, you can join the singles group at your new church?"

"Adele, I would not be here if I was not convinced that God's plan for me is to be with you."

"I have a different conviction."

Even though Adele sat next to him, Debo could sense that emotionally, she was still somewhere far away. He heard a clear directive.

Wait.

Debo changed the topic. "Maman said you found a job?"

"Yes. I finally found a substitute teaching position at a nearby elementary school."

"That's great news."

"I wouldn't say it's great news. It feels like a demotion."

"Sometimes, we have to be pulled back for the momentum to move forward," he said.

"Like arrows."

"Yes. In His hands. Arrows for kingdom work."

Adele frowned. "You sound different."

"I'm learning not to walk by sight," he said. "Pastor Iginla was right. I needed to be in Moose Jaw at least for a season."

Adele didn't respond. He didn't know what she was thinking. Her face was a mask of unpredictability at this point.

"Lately, I've been thinking about doing some missionary work."

That got Adele's full attention. "Where?"

He didn't know. "I'm waiting on God for direction."

Adele's eyes held a distant look. "It must feel good to know your purpose."

"It was what you wanted, too," he said, reminding her of who they once were.

"That's what the old me wanted. This Adele is too jaded and worn out to make a difference in anyone's life."

As he opened his mouth to tell Adele she had something to offer, he heard the directive a second time.

Wait.

"The boys should be home soon," Adele said. "I have to wait for them at the bus stop."

Debo stood. "I don't want you to be late."

Debo's excitement grew when he sighted the school bus.

Given that he hadn't seen them in months, he had expected the boys to jump all over him. The younger three did while his Number One hung back. Puberty had hit in the months they had been apart. Debo was surprised to see he was the same height as his mother. He forced himself not to walk over and pull his son into an embrace.

The younger ones raced towards the house. Adele hurried after them. Debo waited for his oldest son to catch up.

"Hi, Dad."

Debo blinked back tears at the sound of the breaking voice. His boy was in the process of becoming a man, and he wasn't here for him.

He wanted to hug his son, but from the stiff way he held himself, Debo knew he didn't want to be touched. "Hey, kiddo."

"When are you leaving?"

Hurt by the question, Debo had wanted to point out that he just arrived. "I'm here for four days," he said. "So, we have the weekend."

He was rewarded with the promise of a smile. Debo had not expected to see that. It was fleeting, but it had been there.

He shrugged. "Cool."

As they walked towards the house, Debo thought he couldn't agree more.

Chapter Sixty-One

Sam growled into his ear. "Oh, Oh, Oh, Happy Thanksgiving!"

He settled against the couch and placed his feet on the ottoman. "You have your holidays mixed up."

"I'm just counting down to Christmas. You should see the giant, lighted reindeer I ordered. The neighbors will love it."

A cheerful Sam took some getting used to, Debo thought as he chuckled. "And you wonder why I've refused to move back to Brampton. Dealing with you on the telephone is bad enough."

"A few more winters and you'll change your mind about coming back to the warmer side," Sam said. "I'm a patient man."

"Nah."

"We have a full house so I thought it best we say our Happy Thanksgiving greetings now."

"Thanks, Bro. How are your ladies?"

"They're doing great. Hold on for Moni."

He hadn't expected to feel so nervous about talking to her. "Happy Thanksgiving," Moni said when she came to the phone. "How are you doing?"

"I'm fine. It's been a long time."

"Yes, it's been a while. I hope you're keeping in touch with Adele and boys?"

"They're on their way to Moose Jaw as we speak."

Moni's surprise was obvious. "What a nice way to spend Thanksgiving."

When Adele had called to let him know they were coming, he would have done a cartwheel if he hadn't been afraid of tearing a ligament. "It is."

"Great news. My greetings to everyone."

"Will pass them on," Debo replied. Next, he heard Shekinah's voice. "Hey, you. You forget about your old godfather?"

"I'm sorry," Shekinah said. "But you'll be proud of me. This year, I have lots to be thankful for."

They all did. "I'm happy to hear that. You say hello to the Ontario turkeys for me."

Shekinah giggled. "Bye, Uncle."

"Bye, Miss Glory."

"Did I just hear Adele is coming to Moose Jaw?" Sam asked. "Why didn't you tell me you guys are back together?"

"We're not. She's just bringing the boys for a visit."

"Regardless, I'm glad they're coming," Sam said. "I was worried you were going to spend Thanksgiving by yourself."

"I wouldn't have been alone. The Friendship Centre will be serving a warm meal for anyone who wants to come."

"How long are they staying?"

"A week. I'll make sure to Skype before they leave for Montréal. I know the boys will be happy to see their Uncle Sam's face."

"That would be awesome. God bless."

"God bless you, too."

Debo ended the phone call and then for about the hundredth time, he walked through the apartment to make sure he had not missed anything. The house was spotless, the fridge stocked and he had a list of tourist attractions drawn up.

Adele told him she had booked a hotel room but he was hoping that he would be successful in changing her mind since he wanted his family under the same roof. He was perfectly fine sleeping on the couch.

Excited, he arrived at the airport in Regina an hour earlier than needed. It wasn't until the boys piled into the van he'd rented for the duration of the visit that his racing heart settled. A part of him had been worried Adele would change her mind.

Once they were settled, he looked at Adele. She'd cut her hair. The new short cut framed her face nicely. "You look so good." It was painful being so close and not being able to wrap his arms around her.

Adele's hand went to her hair. "You like it?"

"It suits you." He wanted to tell Adele he loved everything about her, but he was afraid the unwanted words would widen the space between them.

She looked down for a minute before changing the subject. "The boys did great during the flight. I had told them there would be no whale watching if they didn't behave."

Number Two had asked him if they could ride the whale. Debo chuckled. "And Maman?"

"She sends her love."

"Boys, it's a long ride to my house. Do you want to get something to eat before we start the last part of your trip?"

He heard a resounding yes from the back. "Okay. Some hamburgers and fries coming up."

***

It took a couple of hours before they made it back to the apartment. They settled the boys in front of the television before he asked to speak with Adele in his one of his guest bedrooms.

She gave him a wary look as he begged her to stay. "Why?"

"I don't have any ulterior motives. I just think it would be good for us to all spend this time together. If after tonight you can't bear to be in my presence, you'll be free to stay at your hotel. Deal?"

"Fine. Remember, I'm here for the children's sake. So don't get any funny ideas."

Debo stared at her. There had been many times when he had been so frustrated by the lack of progress. Times when he had wondered what more he had to do, how else he was going to prove himself worthy to Adele.

He had clearly heard the directive to wait, so, he would wait and seek Him first. Debo raised his right hand as if swearing an oath. "I promise to behave myself. So help me God."

Chapter Sixty-Two

Akiak welcomed Adele and the boys to the Friendship Centre with big hugs and wrapped presents. Debo watched with an opened mouth.

"Something to remind you, you have family in Moose Jaw," Akiak said as he handed over the gifts.

Adele's face turned red, and she flashed Debo a glare heated with embarrassment. "I didn't know we were exchanging gifts."

Debo shrugged. "I'm as surprised as you are."

"Please don't feel bad," Akiak said. "Your presence here is my gift."

He was touched to find Akiak had also reserved a table for them. Their relationship reminded him of the proverb which said a friend loves at all times and a brother is born for adversity.

"We're serving a family style dinner with dessert stations," Akiak said.

Debo wasn't surprised when Adele sat a child between them. "Thank you. Are you sure you don't need me to help out in the back?"

Akiak shook his head. "This is where you're most needed. I'll see you all before you leave."

Debo took the boys with him to get drinks and returned to find dinner served. Adele quietly stared at the platters of food. On one, there was more stuffing than turkey meat.

"What's on your mind?" he asked.

"I was thinking about last thanksgiving," she said. "This is different."

Debo gulped. Their life had changed.

Number One spoke up. "Mom, do we still have to eat this?"

Adele nodded. "Different doesn't mean it's not nice."

"Thanksgiving is much more than expensive clothes and food," Debo said. "It's about saying thank you to God for all the wonderful things He does for us. For our family."

"Are we still a family?" Number Two asked. "You know, with this divorce thing?"

The concerned look on his son's face brought physical pain to Debo's body. He had not wanted Adele to tell them. She had said he didn't have to deal with their questions on a daily basis.

"You'll always be my family," Debo replied. "Nothing can change that."

Akiak had told them each table was free to decide how to say their thanks. "Boys, we have to pray before we eat." Debo stretched out his hands. "We are no longer going to thank God for digested food."

He and Adele exchanged a long look as the boys laughed. "I'm still thankful for you," he said. Her cheeks blushed red, but she didn't respond.

They linked hands and bowed their heads. Looking back over the past year, Debo was grateful to be alive, for another second chance.

Peace I leave with you, my peace I give unto you: not as the world giveth, give I unto you. Let not your heart be troubled, neither let it be afraid.

God's word brought a smile to his face and his spirit. In the midst of life's busyness, he had learned to listen for God's voice. Oh, what a beautiful sound it was.

Chapter Sixty-Three

Moni listened to her nephews and Shekinah kick up a ruckus in the living room. Shekinah had introduced them to the Monopoly game their grandfather brought back from Lagos. Her brother's surprise visit had brightened up their weekend.

As she tossed a large bowl of Caesar salad, she heard her sister-in-law, Aileen, tell them to settle down. The noise level went down, only to rise again. Moni didn't mind. She loved hearing them play.

She placed the salad bowl in the fridge before getting some ripe plantains from her pantry. Their Thanksgiving dinner wasn't complete without a side dish of the fried plantain slices. She also knew they were her nephews' favorite.

The plantain slices were sizzling inside hot oil when her mother walked into the kitchen.

"Madam Chef. Are you sure there's nothing for me to do?"

To her surprise, Mummy had told her she could host the family Thanksgiving dinner. As the host, she had turned it into a thanksgiving, slash house warming party since it was their first celebration in the new house.

Moni shook her head. "I'm almost done."

Mummy surveyed the platters of food she had arranged on her kitchen island. "Moni, the aroma from your cooking brought me here."

"I learned from one of the world's best cooks."

"I see you've inherited your father's sweet tongue."

Moni grinned. "Go and enjoy your grandchildren."

"My quiver is full again." Mummy's voice trembled. "Isn't our God good?"

As she opened her mouth, it struck her that the expected response had become automatic, even flippant. God *was* good all the time. "Yes, He is."

Mummy gave her a pat on the arm before leaving the room.

***

Later in the day, as they stood around the dining table with linked hands, her father asked each person to state one thing they were grateful for. Her youngest nephew made them laugh when he said he was thankful Aunty Moni had made two big turkeys since he was starving, but as the speakers got older, the things they were grateful for were more serious.

Moni was the last person to speak. She looked at the faces around her. It was impossible to put in words the depth of her gratitude to God.

Overwhelmed, she sang a medley of choruses as the others clapped along. As the words sank into her spirit, Moni's heart expanded. Sam, who stood next to her, wrapped his arm around her waist. Always watching, Shekinah rolled her eyes. The half-smile gave away her joy.

Over the past year, they had completed both couple and family counseling. Moni had learned how not to use her words like a knife. She had also discovered that rebuilding trust was much harder than she had thought. Sam had begged her to hold him accountable. She had asked for the same. Their computer stayed in an open place, the passwords for their phones and computers exchanged.

At first, she had wondered if their actions were more like policing each other. Marriage shouldn't feel like a prison. The counselor had told them being partners in marriage was like serving in the Marines. They had to do everything they could not to leave each other behind. They had too much at stake.

She was ecstatic when Shekinah completed the diversion program. They had stayed on at the soup kitchen. It provided a good atmosphere for them to work and laugh together.

There were times when she found it difficult to listen as Shekinah rambled on about things she considered frivolous. But the counselor had pointed out the constant chats were more about keeping a communication line open. The days for serious conversations would come, and Shekinah needed to be comfortable enough to initiate them.

Her mother's face blurred because of her tears.

To remind them all of what was important, Mummy had gifted them the customized plaque Moni placed above the front door of their home. Every day, it was what she saw before she stepped out to face her day.

Inscribed with a quote from Oswald Chambers, the plaque read, *The best measure of a spiritual life is not its ecstasies, but its obedience.*

Once in a while, thoughts from the past came rushing back, but she had learned how to set boundaries for her imagination. It was meant to serve her, not the other way around.

There were days when she needed to stop herself during the middle of the day to pray. For Sam, for Shekinah, for herself. But, despite their difficult times, she had come to believe that what God promises, He also makes good.

Moni let out a long breath. Restoration. Against all odds.

AUTHOR'S NOTE

Dear Readers,

I decided to write this note due to questions raised when I announced I was writing this novel. Some people felt *Secret Places* would be perceived as a deliberate ploy to court controversy through an exposé on the church. Others were of the opinion since swinging or wife-swapping, is practised by such a small percentage of Christians that it's a non-issue.

The reality is we Christians, like everyone else, live in a fallen world. There are some of us who battle daily with addictions, either to illegal drugs, food or sex. My prayer as I wrote this book was for it to minister to the few or many looking for a way out. I know without a doubt, there is restoration through the grace and mercy of Jesus Christ. Seeking help is a hard step. But for those who persist, victory is assured.

The discussion questions were provided to enhance the conversations I hope would arise as a result of reading this book. May God, help you discover how to live a life of integrity and obedience as you weigh the words of this book under the light of his life-changing word.

Thank you for coming along on this journey with me.

Vivian Kay

BOOK CLUB DISCUSSION QUESTIONS

1.   What are some of the major themes of the novel *Secret Places*? Do you feel the themes were effectively developed by the author?

2.   What are your thoughts around the practice of swinging/wife swapping? Is it an issue that should be addressed by the church?

3.   Given that the novel is based on Christian principles, how effective was the author in presenting the Christian faith in a way relevant to the lives of the characters?

4.   Do you think Moni's unforgiveness contributed to the problems in her marriage? How does unforgiveness impact relationships?

5.   Why do you think Moni agreed to explore a swinging lifestyle with her husband? How far should one go in trying to save a relationship or marriage?

6.   What do you think was behind Sam's restlessness? How does discontent impact faith?

7.   What did you think of Debo's redemption? Do you feel it was genuine?

8.   Were you disappointed that Adele and Debo did not get back together? What would you have liked to see happen?

9.   After their reconciliation, Moni and Sam went back to their old church. Would you have stayed or moved to a new church?

10.   Secret Places is a redemptive story. What brings people to redemption? Do you feel the author was successful in presenting different paths people walk?

EXCERPT FROM KNIT TOGETHER

Marigold sat on the couch with her legs tucked under her as she dialed Archibong's number. She had to let him know that weekend wouldn't work for their movie date.

"Why not?" Archibong asked in a gruff voice.

"Logan's taking me to out to dinner. March 21st is our return to Canada anniversary."

"I can come along to even out the numbers," Archibong said.

"Alena isn't coming."

"Really?"

"Yes. It's not their anniversary."

Archibong snorted. "She must be a very understanding wife."

Marigold frowned. "What do you mean by that?"

"Well, if you were my girl, I wouldn't be comfortable with the amount of time you spend with Logan."

"Then it's a good thing I'm not," she said.

"Marigold."

"A man and a woman can just be best friends."

"That is true," Archibong said in a conciliatory tone.

Marigold took a deep breath. "You just like to get me all riled up, don't you?"

"It shouldn't be so easy to get under your skin."

"And there you go again. Goodnight."

Archibong laughed. "Sweet dreams."

Marigold dropped the cell phone on her lap. Number two reason why Archibong needed to stay in the friend zone. She didn't like the way he could get past her defenses.

Saturday morning, Marigold woke up, brushed her teeth, and went to the gym. After a hot shower, she did some grocery shopping and picked up her red cocktail dress from the dry cleaners. She still didn't understand why a blind dining restaurant had a black-tie dress code.

Marigold was ready by the time Logan called to say he was waiting in the lobby. She grabbed her purse, faux fur wrap, and went downstairs.

Logan gave a low whistle when she stepped out of the elevator. "Hello, gorgeous."

He was dressed in a navy tuxedo. "You don't look half bad yourself."

When they arrived at Sentir, a hostess welcomed them at the restaurant's waiting area. A pair of night vision goggles was strapped to her forehead. "Thanks for honoring the dress code. At Sentir, we want to engage your other senses, so it's not about how you look in a dress or suit, it's about how you feel in it."

Logan grinned as he adjusted his tie. "I feel ready for an adventure," he said.

"Then you should order a meal from our "Surprise Me" menu."

"Done," Logan said.

The waitress turned in her direction.

Marigold smiled. "I'm going with the steak."

"Great choice. Please follow me. My colleagues will seat you at your table."

They were each paired with a waiter who led them by hand into the pitch dark dining room. Disoriented, Marigold was grateful when she reached out and felt a wall.

As they made their way through the room, she noted that the conversation was louder than she was used to at a restaurant. Perhaps people were compensating for the temporary sight loss. She sat and the stiff edges of the linen tablecloth draped across her lap.

"You're okay?" Logan asked after she sighed.

"This feels unsettling," she said.

"Just relax. Once in a while, it's good to live on the edge."

She'd been living on the edge for as long as she could remember. If she moved just one more inch, she was sure to fall over. She explored the table with her hands. "They gave us plastic cups."

"They probably don't want guests hurting themselves with glass shards," Logan said.

"True."

When the waiter brought a basket of warm bread rolls, Marigold managed to open the small butter container without getting it all over her hand. "This experience gives me a better understanding of the challenges blind people face."

"The website said all the waiters are blind or visually impaired," Logan said.

"That's a great idea."

"So, how's your food?" he asked after the waiter had served their meals.

Unable to see her plate, she'd concentrated on the flavors and textures. "Very good. How's the surprise meal?"

"There are potatoes on my plate, but I'm not sure if this is a chicken breast or veal. Whatever it is, I'm open to seconds."

Marigold's ears perked up when Rod Stewart's, "Beyond the Sea" began playing over the restaurant's sound system. "Remember that song?"

She heard the smile in Logan's voice. "Of course."

One year, she and Logan had worked in the entertainment department of an adults' only cruise ship. They had a live band on board. She remembered the old men who had to be told to keep their hands on her waist during ballroom dancing. "Do you miss our old life?"

Logan took his time to respond. "I'm where I'm supposed to be," he said.

Marigold was sure she wasn't. Even though she'd become accustomed to the ship's movement, each day she wasn't sure where she'd been the day before. Now it felt as if she was stuck on a carousel, same people, same pace, and the same boring views. "I've been thinking of going back."

"Why?"

"There's nothing to keep me here. You're all settled. And, I'm sure your wife would love to have you all to herself."

"Alena doesn't see you as a threat," he said.

Marigold gave a wry smile. "If you say so."

"I'm serious. Remember, you'd asked if there was anything you could do about the baby issue?"

"Yes?"

She heard Logan exhale. "Well, Alena and I were wondering if you would act as our surrogate mother."

Marigold dropped her cutlery against the plate. They wanted her to carry their baby?

"Are you still there?"

"I didn't see that coming."

"Mari, I know it's a huge commitment. It's almost a year of your life."

Logan was worth more than that to her. She had heard of people using donor eggs. "The baby would be yours and mine?"

"No. Our baby, your womb."

Speechless, Marigold stared into the darkness. When she had asked Logan if there was anything else she could do to help, surrogacy had not crossed her mind.

"I shouldn't have asked in the middle of dinner. I'm sorry."

"Logi, I don't know what to say."

"I wasn't expecting you to give me an on the spot answer. At the very least, sleep on it."

The tight feeling in her chest eased. "Okay."

"Don't feel bad if you have to say no. You have to think about yourself."

Marigold's fingers clenched around her plastic cup. During a heated argument with Ixora, her sister had declared that Marigold had a hard time with relationships because she was selfish.

There wasn't anything bad about being focused on her needs and priorities. Why should she love someone on their own terms? "According to Ixora, that's all I do," she said. "I want us to enjoy the rest of our dinner. So, no more talk about babies and little sisters. Deal?"

Marigold took a deep breath. "Deal."